THE
BABY

BOOKS BY A J MCDINE

THE
BABY

A J MCDINE

bookouture

Published by Bookouture in 2024

An imprint of Storyfire Ltd.
Carmelite House
50 Victoria Embankment
London EC4Y 0DZ

www.bookouture.com

ISBN: 978-1-83525-012-9
eBook ISBN: 978-1-83525-011-2

To my two babies, Oliver and Thomas, now handsome young men.

I'm jolted awake by a noise I can't identify. Birdsong? The cat? I can't tell, because the minute I try to focus, everything is quiet again. The only sounds are a familiar thrumming in my head and a pounding in my chest.

I grasp my phone from the bedside table and stare blearily at the screen. My heart sinks. There are four missed calls from Miles. I open the call log to see when he made them. The first at midnight, then every fifteen minutes until one o'clock, when it appears he gave up trying. Miles hates it when I don't answer my phone. He's such a worrier. And now he'll be going out of his mind. How the hell didn't I hear the bloody thing ringing?

I wriggle to a sitting position, wincing at the resulting stab of pain, and call Miles, the phone pressed close to my ear as it rings. It's moments like these I'm glad my husband hates Face-Time. He'd take one look at my pale face and assume I was sick. Even though I know he can't see me, I still tug my pyjama top straight and paste a smile on my face. But the smile fades as his voicemail kicks in. I consider leaving a message, but am momentarily tongue-tied, so I end the call. He'll know I've tried phoning him, which is the main thing. He'll call me when he can.

And what will I tell him when he asks where I was last night, when I can't even remember myself?

I check the calendar on my phone for clues. There is only one entry for yesterday. *Dentist 11.40 a.m.* That's right, I remember now. I drove into Canterbury, leaving my Mini in the multi-storey car park because I was running late. After the dentist, I bought a sandwich and a drink and took them down to the Westgate Gardens so I could sit and eat on the banks of the Stour. The gentle burble of the river must have made me sleepy as I recall waking up to raised voices and the sound of a baby crying. And then nothing until this morning.

Nothing.

Dread squeezes my intestines. I swing my legs out of bed and hobble over to the window. The space where I normally park is empty.

How the hell did I get home?

I turn back to the bed and scrabble through the odds and sods on my bedside cabinet, finding a crumpled business card for a local cab company in my purse.

One mystery solved, at least.

I long to climb back into bed and sleep away the morning, but sunlight is flooding this long, narrow room in the eaves of my grandfather's house. It's a beautiful day and I won't waste it. Anyway, the cat needs feeding, the fridge is empty, and I promised myself I'd pick the redcurrants and raspberries before the blackbirds eat the lot.

After a shower, the violent thumping at the base of my skull eases to a dull ache behind my eyes. A pint of water and a couple of ibuprofen will help. Let's face it, I've felt worse.

Percy pads across the landing towards me, winding himself around my ankles and mewing piteously.

'I know. I'm sorry,' I tell him, bending down to tickle his

chin. Too late, I realise my mistake. My head swims, and for a second, I lose my sense of what is up and what is down, and I can feel myself pitching forwards.

'Christ.' I shoot a hand out to grip the banister. It is only once the dizziness has passed that I trust myself to follow Percy down the stairs to the kitchen.

I inherited the ginger tom when Grandad died. Along with Grandad's house: a two-bedroomed cottage surrounded by an acre of garden on the outskirts of Chilham, a pretty village on the Kent Downs.

Percy miaows again, but when I reach into the cupboard for his food, I realise I must have used the last pouch yesterday. A memory drifts to the surface, like oil in water. I had planned to drop in to the supermarket on my way home from the dentist. Obviously, that never happened.

'I'm sorry, Perce.' I drag my hands down my cheeks. Thirty-two, and I can't be trusted to look after a cat, let alone myself.

I find a solitary tin of tuna at the back of a cupboard. The expiry date reads 2018 but Percy doesn't care. He wolfs the lot in seconds, then disappears through the cat flap with a swish of his ginger tail.

I run a glass of water, and down it in one. I run another glass, pop a couple of ibuprofen from their blister pack and swallow. The kitchen is a mess. Clutter on every surface; an overflowing bin. Tea first, then I'll tackle it. I can't face breakfast, not this morning.

I flick the kettle on and gaze out of the window while I wait for it to boil. Even though I can see Percy stretched out in the sun by the greenhouse, I could swear I'm not alone. I get that feeling every so often. It's almost as if Grandad's spirit is sandwiched between the plasterboard and the brickwork, like insulation. Sometimes I feel his presence so keenly it's as if he is standing beside me, just out of sight.

But today it's more than that. I can hear something. A

rustling noise, coming from the living room. Not rustling. More like snuffling. I stiffen, my hand gripping the worktop, my head cocked to one side. Hoping to God Percy hasn't brought in a rabbit – I can't deal with that, not today – I make my way along the hallway to the front of the house.

At the door to the living room I stop in my tracks. The bottom drawer of Grandad's old oak bureau, the one with the barley twist legs, has been tipped onto the floor. Diaries and birthday cards, envelopes and notebooks, old seed packets and pens, sticky tape and gardening twine have all been upended on the carpet in a jumble.

But this is incidental. Because it's what's lying in the upturned drawer that's holding my attention.

Tiny fists waving in the air. Chubby legs encased in a white sleepsuit. A fuzz of dark hair.

A baby.

And this makes no sense, no sense at all. Because I, Lucy Quinn, might well have a husband called Miles and a cat called Percy and a cottage that once belonged to my grandad.

But the one thing I don't have, the one thing I've *never* had, is a baby.

2

I have no idea how long I stand in the doorway staring at the baby. One minute? Ten? I am fixed to the spot, terror turning my legs to ice and my insides to jelly.

It is only when the baby's snuffles turn to whimpers that I'm able to force my legs to move. I crouch over the drawer and tentatively reach out to touch the baby's cheek. I am half expecting the whole room to vanish in a puff of smoke, for this all to be a figment of my imagination. But the baby's cheek is soft and warm and real.

Whatever this is, it is not a dream.

I jerk back up to my feet and pace the room, my hands laced behind my head.

What happened yesterday, after I left Westgate Gardens? Before I can even start excavating the memories I've buried deep in my subconscious, my phone rings from the kitchen. It'll be Miles, returning my call.

Shit.

I spy a rattle, shaped like a crab, stuffed down the side of the drawer and hold it out to the baby. As tiny fingers curl around the handle I whisper, 'I'll be right back. And please, *please* be quiet.'

My phone is vibrating on the worktop by the kettle. I grab it, take a calming breath and answer with a cheerful, 'Hey.'

'Luce, is everything OK?'

'Of course. Why wouldn't it be?'

'I called last night. You didn't answer.' There's no anger or reproach in his voice, just concern, and guilt prickles my skin.

'I thought I was coming down with something, so I switched off my phone and had an early night. I'm sorry. I didn't mean to worry you.'

He is quiet for so long I wonder if we've been cut off. Finally, he says, 'Well, I was worried. Is everything OK? Are *you* OK?'

What am I supposed to tell him? That I have absolutely no memory of the last eighteen hours of my life? That I have woken up to find a baby in our living room?

And what can Miles do, anyway? He works on an oil rig a hundred miles off the coast of Aberdeen. There's no point worrying him. I'll tell him once I've figured this out because there's bound to be a rational explanation. Isn't there?

'I'm fine. A Lemsip and an early night did the trick. I'm just about to head out into the garden, actually.'

'Oh, well, if you're too busy to speak to me—'

Now I've upset him. I run a hand through my hair. It feels limp. Greasy.

'Of course I'm not too busy. I was only going to net the fruit.' I scratch around for something interesting to say. 'The fox cubs have been back. I watched them playing on the lawn for almost half an hour last night. The little one seems to be catching his siblings up, thank goodness.'

'Last night?'

'That's what I said.' It's only a white lie. The vixen and her litter of four cubs actually came the night before but Miles can hardly call her to check. 'I left some cat food down for them.'

'They're vermin, Lucy. You shouldn't encourage them.'

'I know, but they're so sweet. And they'll pay me back in spades by keeping the rabbits down.'

I hear a whimper from the living room and I grip the phone tighter. 'Let's have a proper chat tonight, shall we?'

'I can't tonight. I've arranged a card game with the lads.'

'Tomorrow, then?'

He sighs. 'It'll have to be.'

I wish we were having this conversation face to face, so I could read his expression, work out if he's really mad at me or just knackered.

'I love you, Miles.'

'I know.' His voice softens. 'I love you too. Listen, I'm about to miss a safety briefing. Talk tomorrow, yeah? I'll call you,' he says, and the line goes dead.

I scuttle back to the living room. The baby looks up and its face crumples. Clearly, I'm not the person it was expecting, or hoping, to see. The whimpers are gaining momentum, and, as I stand dithering by the sofa, the baby starts crying in earnest. I look around helplessly, as if the answer to this mystery is hiding in plain sight. I'm not sure what exactly I'm hoping for. That the baby's mother lives up the lane and dropped by to say hello? That she left me in charge while she popped to the loo?

Even as I picture the scenario, I know it's not true. There are just two of us in the house. Me and the baby.

My gaze falls on a large black bag I don't recognise, propped up against the bureau. I drop to my knees and riffle through the contents. There are half a dozen disposable nappies in the main compartment, along with a bag of wipes, a tub of nappy cream, a spare sleepsuit and three small plastic cartons of formula milk. In a side pocket, I find three empty feeding bottles.

Of course. The baby must need feeding. I can't think why

this hasn't already occurred to me. The poor thing must be starving. No wonder it's crying. I scoop up a carton of formula and one of the bottles and take them into the kitchen.

I have no idea how much a baby needs, so I fill the bottle to the eight-ounce mark, just to be on the safe side. I check the carton.

A complete breast milk substitute... Suitable from birth... Wash hands... Sterilise all utensils according to manufacturers' instructions... Can be fed at room temperature.

It's just as well, because the baby's cries are louder than ever.

Back in the living room, I place the bottle on the arm of the sofa and reach gingerly for the baby. Its little body is squirming and its face is red and puckered.

'There, there,' I say self-consciously, even though I know we're alone. The wailing ramps up another decibel. I perch on the sofa, place the baby in the crook of my left arm and pick up the bottle.

I may not know what I'm doing, but it soon becomes apparent the baby does. The second it clocks the bottle it reaches out and opens its mouth. Seconds later peace has descended. The baby's eyes lock onto mine and I find myself smiling back.

'Who are you?' I whisper. 'Where did you come from?' But, of course, the baby doesn't answer. And the questions spiral endlessly in my head until I feel as though I'll burst.

3

When the baby seems full I rummage around in the changing bag for the wipes and a clean nappy. There's a changing mat in the bag too, just a small fold-up one, so I lay the baby on it and undo the poppers on the sleepsuit.

I have never changed a baby's nappy before. I haven't had much to do with babies at all, but how hard can it be? At least figuring it out gives me something to focus on as I try to get my head around all this. I know I should be alerting the authorities to the fact that I have acquired a baby – a baby that I know absolutely nothing about – but the authorities can wait. This baby can't.

I ease the baby's small feet out of the sleepsuit and peel open the sticky tabs on the front of the nappy. The minute I do, I am sprayed with a jet of wee. I can't help but laugh, and the baby gazes at me, wide-eyed.

A boy, then. I should have known. Something deep inside me shifts and settles.

'Wren,' I say softly.

He grabs my finger and squeezes.

'You like that name, do you?' A lump has formed at the back

of my throat. I need to get a grip. 'Shall we call you Wren, just while you're here?'

He doesn't protest and, the matter settled, I reach for the wet wipes. 'Let's get you all cleaned up, shall we?'

It's only when the clean nappy is on that I realise urine has seeped into Wren's sleepsuit. He is so wriggly it takes an age to change him into a clean one, and by the time I have, his eyelids are drooping.

The bureau drawer is lined with a soft fleece blanket the same shade of yellow as wild primroses. Holding Wren awkwardly in one arm, I refold the blanket and lay him back down. He sticks his thumb in his mouth and I stroke his cheek until his eyelids start to close.

Once he falls asleep, I head into the kitchen and busy myself finding a clean mug and a teabag. Tea made, I clear a space on the kitchen table and sit down.

Miles would have a fit if he saw the state of the place. It's always immaculate when he comes home. He works four weeks on the rig, two weeks off, and two days before he's due back I clean the house from top to bottom. When he arrives home, tired and grumpy – more often than not – he is greeted with sparkling surfaces, fresh flowers and the smell of something delicious bubbling away in the oven.

I give myself a spring clean, too. He has never seen me in grubby jogging bottoms with a face bare of make-up and dirty hair scraped back in a ponytail. I wax and buff, pluck and polish, in the hope I'll vaguely resemble the girl he fell in love with all those years ago, albeit slightly puffier around the eyes and thicker around the waist.

Miles has two lives: one here with me, and one offshore. Offshore, his life is hard. Punishing twelve-hour shifts, tough, physical work in harsh conditions and little or no privacy or downtime. But it's also an exhilarating, exciting life. Crews are tight knit, their camaraderie borne out of the long hours they spend together and the knowledge that a single mistake can have disastrous consequences for them all.

Back home, his life is safe. We go for walks and watch home improvement shows. We treat ourselves to lunch at the pub and debate whether or not we should invest in a conservatory. It's all very tame compared to dodging storms and wrangling with complicated machinery on a towering rig in the middle of the North Sea.

I worry the drab reality of home never lives up to the dream. Sometimes, when Miles doesn't realise I'm watching him, I catch a closed expression on his face, like his mind is somewhere else entirely.

And I get it, I really do, because it's the same for me.

For four weeks out of every six, Percy and I have the cottage to ourselves. I can rise with the dawn or lie in until lunchtime. I can spend all day in the garden and eat cereal for dinner. I can drink wine on a weeknight without being lectured about my alcohol intake. I can even have a sneaky cigarette or two. In short, I can please myself.

And for the other two weeks, once I have scrubbed and polished, plucked and buffed, I play the part of the perfect wife.

But right now, I have more important things to think about than my husband; I need to decide what to do about Wren.

I pick up my phone, my finger hovering over the keypad, imagining what I'll say to the operator on the other end of a 999 call.

'I'm phoning to report the discovery of a baby. In my living room. Yep, that's right. Well, it must have been some night, because it appears that while I may have lost my memory, I've found a baby.'

It sounds so far-fetched the call handler will probably hang up, assuming it's a prank.

Maybe I could take Wren along to the police station in Canterbury. Explaining the situation face to face to someone on the front desk has to be easier than trying to find the right words on the phone.

But gone are the days you can easily find the contact details and opening hours of your local station. Everything on the police website is designed to encourage people to use the online reporting service.

There are links to report crime, domestic abuse, road traffic incidents and missing people, but my attention is drawn to a link to report someone who has been found. I click through to an online form which asks for my name, email address and phone number. I'm about to type in my name when something stops me.

If I fill in my details, there's no going back. I will be on the system, and so will Wren. A report will be filed, an officer will turn up on the doorstep, questions will be asked. Questions for which I have no answer. And how is that going to look?

Self-preservation kicks in and I close the form. It makes sense to do some checking of my own before I contact the police. I need to see if I can work out where Wren has come from, who he belongs to, and, more importantly, what part I played in it all.

4

I start by googling *Missing baby, Kent*, and am shocked by the sheer number of children who have been reported missing in the last few months. Teens, mainly, although a couple are under ten. When I click through to each appeal, I'm relieved to see most of them have since been found *safe and well*.

I hope this really is the case, but I can't help thinking how desperate these kids must have been, how hopeless they must have felt, to have decided that walking out of their lives was their only option.

I keep scrolling as my tea grows cold beside me. The further down the web page I get, the more the knot of anxiety in my chest eases. This is good. If a baby had been snatched yesterday it would be all over the news. I'm about to check the *BBC News* website just to make sure when a headline catches my eye.

Police enlist public's help in search for missing toddler in Kent County.

Even as I click on the page and wait for it to load, I tell

myself it can't be Wren. I'm hardly an expert on babies but he must only be three, maybe four months old at most.

It doesn't stop my heart rate rocketing, until I see a photo of a little blond, blue-eyed boy wearing dinosaur pyjamas and a goofy grin.

I scan the story. Dylan Holdstock went missing from his home in Kent County after breakfast two weeks ago and hasn't been seen since. The Sheriff's Office is asking anyone who saw him to contact them immediately.

The Sheriff's Office?

I bang my palm against my forehead. Of course. This rosy-cheeked toddler didn't go missing here in the UK, he disappeared from his home in Kent County, Michigan, nearly four thousand miles away.

I check every local news website. I even turn on Grandad's ancient transistor radio and listen to the ten o'clock news.

There are no stories about babies, missing or otherwise.

I pour my cold tea down the sink, rinse out the mug and stack it on the draining board, my thoughts bouncing between Dylan and Wren.

Two little boys: one missing, one found.

Dylan's poor mother must be going out of her mind with worry. Which makes me wonder about Wren's mum. Does she even care he's gone?

Because one thing's clear. No one's reported him missing, have they?

Wren is still asleep when I tiptoe into the living room to check on him later. His arms are flung above his head and his lips are pursed as if, even in sleep, he disapproves of the situation he's found himself in.

I can't say I blame him. How must it feel, to be uprooted

from one life and planted in another, placing your trust, your life, with a woman who can barely look after herself?

I still haven't contacted the police. I know that with every hour that passes, the harder it's going to be to explain how Wren came to be here. Especially as I don't even know the answer myself.

I've decided to give myself until the morning to see if I can stitch the broken pieces of my memory together.

I return to Wren's changing bag, tipping the contents onto the carpet and sifting through every item, looking for anything that might tell me who it belongs to.

The bottles sport the logo of a leading brand. As do the wipes and nappies. You can buy nappy cream from every super-market and chemist in the country, so that's no help. Nor is the sleepsuit which, according to the label, is from a well-known chain of shops.

I pick up the bag and peer inside, just in case I've missed anything. There's another zipped compartment, one I hadn't noticed earlier. I pull the zipper open, and my fingers close around a set of keys. One brass key for a mortice lock and one smaller silver-coloured one for a uPVC door. House keys. But it's the keychain that makes the hairs on the back of my neck rise.

It's a thin loop of green plastic with *Blood Donor – Group O negative* printed on the side. They're given to people the first time they give blood. I know this because I have one too.

I scramble to my feet and hurry into the kitchen to check the key rack by the back door, half expecting mine to be miss-ing. And if it is, wondering what that could mean. But mine is exactly where I left it, hanging from its usual hook, the key to the shed attached to it.

Back in the living room, I stare at the two keychains. The one from Wren's bag is much newer. Mine is worn and faded.

I've been giving blood for years. O negative blood isn't the rarest blood type, but it's not common either. Around one in seven people are O rhesus negative. It's known as the universal blood type because people with any blood type can be given our blood.

Conversely, O negative people can only receive O negative blood. It's why I became a blood donor. You reap what you sow.

The UK has a population of sixty-seven million, which means more than nine and a half million people have the same blood type as me. And one of them is likely Wren's birth mother.

Birth mother. I catch myself. Wren isn't mine and I need to remember that. I need to think of him as a child needing emergency foster care. I'm looking after him while I find his real mum, and as soon as I do, I'll give him back.

He stirs in his sleep. I stroke his head. His hair is as soft as a feather. There's a small diamond-shaped depression on the top of his head. For a moment I panic, but then I remember all babies have them. I read about them once. It's the soft area in a baby's skull that allows their heads to narrow during birth. They close up on their own. Fontanelles. I remember thinking they sounded like a type of pasta.

I run my thumb over the soft spot, feeling a tiny pulse. Wren's eyes flutter open, and he gazes blearily at me.

'Shush,' I murmur. I stroke circles, round and round. After a while he closes his eyes and his breathing deepens again. I rock back on my heels.

Come on, Lucy. Think.

I pick up the changing bag and weigh it in my hands, considering what it tells me. It feels and looks expensive and everything in it is immaculately clean and neatly packed. Organised. It's not the bag of someone with a chaotic lifestyle, the kind of blank-eyed mother you see on the news after the death of a neglected child. This bag belongs to someone who cares.

But if she cares, why hasn't she reported Wren missing? She has lost her baby, but she's also lost the keys to her house. It doesn't make sense.

Unless something else is going on here. Maybe she fears she'll be arrested for some past misdemeanour if she contacts the police, or is protecting her baby from a violent partner. What if it's not that she hasn't bothered to report Wren missing but she *can't*? What if something has happened to her? She could be lying in a ditch somewhere, badly injured or even dead. Did I come across a baby in a pram while I'd had one too many, not knowing his mum was lying injured nearby?

Did I take him home to keep him safe?

5

I press the heels of my hands against my eyes and groan softly. I *need* to remember what happened yesterday.

I begin with the things I can remember. I woke with a headache and a dry mouth just after eight. I stumbled downstairs to feed Percy and make a cup of tea, which I took into the garden to drink.

It was already warm, and the scent of the honeysuckle on the trellis by the back door evoked memories of Grandad so strongly I felt as raw as I had the day of his funeral.

Fortified by a couple of sips of whisky from my uncle Bob's small silver hip flask, I'd shuffled up to the lectern, fixed my gaze on a simple wooden cross on the back wall, and done my very best for my favourite person in the world.

Do not stand at my grave and weep. I am not there. I do not sleep.

Miles and I were in the process of moving back to the UK from Dubai when Grandad died. While part of me misses the cloudless blue skies and shimmering skyscrapers of Dubai, I have never felt more at home than here, where Grandad's presence is all around me.

I would have quite happily holed up at the cottage all day, wallowing in self-pity, but I'd been having niggles with one of my fillings and I didn't want to end up with an abscess, so I showered and dressed, forced down a piece of toast and drove into town.

The dentist X-rayed my teeth and, after declaring the filling was holding up, gave me a scrape and polish.

As he handed me a plastic cup of mouthwash, he said, 'How many units of alcohol a week would you say you drank?'

I swilled the pink liquid around my mouth, spat it out and wiped my lips with the tissue he gave me before I trotted out my stock answer.

'Fourteen.'

It's the Government guidance, a safe number to pick when speaking to health professionals and husbands. I ignored the little voice in my head whispering spitefully, 'Fourteen a week? Pur-lease.'

'Why are you asking?' I asked, a little defensively.

'Do your gums bleed when you brush?'

'Sometimes, I guess.'

'Switch to a toothpaste for sensitive teeth and maybe cut down a bit on your alcohol intake. Book in for a check-up in six months so we can keep an eye on that plaque. We don't want you losing any teeth, do we?' he said with a chuckle.

Patronising dick. I smiled tightly, gathered my jacket and bag and left without making another appointment. Screw him. I'd find a dentist who knew what they were talking about. My teeth were perfectly fine.

I was still fuming as I bought my lunch, which is probably why I picked up a couple of cans of Zinfandel to have with my sandwich. Just to take the edge off.

Westgate Gardens was packed with families and office

workers enjoying the sun after an unseasonably cold May. I found a spot overlooking the river, and checked my phone before tugging the ring pull on the first can.

There was a message and photo from Tess, my best friend back in Dubai. A cocktail glass with an olive on a stick, taken on a rooftop balcony overlooking the glittering metropolis of Dubai at night.

> *Miss you, Luce. Call me when you get a minute, yeah? We have news! PS Did you trim your bush or whatever it was you were doing?!*

Tess is a big-hearted Aussie with a filthy sense of humour. We clicked the moment we were introduced during a barbecue at the beach club. Like Miles, Tess's husband Charlie works for one of the major oil companies, although he has an office job whereas Miles is an engineer on the rigs.

I checked the time before calling her. Dubai is four hours ahead of the UK so it was getting on for five o'clock there, but Charlie works silly hours and is rarely home before seven.

'Miss you too,' I said when she picked up. And then I added primly, 'And I wasn't trimming my bush. I was netting it. That's different.'

Tess snorted with laughter. 'You poms. Whatever floats your boat. How are you, mate?'

'Good. I'm good.'

'And Miles?'

'He's offshore. Back in a fortnight.'

'You lucky bastard.' Tess sighs. 'What I wouldn't give to have a couple of weeks with only myself to think about. Oh, the bliss.'

'Charlie been leaving the loo seat up again, has he? You poor thing.' Charlie is the nicest man I've ever met. He's kind and funny and good-looking in a geeky kind of way; yet Tess is always moaning about him. She doesn't realise how lucky she is.

'D'you know what he did the other day? We'd agreed not to make a fuss for our tenth wedding anniversary, and over breakfast he hands me tickets for a weekend at the Qua Spa at Caesars Palace. I felt terrible.'

'My heart bleeds.'

'I know, right? He's infuriating. Anyway, I didn't call to whinge about my husband. I have news,' she said.

'Are you coming over?' I asked hopefully. She'd been threatening to visit since we moved back to the UK.

'No, it's not that.' She paused, and I remember feeling a shiver of unease.

'I'm pregnant,' she announced.

'*Pregnant?*'

'Four months. I wanted to tell you before, but, you know...' She trailed off.

'That's... that's amazing.' I frowned. Tess never wanted children. She always maintained kids would piss all over her jet-set lifestyle. Her words, not mine. '*Is* it amazing?' I checked.

'It is. After you left, everything seemed so... I don't know... so vacuous. Superficial. Going to parties, drinking too much, waking up with a hangover. Rinse and repeat. It felt like something was missing.'

'That's... that's fantastic news. Congratulations. I mean it,' I added, more to convince myself than Tess. 'When are you due?'

'November. I've had the most diabolical morning sickness, you wouldn't believe.'

I let her natter on about acid reflux and constipation while I sipped my wine and considered how I felt about her news.

A day later, now the shock has worn off, I'm genuinely happy for Tess and Charlie. I always thought it was terribly sad they'd never wanted children because I knew they'd make amazing parents. Who knows, they might even ask Miles and me to be godparents, which would be wonderful.

But yesterday I'd been awash with self-pity and Tess must have sensed this, because she said, 'Sorry, Luce, I know this must be hard for you after everything you and Miles went through.'

I'd tried to snap out of it then, telling her not to be so silly, that I was fine, in fact I was more than fine, I was over the moon for her and Charlie. That it was the best news ever and I was so, so happy for them both.

And we'd ended the call with promises to be better at keeping in touch, and I'd placed my phone carefully in my bag and stared at the river as it gurgled past until I couldn't see through my tears. And I realised I wasn't crying for the baby Tess was having, I was crying for the baby I had lost.

What happened next? I remember I sat on the riverbank feeling sorry for myself for a while. I drank the second can of wine and nibbled at my sandwich, but my appetite had disappeared. I think I must have dozed off, because the next thing I remember is waking to the sound of raised voices.

I ran my fingers through my hair and looked around. A couple were sitting on the bench behind me, engaged in a heated argument, not caring that everyone in the vicinity had stopped their own conversations to listen.

'I don't care what you say, I saw you with her,' the girl screeched.

'Nothing happened,' her boyfriend snarled back. He was wearing a black Nike T-shirt, grey joggers and a baseball cap. He looked about nineteen. His girlfriend, dressed in black leggings and an off-white T-shirt, looked even younger.

'Then what the fuck were you doing with her?' the girl cried.

'She was selling weed. I had an eighth off her. It was only twenty quid.'

'We don't have twenty quid.' The girl stood and bent over a pram I hadn't noticed. She pulled out a bundle wrapped in a stained yellow blanket and hugged it to her chest. Her arms were as skinny as an addict's and covered in tattoos. Her face was stretched tight as she squared up to her boyfriend. 'We have a baby,' she hissed. 'In case you forgot.'

'How can I forget? Bloody thing never stops crying and you never stop nagging. I've had enough. I'm gonna sleep at my mum's tonight.' He produced a roll-up from a tin, lit it, and swaggered off towards the centre of town in a cloud of pungent-smelling smoke.

'Reece!' the girl cried. 'Wait up!'

She put her baby back in its pram and hurried after him. 'Reece, I'm sorry. Just wait up, will you? *Reece!*'

Once she'd gone, an elderly lady on the bench next to me caught my eye and tutted.

'Some people shouldn't be allowed to have kids,' she said.

'They shouldn't,' I agreed, and I packed away my lunch things and got unsteadily to my feet. The argument, on top of Tess's news, had soured the sunny afternoon and I wanted to be anywhere but there.

I remember dropping the empty cans and half-eaten sandwich in the nearest bin and retracing my steps back into town.

I press pause on the scene and replay it carefully as I try to work out how old the baby was. It's hard to tell because I didn't see its face. But it was, I realise with mounting horror, around the same size as Wren.

Did they say whether it was a girl or boy? Not that I recall. And the yellow blanket it was wrapped in gave no clues. Is it possible I came across the girl and baby on my way back to the car park and she either gave the baby to me... or I took it?

I close my eyes and replay the scene a second time. I remember waiting for the lights on the pedestrian crossing to turn green before I crossed the road to the high street. I was alone. And then... nothing.

I growl with frustration, and the sound wakes Wren, who opens his eyes, sees me and whimpers. I check my watch. It's almost twelve, three hours after his last bottle. I have no idea how often you're supposed to feed babies but little and often makes sense, so I head into the kitchen to fill a bottle with another carton of formula, which leaves one left.

He reaches for the bottle the moment he sees it so I give him the lid to play with while I settle him on my lap and lay a clean tea towel over his sleepsuit.

'If you're staying till the morning, we need supplies,' I tell him, stroking a wisp of hair away from his face as he feeds.

I also need to retrieve my car. God only knows how much it's racked up in parking charges. But first, we need to get to Canterbury, seven miles away. It's either a taxi, a train, or the bus. I weigh up the options. The train would be quickest, but it's a long walk to the multi-storey from the station. A taxi would be easiest and there's a card for Canterbury Cabs in my purse. But what if they send the same driver who brought me home last night? My skin crawls with shame at the very thought.

You could find out if Wren was with you, a voice whispers in my head.

And what if he was? What then?

I check my phone. There's a bus from the village at ten past three. We'll catch that.

My next problem is working out how the hell I'm going to carry Wren. I turn to the internet for help.

Turns out, whipping up a DIY baby sling from a bedsheet is a cinch. I grab a clean sheet from the airing cupboard and, watching a video on YouTube, practise a few times with a cushion as a makeshift baby. Once I've got the hang of it, I hoist Wren onto my shoulder and slide him into the sling.

He immediately starts to grizzle, his face squashed up against my collarbone, so I take him outside and walk around the garden singing softly to him until he quietens.

Back inside, I make a mental list of all the things we need, then reach for the tin caddy in which I keep the peppermint tea. Miles hates the stuff, so I know he'll never find the bank card I've stashed in there.

The card is for an account I opened when I first started working. There isn't a fortune in there: just a few thousand pounds. I suppose I should have told Miles about it when we got married, but I once read an article in a women's magazine that said everyone should have a running away fund. It's like taking out an insurance policy. You hope you'll never need it, but if things go pear-shaped you know you'll be all right.

All our other accounts are in joint names and Miles handles the finances as I've never had a head for figures. He knows to the nearest tenner how much we have. That's not to say he's mean. Not at all. He just likes to keep a close eye on our income and outgoings. A big spend in a baby shop will stand out like a sore thumb, and he can't find out about Wren, not yet.

At half past two I pack Wren's changing bag, retie the sling and pop him in. It's a fifteen-minute walk along the lane to the village. The verges are bursting with cornflowers and heads of frothy white cow parsley. The sun is shining, with barely a cloud in the sky. Birds chatter in the hedgerows and high overhead a buzzard rides the thermals, its plaintive mewing almost cat-like.

The heat of Wren's body pressed against my chest is as comforting as a hot water bottle on a cold January night, and as I stride up the lane a feeling of contentment envelops me.

Is this serenity, this sense of completeness, what it feels like to be a mother? I can only hazard a guess.

Wren reaches up to grab my locket, his hand closing around the chain like a clamp.

'Oh no you don't,' I laugh, gently prising his chubby fingers apart. I slip the necklace under my T-shirt and dig around in the changing bag for his rattle. I'm about to give it to him when someone shouts my name and the blood drains from my face.

7

I turn slowly to my left. A woman with short, curly grey hair is watching me from her front garden, a pair of secateurs in one hand and a basket filled with blown roses in the other.

'It is Lucy, isn't it?'

I paste a smile on my face. 'It certainly is. Hello, Claudie, how are you?'

She doesn't answer my question. She's too busy staring at Wren with a look of astonishment on her face.

'I didn't know you had a baby.'

Claudie was the village postmistress until she retired on her eightieth birthday. This must have been over a decade ago, but she could still pass for seventy-five. Grandad said she used to know everything about everybody.

I stroke Wren's head and think on my feet. 'Oh, she's not mine. She's my goddaughter. My friends Tess and Charlie are over from Dubai. They've left me holding the baby. Literally.' I tinkle with laughter, but Claudie just frowns. 'They've gone to a wedding,' I explain.

'A wedding?'

'In Tunbridge Wells.'

'And they've left the baby with you?'

'The invite said no children,' I embellish. *Keep it simple, Luce, or you'll trip over your own lies.*

'They're back in the morning. Not sure I'm going to get much sleep tonight. Anyway, I'd better go, or we'll miss the bus, won't we, Rosie?' It's the first name I come up with. My eyes slide to the basket where the blooms Claudie's been dead-heading are wilting in the sun. I hope she doesn't make the connection.

Fortunately, I'm saved from further questions by the sound of a phone ringing inside Claudie's cottage.

'My son,' she says, nodding towards the house. 'Best answer it. Mind you, he only ever phones when he wants something.'

'Anyway, it was lovely to see you,' I gush, as she makes her way to the front door. I bend down and kiss the top of Wren's head. 'Come on, little Wren, or we'll miss the bus.'

'Thought you said she was called Rosie?' Claudie has stopped on her doorstep and is looking at me with narrowed eyes.

'She is,' I agree amiably. All this smiling is making my jaw ache. 'Wren's just my nickname for her, isn't it, Rosie, darling?' I add.

After an age Claudie nods and disappears into the house. I set off towards the bus stop, but I can't stop myself from glancing over my shoulder. Claudie is watching me from a downstairs window, a phone pressed to her ear and an unreadable expression on her face.

To my relief there's only one other passenger on the bus, an elderly man with a tartan shopping trolley who is sitting in the disabled seat by the doors.

I find a seat halfway down and take Wren out of his sling so he can watch the countryside flash past. When his arms and legs pump in excitement I wonder if this is his first ever bus ride.

After twenty minutes the driver pulls into the bus station and I head straight to the big pharmacy to find nappies, wipes and formula. I spend an age choosing a steriliser, then scoot over to the clothing aisle where I pick up bibs and a couple of packs of sleepsuits, one plain white and one with little tigers printed on them.

Before I know it, I'm putting the cutest dinosaur dungaree and T-shirt set, a Peter Rabbit comfort blanket and a zebra soft toy into my basket. Wren may only be with me for another few hours but that's OK, he can take his new things with him when he goes home. It's only money.

As I pay, I ask the cashier where I can buy a car seat.

'There's a great little independent baby shop on the Sturry Road.' She hands me my receipt. 'How old's your little one?'

For a moment I freeze. I have no idea. All I have to go on are photos of other people's babies on the internet.

'Nearly four months,' I say, frantically doing the calculations in my head. 'He was a Valentine's Day baby.'

'Was he?' The woman's eyes light up. 'That's so sweet! Did you call him Valentine?'

I shake my head. 'Wren.'

'Wren? That's an unusual name.'

'It's because he was so small.' Suddenly I'm overcome by a rush of emotion and find myself unable to speak. A tear leaks out of my eye and drips onto Wren's head.

The woman reaches out and touches my arm. 'I'm so sorry. I didn't mean to upset you. He's doing amazingly well for a preemie. You're obviously doing everything right.'

I thank her and head out of the shop, shame corroding my earlier happiness. I marvel at just how mistaken the cashier is. I'm not doing anything right. I'm doing everything so, so wrong. What am I even doing with Wren? I should have called the police the moment I found him in the house. I have no right to keep him, no right at all. His birth mother – his *real* mother – must be out of her mind with worry, preparing herself for the worst possible news.

I find myself back on the pavement opposite the bus stop. I can't see the police station from here but I know it's just the other side of the city wall, less than a five-minute walk away.

I should go straight there and hand myself in. If it turns out I stole Wren yesterday, they can arrest me and I'll face the consequences. What other choice do I have? My mind made up, I start walking.

With Wren in the sling, the strap of the changing bag over one shoulder and a carrier bag of shopping in each hand, I'm physically laden down, but it's nothing compared to the heavy despair pressing down on me.

In the few short hours since I found Wren, he has become a part of my life, part of *me*. It sounds absurd to say, but it's true.

I cross the road and am about to turn left towards the underpass when Wren starts squirming. I realise it must be gone four o'clock. I'll feed him before I take him to the police station. It won't take long.

I change direction and head through the gates to Dane John Gardens – a small park inside the city walls with a fountain, a bandstand and often gaggles of loitering schoolkids. I walk along the avenue of lime trees until I find an empty bench and drop the bags of shopping on the ground with a grateful grunt.

Wren has started sucking his fist and I'm glad I had the foresight to pour the last of the ready-made cartons of formula into the last clean bottle.

I drink Wren in as he feeds. Already, his face is almost as familiar to me as my own. But it's more than that, I realise suddenly. I straighten sharply, causing his eyes to widen.

'Sorry, my love,' I murmur.

My head spins as a possibility occurs to me. What if Wren

is my baby?

It's not as crazy as it sounds. Last night wasn't the first time I've blacked out. Once, not long after we moved back to Kent from Dubai, I lost almost forty-eight hours. It was a week after my grandfather's funeral. Miles was offshore and I was in a fog of depression, devastated I hadn't been able to fly home in time to see Grandad before he died.

I woke up fully clothed on the sofa one morning, Percy kneading my chest, with absolutely no recollection of how I'd got there. When I checked the date on my phone, I thought it must have malfunctioned. I'd lost two whole days. I told myself it was the grief but I was kidding myself. Grief doesn't cause blackouts. Neat vodka does.

What if my memory is so screwed up that I can't remember being pregnant, giving birth? What if I am Wren's mother? Hope surges through me as I gaze at his features, trying to match them to my own. His wispy hair is brown like mine. Miles and I both have brown eyes. Wren's are the blue of new denim, but all babies are born with blue eyes, aren't they?

There is definitely something familiar about his face even though I can't put my finger on it.

What if I were to walk into the police station and announce that Wren is a foundling, only for their subsequent enquiries to reveal he is actually mine? At best they'd involve social services, who'd probably declare I was an unfit mother. At worst, I'd be classed as a danger to both Wren and myself and carted off to the nearest psych ward.

Whatever happened, the outcome would be the same: I would lose him.

He is falling asleep with the teat of the bottle still in his mouth. I carefully extract it and set the bottle on the bench beside me, then sit him on my lap so I can rub his back.

As he gives a milky belch, I have a moment of clarity. I can't take him to the police until I'm absolutely certain he isn't mine.

8

I slip Wren back into his sling, climb stiffly to my feet and make my way to the multi-storey car park.

In the lift up to the second floor I gaze at my reflection in the mirror. Anxious eyes ringed with purple shadows stare back at me. My hair needs a trim, my lips are dry and cracked and my long-sleeved T-shirt is creased and there's a greasy stain on the shoulder. I'm a mess.

At the ticket machine I tap in the Mini's registration number. The parking charge is almost eighty pounds. I use my secret bank card to pay so Miles doesn't ask any awkward questions.

At the car I open the boot and fling in the shopping bags. I'm going to have to drive with Wren in the sling, which isn't ideal, but until I've bought a car seat, I don't have a choice.

I'm fixing the seat belt when my phone bleeps with a text. I consider ignoring it, but it might be Miles, so I grab the phone from the changing bag on the passenger seat.

Been worrying about you. Are you taking it easy?

I'm about to tell him I'm having a quiet day pottering in the garden when I remember Find My iPhone. He'll be able to see I'm in Canterbury.

Typing around Wren's body isn't easy, but after a couple of false starts, I ping off a reply.

Thought I'd pop into Canterbury for a coffee and a wander. It was just what the doctor ordered. Feeling much better, thanks. Xx

As long as you're OK. Speak tomorrow. Love you, babe.

Absently, I fiddle with my necklace. Miles gave me the delicate silver locket last Christmas, before we moved back to the UK. There's a tiny photo of Percy on one side. On the other is a picture of me and Miles that Tess took at the beach club a couple of summers ago. We're tanned, relaxed and grinning widely at the camera, our arms wrapped around each other.

'You like it?' Miles asked, as he took it from the box and carefully fixed the clasp around my neck. It was early on Christmas morning and we were still in bed.

'I love it. You're so good at presents. It makes me feel bad that you're just getting socks again.'

Miles laughed, because he knew as well as I did that there would be more than socks in his stocking. I'd been squirrelling away chunks of my housekeeping money all year so I could buy him the beautiful Tissot watch he'd admired in the window of a jeweller's down the road from our apartment.

'How does it look?' I said, swivelling around to show him.

'Beautiful.' He dropped a kiss on my neck, sending a shiver of desire rippling through me. 'Even better with nothing on.'

We'd barely left our bed all day.

As I turn the locket over, I'm hit by a wave of longing for Miles. I'm used to him working away but I miss him. When we're apart, it's like I'm living half a life. When he's home, I'm complete. I stare at my phone, then tap a reply.

Love you too. Good luck tonight. Xx

For once luck is on my side and I've timed the journey perfectly between school pick-up and rush hour and it takes a little over ten minutes to reach the baby shop on the other side of the city.

A middle-aged woman is attaching sale stickers to a line of prams as we walk in. She breaks off to ask if I need any help.

'I'm looking for a car seat. We've just moved back from Dubai and all our stuff is on a container somewhere in the Gulf of Oman.' The lies are tripping off my tongue but I need to be careful. I'll end up tying myself in knots.

'What's your budget?' the woman asks, leading me towards a display of car seats at the back of the shop.

I don't have the faintest idea how much a car seat costs. Fifty quid? One hundred and fifty?

'Um, mid-range, I guess. And I'd like one of those ones with a handle.'

The woman spends the next fifteen minutes guiding me through the various car seats and their fittings. It's more complicated than I'd have dreamt possible, but eventually I settle on a smart grey rear-facing one which, she tells me, will last until my little one reaches 13kg or 83cm, whichever comes first.

As I plan to take Wren to the police station in the morning, this is irrelevant, so I tell her it's just the job.

On the way to the till we pass a couple of Moses baskets. Wren can't spend another night in a drawer. 'I'll have one of them,' I tell the woman. 'And do you have any baby carriers?'

'We certainly do. These are very popular. They're forward-facing. Babies love them.'

I catch a glimpse of the price tag as she hands one to me. It's over a hundred pounds, but I don't care. 'Perfect.'

'I love your sling,' she says, as she tots up my purchases. 'Is that how they carry babies in Dubai?'

'It is,' I lie.

'How marvellous. That'll be three hundred and twenty-five pounds, please.'

Once I've paid, she carries the car seat out to the Mini and shows me how to fit it properly. Wren safely strapped in, I stow the Moses basket and carrier in the boot.

'What a lovely little boy you have,' she says. 'He looks a lot like you.'

My face breaks into a smile. 'Do you think?'

She looks from me to Wren and back again. 'Absolutely.'

'Thank you,' I say, and there's a catch in my throat. Because if a stranger sees a likeness between us, maybe Wren really is mine.

9

We stop at the supermarket on the way home. It's the last place I feel like visiting, but there's no food in the house and although I have enough formula for Wren and Percy can catch his own dinner, I can't live on air.

I pull up in one of the parent and child parking bays and skim-read the instructions for the new baby carrier. Once I've worked out how to strap it on, I lift Wren out of the car seat and ease him into it.

His head swivels left and right as I find a trolley and head into the supermarket. The hair on the back of my neck stands on end when a security guard just inside the doors holds his radio close to his mouth and starts talking rapidly into it as we pass.

My grip on the trolley tightens. Has he recognised Wren? I realise with a sinking feeling that I haven't checked the news websites since this morning. How stupid. Wren's face could be plastered everywhere by now and I'd have no idea.

I lower my gaze and veer left towards the toilets and tobacco kiosk. A second security guard appears, and I feel a swooping sensation in my stomach. They're on to me, I know it. Fear is replaced by a wave of sorrow. All I wanted was a few more hours with Wren. Is that too much to ask?

I watch in horrified fascination as the two guards whisper urgently to each other, throwing an occasional glance in my direction. I drop another featherlike kiss on the top of Wren's head and brace myself for the shit to hit the fan.

But the two guards turn their backs on me and approach a woman about my age pushing a buggy out of the store. Her baby, a little boy, judging by his denim dungarees, can't be much older than Wren, and for one crazy moment I want to tell them they've got the wrong woman, the wrong baby.

'Excuse me, miss,' the older of the two guards says, stepping in front of the buggy. 'I have grounds to suspect you've been shoplifting. Would you mind if I had a quick look in your pushchair?'

The woman's face drains of colour.

'Shoplifting?' she stutters.

He crouches down and riffles through the basket under the baby's seat. A small crowd of shoppers have gathered now, and there is a collective intake of breath as he pulls out a bottle of supermarket-brand gin.

'Do you have a receipt for this, miss?' he asks.

The woman bites her lip and shakes her head. As the security guard confers with his colleague, she catches my eye. I am blindsided by the desperation on her face. Can't he see there's obviously been a misunderstanding?

This woman, with her Bugaboo pushchair, cashmere cardigan and designer jeans, isn't the kind of person who shoplifts, just as I am not the kind of person who steals a baby.

I want to stride over and tell the cocky security guard to lay off her, but I don't, just in case her guilt is infectious.

10

Wren is asleep before I've left the supermarket car park, and I leave him in his car seat on the kitchen floor while I unpack the few bits of shopping I picked up. It's enough to keep me going for a couple of days. I can't think beyond that.

Once I've figured out how the steriliser works, I make up three feeds which I reckon should see us through the night.

Percy saunters in, doing a comedy double-take when he sees the sleeping baby. If cats had thought bubbles, his would read, 'WTAF???' No word of a lie.

I spoon Whiskas into his bowl and he wolfs it down, throwing the occasional look of horror in Wren's direction. If Wren *was* mine, he wouldn't turn a hair. Even so, I leave the two of them in the kitchen and trail from room to room looking for any sign that a baby lives here.

There aren't any.

Percy has disappeared through the cat flap when I troop back into the kitchen. Wren is stirring, and I lay a folded quilt on the floor and settle him on it while I make myself cheese on toast.

As the grill heats up, I think about the woman with the

Bugaboo buggy. Perhaps she has a controlling husband at home, a husband who checks her till receipts, and that's why she tried to steal the bottle of gin. I find myself pitying her. How desperate must you be to risk a criminal record just for the sake of a drink?

I'm not touching a drop, not while I'm responsible for Wren. What if I blacked out again and something happened to him? It doesn't bear thinking about.

He babbles away, chuckling to himself every now and then when he manages to grab one of his own feet. I marvel at how he has taken everything in his stride. He's the original contented little baby.

I pop back upstairs in search of cotton wool and a couple of towels, then run warm water into the washing-up bowl and set it on the floor beside Wren. Soon he is splashing about in his makeshift bath while I wash him with the cotton wool. I dry and dress him, then take him into the living room and let him have another half an hour on the quilt while I check the news websites on my phone, then turn on the TV for the six o'clock news.

There is still no mention of a missing baby.

When Wren starts to grizzle, I pick him up and cuddle him until his eyelids grow heavy. Once he's asleep, I settle him in the Moses basket on the floor by my feet. I mute the TV, leaving the news channel on so I can keep half an eye on the rolling head-lines, but it's not long before a wave of exhaustion hits me. I reach for the throw on the back of the sofa and curl up under it.

Just as I'm drifting off to sleep, I have another flashback.

Yesterday. Late afternoon.

I was sitting at a table in the corner of the ABode, a posh hotel and bar in Canterbury High Street, nursing a double gin and tonic, when I heard my name being called.

'Lucy McKinley, as I live and breathe! Is it really you?'

I turned around to see a tall man in a dark grey suit striding towards me. For a moment I couldn't place him, but something about the way he walked stirred a distant memory, and a grin spread across my face.

'Oh my God.' I jumped to my feet. 'Pete O'Neal. What are you doing here?'

'Meeting.' He patted his laptop bag, then looked at my drink. 'Want another, for old times' sake?'

'Why not?' I said. 'G&T, please.'

As he disappeared towards the bar, I surreptitiously combed my fingers through my hair and peered into my compact to check my mascara hadn't run.

Pete O'Neal was the object of my teenage desires for about three years, on and off, at secondary school. Fifteen years later I could still feel that exquisite pain of unrequited love. We once shared a lingering kiss at a mutual friend's party when we were sixteen, but we were both going out with other people at the time, so it never went any further. The last time I saw him, at the leavers' day disco, he enveloped me in a bear hug and whispered in my ear, 'Keep in touch, eh?'

But I was too busy partying hard, first at uni and then when I moved to London, to stay in touch with any of my friends from school. Every once in a while, usually when I was between boyfriends and feeling sorry for myself, I would think about Pete O'Neal and wonder what my life might have looked like if we had hooked up. But then Miles had whisked me off my feet and I'd forgotten all about him.

And suddenly there he was, all six foot two of him, walking towards me with a gin and tonic and a pint of lager, a look of surprised delight on his face.

'Cheers,' he said, handing me my drink. We clinked glasses and he loosened his tie and undid the top button of his shirt.

'So, Lucy McKinley. What brings you back to Canterbury? Last I heard, you were living abroad.'

'I'm Lucy Quinn now,' I said, waving my wedding band and diamond engagement ring at him.

'Who's the lucky fella?'

'Miles. He's an engineer for an oil company. We've just moved back from Dubai.'

'Dubai, eh? I got as far as Maidstone before I came back.' He laughed.

'What do you do?'

'I'm a graphic designer. I mainly work on advertising accounts. I'd rather be illustrating, but it pays the mortgage.'

I'd forgotten Pete was a talented artist. Even the doodles on his exercise books were amazing.

'I worked in children's publishing before I met Miles,' I told him. 'It was only a small press and I was a lowly editorial assistant on a pittance, but I loved it.' I felt an unexpected pang of loss. I'd adored that job. I'd just been offered a position as an assistant editor when Miles came on the scene.

'Why did you leave?'

'Miles was offered the job in Dubai. It was too good an opportunity to turn down.'

I'd only known Miles for four weeks when he took me out to dinner and announced he'd been offered a transfer to the United Arab Emirates. I'd been absolutely gutted... until he told me he wanted me to go with him.

'Go with you to Dubai?' I'd said, laughing. 'I can't.'

'Why not?'

'Because I have commitments here. My job, my flat, my family—' I had counted them off on my fingers.

'Your job is basically making the tea and proofreading. Rebecca and Maddie can find someone to take your room, and your parents don't even live in the UK.'

Mum and Dad had moved to the Algarve the year I graduated, but my grandad still lived in Kent and I drove down to visit him every few weeks.

'Come on, Lucy, can't you see? This is a once-in-a-lifetime chance to live and work in one of the most exciting cities in the world,' he'd wheedled.

'But we've only known each other for a few weeks.'

'You're saying I'm not enough for you?' His shoulders had crumpled.

'Don't be silly. Of course you are.'

'Will this make a difference?' he'd asked, plunging a hand into the pocket of his jeans and pulling out a ring box. I'd gasped audibly as he'd dropped to his knees in the middle of the restaurant and asked me to marry him.

11

'So why are you back?' Pete said, watching me over the top of his pint glass.

'Long story.'

He smiled. 'I've got time.'

'Miles was offered a promotion. And we were beginning to tire of the ex-pat life.' I remembered Tess's words. 'It all seemed a bit superficial.'

'Do you have kids?'

I took a long slug of my drink before answering. 'Unfortunately, not. What about you?'

'Unfortunately, yes.' His eyes crinkled. 'I'm joking. I love 'em to bits.' He fished about in his jacket pocket for his phone and held it towards me. The screensaver was a photo of a boy and girl with the same shade of straw-blond hair and the same cheeky grin.

'Mia and Lucas,' Pete said. 'They're eight. Twins,' he added.

'Twins? How lovely. They're beautiful,' I said, smiling back. 'But hard work, I should think. No wonder you stopped at two.'

As his gaze dropped to his feet, a breath caught in his throat.

I realised with horror he was trying very hard not to cry. I reached across to touch his hand.

'I'm sorry,' I said gently. 'Is it something I said?'

He gave a little shake of his head. 'It's all right. You weren't to know. Sophie fell pregnant again last year. Another set of twins. But there were... complications. We lost the little girl at twenty-two weeks. And the boy—' His voice broke, and he ran a hand across his face. He was silent as he fought to compose himself. 'I'm sorry. I find it hard to talk about.'

'Don't be silly,' I cry. 'It's me who should be apologising, not you. I shouldn't have asked.'

'Like I said, you weren't to know. But it's all a bit raw, as you can probably imagine.' He looked up at me then, and the desolation on his face moved me deeply. He was right, I *could* imagine.

'I'm so, so sorry, Pete.'

He squeezed my hand. 'Thank you.'

I racked my brains for something neutral to say. 'Your wife, Sophie, how did you meet her?'

He looked at me in surprise. 'Didn't you know? I married Sophie Weatherall. We both ended up at Warwick. We had our twelfth wedding anniversary a couple of weeks ago. Soph's a GP.'

Of course she is. Sophie was the prettiest girl in our year at school. Clever, too. I went to take another sip of my drink, only to find I'd already finished it. I glanced up at Pete. He was frowning and I had a horrible feeling I might have actually voiced my thoughts. 'Only joking,' I added, with what I hoped was a disarming smile. I picked up my glass. 'Want another?'

Pete looked at his watch. 'Better not. Soph's got evening surgery and I've got to pick the kids up from after-school club.'

'What time does it finish?'

'Six.'

'It's only just gone five. Go on, stay for one more. I could really use the company.'

He relented. 'All right, just a quick one. But you stay here. I'll get them.'

He returned a few minutes later with another G&T for me and what looked like a pint of orange juice and lemonade for him.

'Driving,' he said, when he saw me looking. 'What about you? How are you getting home?'

The question drew me up short. I'd forgotten I'd driven. I pushed my hair out of my face. 'Train. It's so convenient for Chilham.'

'That's where you're living?'

I nodded. 'My grandad died last year and left me his cottage. Miles wasn't keen being stuck out in the middle of nowhere but I couldn't bear to sell it.' Now it was my turn to well up and I rubbed my eyes impatiently.

'I'm sorry, Lucy, I didn't mean to upset you.'

'You didn't. It's just we were very close. I still can't believe he's gone.'

Pete squeezed my hand and a jolt of electricity fizzed up my arm. Did he feel it too?

We reminisced about school for a bit. Pete still played five-a-side with his closest friends, although he was injured more than he was fit these days. Sophie still hung out with a group of her best friends from school.

'They've all got kids around the same age as Mia and Lucas so we knock around together quite a bit. We rented a holiday home in France together last summer.'

'How lovely.' I took another slug of my G&T, hoping Pete hadn't noticed the edge to my voice.

It all sounded so bloody hunky-dory. I hadn't exactly hated school, but I'd found making friends hard, and was happy to have been given the chance to reinvent myself when I'd gone to uni.

I doubted Sophie and her friends even remembered me. But Pete did. Big, kind Pete, who cupped my face in his hands at that party all those years ago and told me he'd always fancied me. Pete, who was, I suddenly remembered, a really good kisser. My stomach turned to liquid as I wondered what it would be like to kiss him now, whether the spark was still there.

He sat back in his seat, balancing his drink on his thigh. 'It's so good to see you, Luce. What a coincidence you were here today.'

'I don't believe in coincidences,' I told him boldly. 'I believe in fate. I was meant to bump into you today.' As I said it, I realised I was only partially joking.

He raised an eyebrow, but I could tell he was amused. 'Fate, eh?'

'You know, I often wonder what would have happened if we'd gone out at school.'

'Perhaps we did in a parallel universe.' Pete smiled. 'Who knows?'

The motto of our school was *Carpe diem*. Seize the day. I nudged him with my shoulder. 'You know, it's not too late to see what life in that parallel universe is like, Mr O'Neal.'

'Eh?'

I gave him a cheeky grin. 'We could get a room.'

'A *room*? Lucy, I don't—'

His expression shifted from shock to pity. Shame bloomed in my stomach.

'I'm kidding.' I reached out to pat his arm. He flinched. I forced myself to laugh. 'You didn't really think I meant... you and me?' I pointed up at the ceiling, 'Here?' I shook my head. 'It was a joke. I was *joking*.'

But he was already gathering his phone and laptop bag.

'It's been lovely to see you, Lucy, but I need to pick up the twins.' He stood. Paused. 'You know, Sophie can put you in touch with people who can help.' His gaze slid to my empty glass, then back to me. 'Support groups, counsellors, that kind of thing. She's based at the surgery just up from the police station. She'd love to see you.'

His smile barely reached the corners of his mouth. I clasped my hands in my lap as he scurried out of the hotel bar like a hunted man.

I dropped my head in my hands and groaned. What was I *thinking*, coming on to someone I hadn't seen for fifteen years? I could have screwed everything up. Everything. Just for what? A bit of excitement? Temporary respite from my loneliness? A boost to my ego?

'Are you all right, madam?' a voice said, and I looked up to see the girl who had served me at the bar watching me with concern.

I rearranged my features into a smile. 'I'm fine, thank you.'

She gestured at my empty glass. 'Can I get you another?'

I calculated how much I'd had. The cans of Zinfandel with my lunch, followed by three gin and tonics here. Or was it four? And if they were all doubles, how many units was that? But before I could total them all up, I felt a surge of defiance. Pete was talking crap. I didn't have a problem with drink. Why the hell did I need Perfect Sophie to put me in touch with a support group?

'Yes, please,' I told the waitress. 'And make it a double.'

12

The flashback is so raw it's like I've lived it all over again, minute by humiliating minute. What must Pete have thought of me? Once again, I am flooded with shame as I picture the look of pity on his face.

Try as I might, I can't remember a thing after the waitress brought me that last G&T. It's like someone has shut a door in my brain, and no matter how much I push and pull on the handle, it won't budge even an inch.

I hug my knees to my chest and gaze blankly at the television. An earthquake has killed thousands in the Middle East. Homes, businesses, whole blocks of flats have been reduced to rubble in a matter of seconds.

A mother wearing a shawl soaked in blood stumbles out of a ruined building carrying a young child in her arms. I don't need to turn up the volume to know the woman is wailing. I can tell by the way her mouth twists in anguish. I hold my breath, watching the child for signs of life, but he is limp in her arms. When the reporter holds out a microphone, the woman points to the pile of rubble behind her and shakes her head in sorrow, over and over.

Once again, I wonder why Wren's mum hasn't called the police. Does it mean she doesn't want him? In which case, maybe Miles and I could adopt him? But I know I'm being ridiculous. Firstly, you can't just adopt a kid. There are rules about that kind of thing. And, secondly, Miles would never agree, because he's never wanted children.

He waited until after we were married to tell me, and I'll never forgive him for that. I'd just assumed that, like me, he saw our future not just as a couple, but as a family.

I didn't care if we had one child or four, but I knew I wanted kids, I always had. Miles was the middle child of five. Perhaps that's why he didn't want children. He always claimed his parents were too busy with his siblings to pay him any attention. And then, when he was nineteen and barely out of sixth-form college, his girlfriend fell pregnant and he talked her into having an abortion she never wanted.

I only found out Miles didn't want children the night of our first wedding anniversary. I'd booked a table at a fancy sushi restaurant with a panoramic view over Dubai. Everything had been perfect until I'd brought up the subject of babies.

'I was thinking,' I said, reaching for his hand, 'it's time I came off the pill.'

'Why would you do that?'

'Now you're settled in your new job and we have our lovely apartment, it feels like the right time to start our family.'

'It'll never be the right time, Lucy.'

'What d'you mean?'

'I don't want children, you know that.'

I gaped at him.

'Don't go all puppy dog on me. I told you when we first got together.'

'No, you didn't.'

It was the wrong thing to say. His expression darkened. 'I

did. It's not my fault you can't remember. You were probably pissed.'

I bit back a retort. I was absolutely certain Miles had never mentioned not wanting a family. It's not something I would have forgotten, whether I was sober or steaming drunk at the time. But just as I knew he was lying, I also knew I wouldn't win him round by arguing with him, so I massaged the inside of his wrist with my thumb. 'I'm sorry, Miles. Let's not ruin our anniversary.'

'*I'm* not ruining anything.'

'It's me. I must have misunderstood. I must have thought you meant you didn't want children *yet*.'

'I made it quite clear,' he said, pulling his hand away. 'I have no interest in being a father. At all.'

Miles was uncharacteristically tight-lipped about his own dad. Jack Quinn died when Miles was in his early twenties. They hadn't had an easy relationship, from what I'd gleaned from his mum, Faye.

'Miles always felt Jack was picking on him,' she'd told me during a brief visit to her bungalow in Haywards Heath not long after we'd announced our engagement. Miles had disappeared into the garden to take a work call when she'd patted the chair next to her and asked if he ever talked about his father.

'Never,' I'd said. He rarely spoke about his mum either, but I wasn't about to tell her that.

She'd sighed. 'Miles never saw it from Jack's point of view. He was a bit of a handful growing up, you see. Jack was hard on him, but only because he wanted the best for him. They were cut from the same cloth, those two.'

'You mean Miles takes after his dad?'

She had stared through the patio doors at Miles. He had finished his call and was heading back towards the house. 'He does. But don't ever let him hear you say it, Lucy,' she said. 'He wouldn't thank you for it.'

I had drunk too many gin cups to heed her words as we sat in the restaurant celebrating our first wedding anniversary.

'Do you mind me asking you something?' I asked Miles.

He placed his chopsticks by the side of his plate and wiped his mouth with his napkin. 'Depends what it is.'

'Did something happen between you and your dad? Is that why you don't want children?'

The muscle twitching in Miles's jaw should have been a red light, but the cocktails had given me Dutch courage.

'Miles? This matters to me. I need to understand why you feel like this. Did he... did he hurt you?'

'For Christ's sake, Lucy, can't you get it into your thick skull? I don't want to talk about that bastard. Not now, not ever.'

'OK. I understand. I'm sorry. Do you... do you think you might feel differently in the future? Because I can wait, if that's what you want. I don't just want children. I want *your* children.'

He motioned to a nearby waitress for the bill and we sat in silence as she cleared our plates and set the bill and a couple of steaming lemon-scented cloths on the table. Only when she was out of earshot did he hiss, 'I don't want children and I'm never going to change my mind. So if that's not something you can live with, I'm sorry. You need to make other arrangements.'

Other arrangements? He made unpicking our marriage and finding someone else to spend the rest of my life with sound like taking the train instead of the car.

I didn't make other arrangements, but every couple of years I got drunk enough to broach the subject, and every time I did Miles remained adamant that he didn't want kids and never would. Wasn't he enough for me? Couldn't I see my obsessive need for a baby was poisoning our marriage? Couldn't we just be happy as we were?

As the years went by, I began to realise I would never change his mind. And when he was home, I convinced myself he was enough. It was a different story when he was offshore. I drank to blot out the loneliness, filling the void with Singapore slings, mojitos and Manhattans. Only Tess was privy to my all-consuming desire to have a baby, and she probably saved my marriage, because she helped me see things from Miles's perspective.

'Just because he doesn't want to have children with you doesn't mean he doesn't love you. In fact, it's probably because he loves you so much. He doesn't want to share you,' she said once.

'That doesn't make sense. Love is elastic. I would have enough to go around.'

'Perhaps he doesn't think Dubai is the best place to bring up kids.'

'That's bullshit too. We'd never afford help at home, but we could here, and the international schools are amazing.'

'Perhaps he's worried he might not be a very good dad.'

That was more like it. Miles was worried blood would out and he'd turn into Jack Quinn. Strict, controlling, authoritarian. The man who'd made his life a misery when he was growing up. I suppose it made sense that he didn't want to repeat the mistakes of the past.

So I stopped bringing the subject up and kept taking the pill. I told myself our little family of two was enough, and when we finally moved back to the UK, I would surround myself with cats. Half a dozen of them.

And Tess and I congratulated ourselves every time a fellow ex-pat announced a pregnancy or went into the private hospital to have an elective caesarean.

'Her life's over,' we'd say, clinking glasses down at the beach club or in some rooftop bar. And I'd pretend I enjoyed my freedom too much to have kids, and Tess wittered on about sleepless nights and morning sickness and how pregnancy ruined your figure.

I think we both knew I was lying through my teeth. And it

seems even Tess wasn't immune to her biological clock tick-ticking away.

I was desperate to have a baby, and now I have one. But I didn't conjure him up through wishful thinking, nor did the stork deliver him. He came from somewhere. I just wish I knew where.

13

Perhaps Miles has sensed I was thinking about him, because my phone buzzes, his name flashing up on the screen.

I sit cross-legged on the sofa and press the phone to my ear. 'I thought you had a big card game tonight?'

'I played a couple of rounds but I wasn't really in the mood. I wanted to check you're OK.'

'I'm fine. Why wouldn't I be?'

'I don't know. You seemed distracted earlier.'

'I was just trying to find some change for the parking machine.'

'Yes, I saw you didn't use your card.'

My eyes widen. Miles must have been on the banking app. Just as well I didn't use our current account debit card to pay the £80 ticket. Let alone Wren's car seat, Moses basket and baby carrier. 'I had a load of change I wanted to get rid of. How was work?'

'Same old shit. That's what I wanted to talk to you about, actually.'

This isn't good. Every so often Miles talks about handing his notice in and jokes about sending me out to work. But I've been out of the job market so long I'm not sure I could find work if I tried.

'I've had enough, Luce. I'm too old for it all: commuting to Aberdeen, existing on that fucking rig, living two lives. I've quit.'

'You've what?'

'I decided last night. I wanted to talk it over with you, but you didn't pick up, remember?' He sounds aggrieved and I can't say I blame him. He wanted to discuss a life-changing decision and he couldn't get hold of me because I was busy making a move on an old crush. The knowledge I've lied to him sends yet another wave of shame over me.

'What will we live on?'

'You can finish your magnum opus.'

Like just about everyone I worked with at the publishing house, I've always harboured a secret desire to become an author. I started planning a middle-grade time travel detective series almost a decade ago. Moving to Dubai was supposed to give me time to focus on my writing, and while I tell people I'm powering on with the first book and sketching outlines for the next three in the series before I start approaching agents, the unpalatable truth is I haven't got much further than the middle build of book one.

The fact is, I spend more time talking about my novel than writing the bloody thing. It sure as hell isn't going to provide us with an income anytime soon. Yet Miles seems to think I can match his generous salary. He has no idea.

'D'you know how much the average author earns in a year?' I ask. 'Seven grand. Seven!'

'Tell that to J.K. Rowling,' he says. 'And until the books start earning, we've got your grandad's money.'

Alongside the house, Grandad left me his life savings and premium bonds. It isn't a fortune – about fifty thousand pounds

– but it would, I suppose, keep us for a couple of years if we're careful.

'I'm done here, Luce.' Miles hesitates. 'I want us to be together as a family.'

A family? My gaze slides down to Wren, who is sucking his thumb in his sleep, his index finger stroking the soft skin between his nose and top lip. Before I can work out what Miles means, he laughs. 'You, me and Perce. Our own little family of three. It's what you've always wanted, isn't it, to have me home all the time? And I can pick up work locally. There must be people in the village who want jobs done.'

Miles, an odd-job man? It doesn't sit with the man I married, the guy who boasts that he risks his life every day on the rig. I can't see him being happy mowing lawns and replacing washers for Chilham's many pensioners. And another thing. I may have always told Miles I wished he worked a regular job and was home every night, but is it actually true? I love having him home, but I also love the four out of every six weeks when I'm on my own, with no one but myself and Percy to worry about.

Be careful what you wish for, Lucy.

'I'm sure you're right,' I say, reaching down to stroke Wren's cheek. And even if he isn't, it's too late now. Miles has quit. It's a fait accompli.

He clears his throat. 'Oh, I nearly forgot. I need you to stay at home tomorrow.'

'Why?'

'My new phone's arriving and they need a signature.'

'Oh. What time?'

'They haven't said. Why, is it a problem?'

I can't exactly tell him I won't be in because I'm taking the baby I found in our house this morning to the police station. Miles is my husband. I know him as well as I know myself. But even I have no idea how he'd react. I watch Wren as his thumb falls from his mouth and he starts to snore softly. Would it hurt to keep him a little longer? It's not like his mum has reported him missing. And he's safe here. What harm can one more day do?

'No,' I tell Miles, my heart already lighter now he's unwittingly given me permission to keep Wren for another twenty-four hours. 'It's not a problem. Not a problem at all.'

At eight o'clock Percy stalks in and starts scratching the carpet, his passive-aggressive way of telling me he's still hungry. He follows me into the kitchen and sits at my feet as I pour a generous helping of dry food into his bowl.

It reminds me I haven't eaten, but the prospect of a microwaved supper isn't appealing, so instead I make myself a plate of cheese and biscuits. Reaching into the cupboard for a wine glass is such an automatic action that it's only when I'm staring at the glass in my hand that I realise what I've done.

Even though I'd normally consider a glass or two of red wine as vital an accompaniment to cheese and biscuits as my favourite chilli jam, tonight I put the glass back. This is because one glass usually leads to another and before I know it, I've finished the bottle and opened a second. But I'm not making that mistake tonight, not when I have Wren to look after.

I run myself a glass of water instead and take both it and the plate back into the living room, flicking through the channels and settling on a repeat of a cooking show. The celebrity chef has a glass of wine in his hand as he chops and sautés, and I'm gripped by an urge to trot back into the kitchen and open the last bottle of Merlot in the wine rack. But a memory of the woman in the supermarket comes back to me, the look of terrified desperation on her face, and I quash the impulse and take a long draught of water instead.

My relationship with alcohol has always been... complex. I had my first taste of it when I was twelve, when friends of my parents gave me a snowball at a Christmas drinks party.

I'd thought the highball glass of egg yolk-yellow Warnicks and lemonade, complete with cocktail umbrella and crushed ice, the height of sophistication. It tasted as sweet as ice cream and the rush to my head was intoxicating.

My well-meaning parents believed that giving me a small glass of wine with dinner would teach me to drink responsibly. They had no idea that exposure to alcohol as a child leads to an increased risk of alcohol dependency as an adult.

At university, alcohol was a salve to my natural shyness and, as a consequence, my drinking ramped up several notches. But I wasn't alone: we all preloaded with cheap white wine and knocked back shots at the student union like they were water. Getting trashed was a way of life.

I graduated with a 2:1 that would have been a first if I'd spent more time working and less time partying. But it didn't matter. After a couple of unpaid internships, I was offered the job in publishing I'd long coveted. I moved into a flat with my best friends from uni, Rebecca and Maddie, and embraced London life. The drinking culture was insane. We downed tools at the office at six o'clock and headed straight for the pub, often staying till closing time, then I would stagger back to the flat, completely hammered.

Sometimes I woke to find dried vomit in my hair. Occasionally, I lost my purse or my keys. Once, after a particularly heavy night, I discovered angry welts on both my biceps yet had absolutely no memory of how they got there. It was my first blackout, and it frightened me so much I stopped drinking for a month... until I was offered a glass of Prosecco at a book launch. An hour later I was so steaming drunk my boss had to help me into a taxi and pack me off home. Not my finest hour.

I was two tequila slammers on the wrong side of drunk the night I met Miles. Bex, Mads and I were at a new club in Hackney that Bex's workmates were raving about. The floor was sticky, the drinks were warm and the house music was so loud it swallowed you whole. It was every bit as good as we'd hoped.

I was propping up the bar waiting for a round of drinks when I became aware of a man watching me.

He had the kind of dark, brooding looks that suggested he was mad, bad and dangerous to know. The kind of looks I always found irresistible. A strong, square jaw, messy quiff, and broad shoulders that tapered to a narrow waist. A swimmer's physique.

Shamelessly, I ran a hand through my hair and held his gaze until he looked away first. Then the barman arrived with our drinks and Maddie appeared at my shoulder and dragged me to our booth at the back of the club. But later, when we headed onto the dance floor, I glanced over to the bar, unaccountably pleased when I saw him there, still watching me.

Was it lust or the tequila slammers making my head swim? It could have been either, but as I danced to the music I could feel the heat of his gaze on my bare skin and it was electrifying.

Then I stumbled, my ankle turning, and as I flung my arms out to steady myself, I accidentally whacked a guy behind me in the chest.

'Oi, watch what you're doing, you stupid cow!' he yelled into my face. His forearms and neck were inked with tattoos and the white T-shirt he was wearing was at least two sizes too small. He was built like a... like a... what was it?

'Shit brickhouse,' I said under my breath, then swallowed a gurgle of laughter. 'Not shit brickhouse, Luce. Brick shithouse.'

'What did you say?' the man yelled. He wasn't much taller than me but his physical presence was as intimidating as a street fighter's and I took a step backwards, bumping into the couple behind me. I looked around in panic for Bex and Maddie but they must have headed to the bar again. I was on my own, encircled by a mob of strangers who stared at me with the same hungry fascination as a pack of wolves circling their prey.

'Did you hear me, you drunk bitch? I said, what did you call me?'

'Nothing,' I stammered. 'I didn't call you anything. Pinky promise,' I said, offering him my little finger.

'Are you taking the piss?' His breath was hot and sour in my face and I held up a hand in apology, flinching as he batted it away.

And then a figure was by my side.

'Get your hands off her,' the figure growled, and I spun around to see the man from the bar beside me. And I was right about him being mad, bad and dangerous to know, because he looked absolutely enraged as he squared up to the guy with the tattoos. And Tattoo Guy's eyes darted nervously about him as my saviour seized a handful of his white T-shirt and pulled him so close their noses were almost touching.

'If I ever, *ever*, catch you so much as looking at her again I will ram your balls so far up your arse you'll be singing soprano, you fucking coward,' my rescuer snarled.

With a forceful shove, he released his grip and Tattoo Guy beat a hasty retreat, looking less like a wolf and more like a dog with its tail between its legs after a telling-off.

Before I could thank my rescuer, he took my elbow and guided me towards the back of the club.

'C'mon, let's get you out of here.'

'Thanks,' I managed, as we reached the foyer.

'Anytime.' He held out a hand. 'Miles,' he said.

His grip was strong and assured. I peeked up at him, thrown

by the intensity of his gaze. My stomach flipped, and it had nothing to do with the tequila slammers.

'Lucy,' I said.

'Well, Lucy, how are you getting home?'

'Taxi, probably.' I shrugged. 'Depends on my friends.'

'Your friends?' he said, one eyebrow cocked, as if to say, *where were they when you needed them?* 'Where d'you live?'

From any other guy this might have sounded creepy, but this man – Miles – had just saved me from an arsehole. I knew instinctively I would be safe, that he would look after me.

'Fulham.'

'I'll walk you home.'

'But it's miles.'

'Then we'll have plenty of time to get to know each other on the way, won't we?'

He pulled open the door and stood aside to let me through first, and I was touched by this gentlemanly gesture. We chatted the whole way home and by the time we reached the door to my flat, I was head over heels in love.

15

I have no idea if Wren is sleeping through the night. For all I know he could have woken on the hour every hour last night, his crying falling on deaf ears while I lay in bed, comatose. The possibility is toe-curlingly shameful.

Do four-month-old babies sleep through? Is Wren even four months old? I'm only guessing he's around that age after comparing him to pictures of babies online.

That intense feeling of inadequacy rears its head again. What am I even thinking, keeping a baby that doesn't belong to me? His mum would know how many times he wakes in the night. She would know how he prefers to be held, how to comfort him. What if Wren's breastfed? His mother's not suddenly going to stop producing milk just because he's gone. Is she having to express milk, keeping bottles of the stuff in the fridge until he comes home?

Up until now, I haven't given Wren's real mum much thought. She's just a shadowy figure in my mind. An inconvenience, actually, because if she didn't exist, I could keep her baby. I find myself wondering what she looks like. Is she fat or thin, short or tall? Is she blonde, or brown-haired like Wren? Is he her first child or one of many? I don't know why, but I hadn't considered he might have siblings. And what about his dad? Even if Wren's mother was unwilling or unable to report him missing, surely his father would have alerted the authorities by now?

I reach for my phone, checking the news websites for the thousandth time. There's been a large house fire in Rochester. Firefighters have rescued a pensioner and her three cats. Police are appealing for witnesses to a smash-and-grab at a newsagent's in Maidstone, and a couple from the Isle of Sheppey have gone public after winning over eight million on the National Lottery. There's nothing about a missing baby.

On a whim, I check all the Canterbury residents' Facebook groups I can find, scrolling through recent posts. There are moans about parking charges and pleas for recommendations for reliable plumbers and electricians. There are appeals for lost dogs, lost cats and even a lost teddy, though no lost babies.

But Wren has come from somewhere. Once again, possible scenarios run through my mind. Wren's father murdered his mum and dumped their baby somewhere in Canterbury before killing himself. Perhaps Wren's mum is a single parent with a history of mental illness and, unable to cope any more, abandoned him on the steps of the library, where I found him as I staggered out of the ABode.

I wish I'd paid more attention to the couple in Westgate Gardens. Reece and his girlfriend. Was that Wren she'd hugged to her skinny chest? The pram looked tatty and the baby had been wrapped in a stained yellow blanket. But the changing bag I found in the living room looks brand new and expensive. It doesn't add up.

I rack my brains, trying to remember if I've seen any babies in the village recently. A mother and baby group meets in the church hall on the third Thursday of the month, I seem to recall. And a group of mums with little ones often congregate in the cafe in the square after school drop-off, but I would hardly have swiped one of their babies from under their noses, would I?

Of course I wouldn't.

Pete's wife Sophie had been pregnant with twins, I remember suddenly. They'd lost their little girl at twenty-two weeks, but Pete had been too upset to talk about the second twin – a boy – and I hadn't pushed him.

I suppose I'd assumed the little boy died too, but what if he hadn't? When I asked Pete if he had kids, he only mentioned the older twins, Mia and Lucas. What if their baby brother was born prematurely, maybe with profound disabilities? What if Pete and Sophie decided they couldn't cope and offered him up for adoption? Could Wren be their baby?

As I dismiss this possibility as being, frankly, ridiculous, I recall another baby I've been in contact with recently. I can't think why I haven't thought of him before. Probably because the day I met him is one I'd rather forget.

When I told Pete I hadn't caught up with anyone from school since we'd been back in the UK, I wasn't being entirely truthful.

Miles and I had been mooching round a farmers' market at Easter. The kind of place where a loaf of bread costs a fiver and the customers congratulate themselves on shopping sustainably as they drive home in their enormous diesel-guzzling, ozone-wrecking 4x4s. We'd stopped to taste slivers of goat's cheese at an artisanal cheese stall when a woman's ringing voice made me pause, my hand raised halfway to my mouth.

'Lucy McKinley, is that you?'

I stared at the woman bearing down on me. She was wearing the uniform of the country set: an olive-green Barbour jacket, skinny jeans and Hunter wellies. Her wavy chestnut shoulder-length hair was glossy. *She* was glossy.

'Hello, Sarah,' I said, unsure what I should do with the

pungent-smelling goat's cheese going soft in my hand. 'Fancy seeing you here.'

Spotting Miles beside me, Sarah's eyes widened a fraction. It was clear she thought I was punching well above my weight.

'How nice to meet you...' she began.

'Miles,' Miles said, shaking her hand. He looked at me. 'How do you two...?'

'School,' Sarah said before he could finish. 'Lucy was in my English Lit class.' She turned back to me. 'You were going to become an author, weren't you? Did you ever write that bestseller?'

'Still working on it,' I said lightly, but Sarah had already turned back to Miles. 'Where have you two been hiding?'

'Dubai,' Miles said with a hint of pride. He loved the fact we'd led a more cosmopolitan life than most people our age.

'Dubai? Ooh, how exciting.' Sarah was suitably impressed, and as she quizzed Miles about his job, I cast my mind back to the girl she was at school. Bossy, overconfident and overbearing. Head of the debating society, head girl. Destined to marry well and live in a Georgian pile with overconfident, overbearing children who would also go on to become head of the debating society.

We weren't close at school, but the way Sarah was regaling Miles with stories about our antics you'd be forgiven for thinking we were bosom buddies.

'My husband's here somewhere,' she said, looking round. Her gaze fell on a slightly overweight man in a checked short-sleeved shirt and khaki cargo shorts who was carrying a baby in a sling. A tiny baby, judging by a barely visible fuzz of downy hair.

'Darling, come and say hello to these two gorgeous people,' Sarah said so loudly several people turned round to stare.

'Toby, meet Lucy and Miles. Lucy and I were at school

together. And this is little Theo. The others are here some-where. Tobes, where *are* the others?'

'Last seen in the queue for the ice-cream van,' Toby said, pumping Miles's hand. He had an unmistakable public-school drawl. 'Do you have any?' he asked. 'Ankle-biters,' he added, seeing Miles's quizzical look.

'No,' Miles said after a tiny beat. 'How many do you...?'

'Four at the last count.' Toby honked with laughter. 'All boys. Sarah's threatening to make me have the snip but there's no way I'm letting a man with a scalpel near my family jewels. No way, José.' He honked again.

'Or woman,' Sarah said. 'Women can be surgeons too. This isn't the eighteenth century, you know.' She rolled her eyes at us as she said this, and shook her head. 'Apologies for my husband the reactionary. He's stuck somewhere in the nineteen fifties.'

I laughed politely, even though I didn't find men like Toby the least bit amusing.

Suddenly we were joined by a gaggle of small boys clutching ice creams. Their ages ranged from about eight to four.

'Jude, Henry and Freddie,' Sarah said. 'Boys, say hello to Lucy and Miles.'

They ignored their mother and began playing some compli-cated form of tag, darting between shoppers browsing the stalls. Both Sarah and Toby seemed completely oblivious to the dagger looks they were getting.

'Where do you live?' Toby asked.

'Chilham,' Miles said. 'Just while we get ourselves sorted.'

'Super,' Sarah gushed. 'I *love* Chilham. So quaint. Toby's cousin lives in one of those big timber-framed houses in the square. Where are you?'

'Mountain Street,' Miles answered. 'Lucy's grandad left her his little cottage. But we're looking for somewhere bigger.'

This was news to me. For one thing, we didn't have the

money to buy anything bigger, especially in Chilham, where prices were at a premium, and secondly, I had no intention of moving. I loved Grandad's cottage. But I kept quiet, because I knew men like Toby made Miles feel inadequate and he was overcompensating in an effort to impress.

'We're in Sandwich,' Toby said. 'The commute's hell, but it's the price you pay, eh?'

'I know!' Sarah clapped her hands. 'Why don't you come back to ours for supper? Toby's doing something with a chicken.'

'It's lovely of you to suggest it, but we have to get back,' I said.

Miles laid a hand on my arm. 'Nonsense. We don't have anything planned. We'd love to,' he told Sarah and Toby, and my heart plummeted.

Call it a sixth sense, but I knew even then the evening would be a disaster.

16

Miles pulled me over to a stall selling wine from a local vineyard on the way back to the car.

'We should buy a couple of bottles to take to Sarah and Toby's.' He scanned the display, his gaze settling on a case of brut. 'We'll have two of those,' he told the woman manning the stall.

'But they're nearly forty quid each,' I squeaked.

'Don't fuss, Lucy. We don't want our new friends thinking we're the poor relations, do we?' He tapped his card on the card reader as the woman wrapped the bottles in black tissue paper and popped them in a bag.

We found our car and Miles punched Sarah and Toby's address into the satnav. Kings Chase, Upper Strand Street, Sandwich. It sounded suitably grand. I'd been to Sandwich a handful of times as a child. It was a pretty medieval market town on the banks of the River Stour in East Kent; a labyrinth of curling narrow streets stuffed full with Georgian, Queen Anne and Tudor houses.

'It would be nice if you made a bit more of an effort,' Miles said as we headed out of Canterbury.

'What d'you mean?'

'I know you don't want to go to their house, but you spend too much time on your own. It's not healthy. You should be out socialising more, making new friends.'

Miles was probably right, but since we'd been back in the UK I hadn't had the energy for the whole getting to know people thing. It had been easy with Tess. We'd clicked the minute we'd met at a lavish barbecue held to celebrate the ruby wedding of one of the oil company execs. We'd shared a bottle of Dom Pérignon, then strutted our stuff on the dance floor while our husbands watched indulgently from the sidelines.

Tess was the first close friend I'd made since I lost touch with my old flatmates, Bex and Maddie, and I missed her intensely. But I wasn't about to plug the big hole she'd left in my life with Sarah.

'I will,' I said. 'But this doesn't feel right. Sarah and I weren't friends at school. Why would we suddenly become best buddies now? She was a bighead at school, and nothing's changed, by the look of it. And Toby is just as bad.' I pulled a face. 'They're so bloody *smug* with their huge BMW, their mansion in Sandwich and their four Boden-clad boys.'

'Are you sure you're not just jealous?'

I turned to look at him. 'Of what?'

'Oh, I don't know,' he said, tapping the steering wheel. 'Their huge BMW, their mansion in Sandwich and their four Boden-clad boys?'

I didn't reply, and instead stared out of the window as the countryside flew past. We were on the outskirts of Sandwich when Miles spoke again.

'Even if you don't see Sarah as potential friend material – and I really can't see why not because she seems perfectly nice to me – perhaps you could see things from my point of view, Luce. I have no friends in Kent, and I would like the chance to make some. You know how hard it is for me, spending half my life on the rig. It's twice as difficult to settle anywhere. And that's what you want, isn't it, for me to feel settled here with you?'

'Of course it is.' I'd grown up in Kent and moving back was like coming home, but I knew Miles had no emotional ties to the place. It could be anywhere as far as he was concerned. 'I'm sorry, I should have realised. I'll make an effort, I promise.'

'Thank you. That's all I ask.'

We were both quiet as Miles navigated the Mini through the narrow streets and past a small quay. He pulled into a space in the car park at the end of the quay and we followed Toby's directions to Upper Strand Street.

'This must be it,' I said, pointing to a perfectly symmetrical Georgian house with sash windows and stucco columns either side of the smart postbox-red front door. Kings Chase was engraved on a tasteful slate sign to the right of the door.

'I'll drive home,' Miles offered as he tugged at the brass door knocker. 'A couple of drinks might loosen you up.'

I was about to protest but thought better of it. Miles was right. A couple of drinks would help. I could feel the usual mixture of restlessness and anticipation I always felt when I needed a drink, building inside me. Not a craving, because I wasn't an addict. More a hankering, like one might hanker after a mid-morning slice of cake, or some cheese and biscuits after dinner.

I made a bargain with myself. I would stick to two large glasses of wine. Experience told me it was the optimum amount: enough to provide a crutch, a social icebreaker, but not so much that I would end up doing something I would regret when I woke the next morning with a pounding head and a fuzzy memory of the night before.

Sober Lucy was boring as hell. I was self-aware enough to know that Steaming Drunk Lucy wasn't much fun either. There was always the risk she might say something she shouldn't, or fall asleep at the dinner table, which is exactly what happened during one excruciatingly dull dinner party not long after we'd first moved to Dubai. But Tipsy Lucy was vivacious and funny, the life and soul of the party.

Yes, I thought, as we stood on the doorstep of Sarah and Toby's beautiful home waiting to be let in. Two – maybe three – large glasses of wine should do the trick.

17

The front door swung open and Toby ushered us in. He'd swapped the baby carrier for a navy apron sporting the silhouette of a man brandishing some barbecue tongs and the words 'Licensed to Grill'.

'Welcome to our humble abode,' he said, taking the two bottles of sparkling wine Miles gave him and plonking them on a walnut sideboard next to a vase of blousy powder-pink peonies.

'It's lovely,' I said dutifully, because it was. A generous hallway with high ceilings and a black and white tiled floor led into a huge room at the back of the house with an indigo-blue kitchen on the left and a vast modular corner sofa, a wood-burning stove and a wall-mounted TV on the right. Separating them was an ultra-modern dining table big enough to seat about twenty people. Bifold patio doors the width of the room looked out on to a walled garden. Everything was so tasteful, so *curated*, I felt as though I'd just stepped into the pages of an interior design magazine. One of the really upmarket ones.

I glanced at Miles. He was giving a good impression of being completely unfazed by Sarah and Toby's obvious wealth as if we rubbed shoulders with people like them all the time, but I knew that as he chatted to Toby about the unseasonably warm weather, he'd be working out how they'd made their money and just how much they were worth.

'I'm spatchcocking a chicken,' Toby said. 'Hope neither of you are veggie?' He made it sound like being vegetarian was a disability rather than a life choice.

'Sounds lovely,' I said, making an effort. 'Is there anything I can do?'

'You can have a glass of wine. Sarah'll be down in a tick. She's just giving Theo a feed. What's your poison?' Toby said, opening the fridge. 'Red, white or rosé? Or there's beer if you prefer?' He looked at Miles as he said this, but Miles shook his head.

'Something soft for me. It's my turn to drive.'

'Poor chap. Ah well, all the more for us then, eh?' he said, winking at me. God, he really was insufferable.

'Rosé for me, please,' I said, impatient to feel the first buzz of alcohol hitting my bloodstream. He handed me a glass and I took a big sip. It was cold, zinging and delicious.

'Where are the boys?' I asked.

'Upstairs, glued to their iPads, the little scamps. I was out having adventures in the woods when I was their age. They'd happily sit in their bedrooms staring at their screens all day if we let them. But it keeps 'em quiet. And while the cat's away...' He winked at me again, and I took another slug of wine. It was the only way I was going to get through this.

He led us into the garden to a large wicker-style dining table and gave a little bow as he pulled out one of the matching chairs.

'Are you sure there's nothing I can do?' I said, knowing that if I didn't keep my hands busy, I'd end up drinking more.

'No, you park yourself there and I'll bring out some nibbles.'

'I'll give you a hand,' Miles said, following Toby back into the house.

I sat back in the chair and sipped my wine as I gazed around the garden. It was small but beautifully landscaped, with wide steps leading from the patio to a raised area of lawn on which a small football net was flanked by two topiary bay trees in terracotta pots. Honeysuckle and yellow roses rambled over the far wall, and over to the right were a couple of raised vegetable beds in which lettuce and radishes were planted in ruler-straight lines.

The house and garden reeked of money. We'd met plenty of people like Toby and Sarah in Dubai. Rich, privileged couples who thought nothing of upgrading their 4x4 to the latest model or booking a week's skiing holiday in Verbier on a whim. I never coveted what they had, but Miles had always had a chip on his shoulder and a bad case of comparisonitis. I could tell him there were plenty of people far worse off than us until I was blue in the face, but I knew he would still spend the entire journey home bemoaning the fact that we were stuck in a poky two-bedroomed cottage with rising damp and an avocado-green bathroom while Sarah and Toby were living the high life in a gorgeous Georgian home.

'Need a top-up?' Toby said, appearing with a bowl of fat olives and the bottle of rosé.

'Just a small one,' I said, taking the olives from him and placing them on the table.

'Nonsense,' Toby said, filling my glass almost to the brim. 'Get that down your neck. You look like you need it.'

What was that supposed to mean? Was it that obvious I didn't want to be here? I rearranged my features into a smile and complimented Toby on the garden.

'One of the winners at Chelsea designed it a couple of years ago. Cost a fortune, but Her Indoors seems to think it was worth it.'

'What did I think was worth it?' Sarah said, plonking a baby monitor and a pile of plates on the table.

'The exorbitant amount you paid that fella for the garden.'

'Oh, it was worth every penny. Gabe has such an eye for detail. And pecs to die for. Think Constance and Mellors, Lucy.' It was Sarah's turn to wink at me.

Toby guffawed with laughter. 'In your dreams, dear heart,' he said to his wife. 'Anyway, wasn't Mellors a gamekeeper, not a gardener?'

'Toby read English at Durham before he converted to law,' Sarah explained. 'Where did you go again, Lucy?'

'Oxford,' Miles said, squeezing my shoulder.

'Brookes,' I added hastily. I hated it when he let people think I went to the elite University of Oxford and not the former polytechnic a mile down the road. Not that there was anything wrong with Oxford Brookes, but still.

'Miles said you're an author now,' Toby said. 'He says you're going to be the next J.K. Rowling.'

I wished Miles wouldn't do this too. Big up my non-existent writing career. But sometimes it was easier to tell him the book was going well than to admit I hadn't picked up the half-finished manuscript in months. I only had myself to blame.

'I wouldn't hold your breath,' I told Toby, then turned to Sarah a little desperately. 'Are you sure there's nothing I can do to help?'

She gave an airy wave. 'It's all sorted. The chicken's on the barbecue. I've thrown together a salad and there are rosemary potatoes for us and wedges for the boys in the oven. Sit and talk to me. I want to hear all about life in Dubai.'

I gave her the edited highlights: our lovely apartment on the thirty-second floor with its spiral staircase and balcony over-looking the marina; water sports at the beach club; the endless parties.

'It sounds bliss,' she said enviously. And I suppose it did, even though I'd always felt something was missing. 'What brought you back to Kent?'

'Miles was offered a promotion.' While this wasn't the actual truth, it's what Miles liked to tell people.

'What does he do?'

'He works in the oil industry.' Again, I didn't elaborate because Miles preferred to give the impression he had a shore-based executive role, not a hard, physical job on the rigs.

'You've done so much,' Sarah said. 'All I've done is stay at home and have babies.'

It was my cue to ask her about the boys, and as she droned on about their various exploits, her role as chairman of the PTA and the baby fat she was still trying to shift following Theo's arrival on Valentine's Day, I reached for my glass, surprised to see it was empty again.

Noticing, Toby pushed the bottle towards me.

'I'm sure Lucy doesn't want to hear the ins and outs of life in the mummy mafia,' he said, shooting a meaningful look in his wife's direction. Whether it was sparked by compassion or pity, I couldn't be sure, but all of a sudden I felt a wave of self-pity wash over me. Miles must have told him what happened to our baby. Just then, the garden rang with a plaintive wail, making me jump a foot in the air, sending the wine I was pouring into my glass sloshing over the rim.

Miles stiffened beside me. Toby laughed.

'It's only Theo,' he said, pointing to the baby monitor at the other end of the table.

'It's your turn,' Sarah told him, but he waved the tongs he was holding in her direction.

'I can't. I'm cooking.'

'So am I. You might be giving the chicken an occasional prod between sips of beer, but I've done everything else.'

'I'll go,' I found myself saying.

'Are you sure?' Sarah asked. 'He's not due a feed for hours. He's probably just lost his dummy.'

'Of course. I'd like to.' I pushed my chair back and stood unsteadily, shocked at how the wine had gone to my head, even though I'd only had two glasses. Two generous glasses, admittedly. Or was it three? Toby was one of those hosts who topped up your glass when you weren't looking so it was hard to be sure. I was a long way from being drunk. I just felt warm and buzzy.

'Where's Theo's room?' I asked.

'Upstairs, turn right and it's the second door on the right. Will you tell the boys supper's in fifteen minutes? They're holed up in Jude's room, which is the next bedroom along. Thanks so much, Lucy, you're a star.'

I could feel their eyes on me as I crossed the patio, heading for the house. I walked carefully, not wanting them to see I was even a touch tipsy. In the kitchen I took a tumbler from the drainer by the sink, filled it with tap water and downed it in a couple of gulps. I rinsed the glass under the tap and replaced it on the drainer, deciding in that moment that I would make my next glass of wine last the rest of the evening. That way I'd have only gone over my self-imposed limit by one glass – or was it two? – and I'd wake with a clear head in the morning.

I trailed my hand along the wall as I climbed the wide staircase and when I reached the landing I turned right and scooted along to the second door. I pressed my ear against it and reached for the porcelain handle when I heard Theo whimpering.

The curtains were closed, and the room was in darkness bar a rash of moving stars projected onto the ceiling by a small lamp next to Theo's cot.

The whimpers were building up to a full-blown cry and when I peered over the side of the cot and saw Theo's clenched fists and his little red face all scrunched up, something stirred deep in my gut.

'Come here, you poor little lamb,' I crooned, scooping him into my arms and holding him tightly against me. 'I'm here. I'll look after you.'

I walked over to the window, swaying gently from side to side, my hand cupping his crown. It felt like the most natural thing in the world to drop a kiss onto the top of his head.

'Shush, angel, don't cry,' I whispered. His little body felt reassuringly warm against me, and I was sure I could feel the pitter-patter of his heart beating next to mine. 'There, there.' I rocked and swayed and whispered endearments until gradually he stopped crying. I could have put him back in his cot then, but I couldn't bear to break the intimacy, so I continued to pace the room, Theo's head tucked under my chin and my arms wrapped around his little body.

A primeval longing for the one thing I couldn't have rose in me like a scream. I clenched my jaw and tried to shake the feeling away. But I couldn't. Tears rolled down my cheeks, splashing onto Theo's head. When the scream escaped as a sob, he turned his puckered face towards me and blinked.

'Oh, baby,' I said. 'I miss you so much. So, so much.'

18

Three years ago, I fell pregnant. Not intentionally – I would never do that to Miles – but by accident. I was twenty-nine at the time and we'd been living in Dubai for four years.

Tess guessed the day I swapped my usual latte for a pot of tea.

'Not preggers, are you?' she asked.

'Don't be ridiculous, of course not.'

'Then why are you drinking that?'

'I don't know. I didn't fancy coffee. It's not a crime, is it?'

'Are you late?'

I shrugged. 'I don't think so.' But I checked the calendar on my phone anyway, counting back to the date of my last period. And when I realised it was six weeks ago I stared at Tess in disbelief.

'Told you,' she said with satisfaction. 'You're up the duff.'

'But I haven't felt sick.'

'Not everyone does.'

'What'll I tell Miles?'

'Nothing, yet. Not until you've done a test and know for sure. When's he due back?'

'A week on Friday.' I chewed my lip. 'Will you do it with me?'

'Pee on the stick? Not likely. But I'll hold your hand. In a manner of speaking.' She stifled a snort of laughter.

'Tess, this isn't funny,' I wailed. 'This is, this is...' I broke off, because I wasn't sure what it was. The best thing that could have happened or an unmitigated disaster? The last time I'd broached the question of children the previous Christmas, Miles had completely lost his shit, punching the wall in anger.

'He'll think I did it on purpose,' I said.

'Maybe. But d'you know what? Maybe he'll be pleased.'

'Maybe,' I said, but I wasn't convinced.

The next day I arrived at Tess and Charlie's apartment before breakfast. Tess opened the door, still wearing a silk kimono over her nightdress.

'Is Charlie at work?'

'Just left.' She peered at me. 'You look like crap.'

'Couldn't sleep.' I scrabbled about in my bag for the two pregnancy tests I'd bought the previous evening but had been too scared to use on my own.

'C'mon,' Tess said, ushering me along the hallway and pushing open the door of their opulent bathroom. 'Let's put you out of your misery. Want me to stay?'

'No, you're all right.' I gave her a weak smile.

When I saw the result on the first test, I thought it might be a false positive, so I tore open the second. When that also had two clear blue lines I called Tess into the bathroom and handed her both sticks.

She took one look and hugged me. 'Congratulations, Luce. You're going to be a mum.'

I shook my head, letting it sink in. I was pregnant. Miles and I were having a baby.

I clutched Tess's arm. 'What if I've damaged it?'

'Damaged it? How?'

The previous weekend Tess and Charlie had invited me over to theirs for a meal as they often did when Miles was offshore. We'd polished off four bottles of wine between us and I'd ended up passing out in their spare bedroom, waking with a pounding hangover.

'All the booze,' I groaned.

'Millions of women drink before they realise they're pregnant and their babies are absolutely fine.'

Tess was probably right, but I made up my mind not to touch a drop of alcohol until the baby was born.

'When will you tell Miles?' Tess asked.

'When he's home.' It wasn't the kind of bombshell I wanted to drop over the phone. 'He made his first girlfriend have an abortion.'

Tess looked at me in shock.

'She wanted to keep the baby, even though they were only nineteen. But he and her parents talked her into having a termination. He drove her to the clinic and waited outside till she came out.' Without thinking, my hands cupped my belly. 'What if... what if he wants me to get rid of ours?'

'You are not nineteen, and neither is Miles,' Tess said. 'If he tries to talk you into doing anything you don't want to do, you call me and I'll be over like a shot.'

Tess's lips had thinned, as they often did when she spoke about Miles. I wasn't convinced she or Charlie liked him very much, to be honest. Invitations to theirs were much more frequent when Miles was on the rig, at any rate. 'Promise?' she said, squeezing my hand.

'Promise,' I agreed.

I started taking folic acid and stopped drinking. I made an appointment with our GP. In the early hours of the morning when sleep eluded me, I pored over pregnancy websites, absorbing the facts and stats. By the GP's calculations, I was nine weeks pregnant and our baby was the size of a strawberry. She – because I was convinced she was a girl – had eyes and eyelids, a little mouth and even a tongue with tiny taste buds. She didn't have hands or feet yet, and still looked like an alien, but that didn't make me love her any less. I was besotted by the idea of her. Totally and utterly head over heels in love.

As for me, I was noticing changes too. My breasts were bigger and my waist a little thicker. I was constantly tired and had a terrible metallic taste in my mouth, as if I'd been chewing coins. The hormones surging through my body left my emotions all over the place. One minute I was filled with happiness. The next I was in floods of tears. Every sad song on the radio or distressing story on the news made me howl.

I counted down the hours till I saw Miles with a mixture of excitement and trepidation. Mainly trepidation. I had no idea how he would react. We knew a couple at the beach club who'd claimed they were happily child-free and were planning to stay that way. When the wife had fallen pregnant unexpectedly, they'd been over the moon, and had taken to parenthood like ducks to water. They were now expecting their second child.

People change. Just because Miles didn't want a baby at nineteen didn't mean he wouldn't want one now he was in his thirties, happily married with a solid career and no financial worries. He'd make a great dad. Strict, but fair. It might take him a while to get his head around the fact that we were pregnant, but once he did, I hoped he would embrace this new stage of our lives. And if he didn't... well, if he didn't, I wasn't sure what I would do.

The day Miles was due home, I cooked rack of lamb – even though it was the last thing I felt like eating. The morning sickness had finally kicked in, and the thought of anything other than toast made my stomach heave.

He dumped his bag in the hallway and came and found me

in the kitchen, raising his eyebrows at the opened bottle of Châteauneuf-du-Pape and the lamb resting on the worktop.

'What's all this in aid of?'

'You,' I told him, dropping the peeler I was holding and giving him a hug. He smelt of oil and sweat, like he always did when he came off the rig. 'I've missed you. Why don't you take a shower? It'll only be ten minutes.'

When he reappeared, looking impossibly handsome in a white linen shirt and chinos, I pulled out his chair and poured him a glass of wine.

He must have noticed my tumbler of sparkling water because he cocked an eyebrow. 'You're not having any?'

'Not tonight.' I held out my hand for his plate and piled it high. I'd cooked the lamb to perfection, but the sight of the pink meat made the contents of my stomach roil and I had to hand him back his plate and take a slug of water to stop myself from vomiting.

'Are you ill?' Miles said. 'You've gone green.'

'Not ill, no.' I'd wanted to wait until his edges had been soft-ened by the wine but my hand had been forced. I had to tell him now. I didn't want him thinking I was hiding anything from him. 'I'm... I'm pregnant.'

Silence stretched between us for a long moment, and I stared at my empty plate, willing him to jump up from his chair, wrap me in a hug and tell me how happy he was. Instead, he carefully placed his glass on its coaster, adjusted his place mat so it was perfectly parallel with the edge of the table, and cleared his throat.

'How did that happen? Did you forget your pill?'

'No,' I assured him. I didn't want him to think I'd done this deliberately and behind his back. 'It must have been the St John's wort.'

'The what?'

'St John's wort. I've been taking it for a couple of months to help when I'm feeling a bit anxious. It's a herbal remedy, so I assumed that even if it didn't do any good it wouldn't do any harm. But the GP said it can affect the pill.'

'You've been to the doctor?'

'On Monday. He's booked me in for the dating scan in a couple of weeks.'

'And you didn't think to check the label before you took this stuff?' Miles was incredulous.

'It didn't even occur to me. I'm sorry.' I reached out a hand and touched his, heartened when he didn't snatch it away.

'How far gone are you?'

'Nine weeks. It's the size of a strawberry. It'll be as big as a small apricot next week, and fig-sized in a fortnight. Why they use soft fruit as a metric for measuring babies I'll never know.' I laughed, but it sounded forced, like someone had their hands around my neck, squeezing my windpipe.

'It's not a baby, not yet. It's a mass of dividing cells.'

'It has eyes. And taste buds,' I counter. 'Eat up. Your dinner's going cold.'

Miles drew his hand away and picked up his knife and fork.

'What are we going to do about it?' he said, spearing a piece of lamb.

I felt a swooping sensation in the pit of my stomach. 'What d'you mean?'

'I thought we agreed we weren't having children.'

You agreed, I thought. I never signed up for it. But I knew better than to point this out.

'I know,' I said. 'But accidents happen. Perhaps it's fate. Perhaps we were always meant to be parents.'

'Fate? Is that what you're blaming? You should have read the side effects of this herbal crap you've been taking. This is on you, Lucy.'

'I know, and I'm sorry. But I can't get rid of her, Miles. I just can't,' I said thickly.

Miles massaged his temples, took a long sip of his wine and gave me a calculating look.

'Miles? I said I'm sorry.'

He gave a small shake of his head. 'I know. And maybe you're right. Maybe we are meant to be a family.'

'You mean it?'

He nodded. A smile played on his lips, as if he was picturing himself as a first-time dad and liking what he saw. Then a shadow crossed his face. 'But you should have told me sooner, Luce.'

'I know.'

'No more secrets, OK?'

'No more secrets,' I assured him. 'I promise.'

19

Maybe it was the wine, maybe it was Theo's warm proximity, the baby smell of him, but all of a sudden I found it impossible to stop the memories I'd locked up so tightly from pouring out like water from a storm drain.

The antiseptic smell of a Dubai hospital. A gentle midwife explaining the difference between a late miscarriage and a still-birth. A doctor in scrubs telling me I had no option but to go through labour to have my baby. Being taken into a room and handed pessaries and a box of tissues. My waters breaking. The same midwife holding my hand because Miles was too trauma-tised to stay with me.

I have no recollection of the birth itself after half a dozen medical staff rushed in when I started haemorrhaging. When I woke, I was tucked into clean sheets and Miles was sitting by my bedside holding my hand and gazing at me with red-rimmed eyes.

'What happened?' I asked him blearily.

'I'm so sorry. We lost the baby, Luce.'

I knew that. How could I forget? The baby I'd longed for had died inside me at eighteen weeks. She was just over fourteen centimetres long, as big as a sweet red pepper. She had mastered the art of yawning and hiccupping. She could suck and swallow and twist and roll. I had started to feel her moving inside me, the fluttering sensations the midwives and baby books called quickening. And now she was dead. She would never be nineteen weeks, the size of a beef tomato. I would never know if she had inherited Miles's beautiful brown eyes or my freckly skin.

'Can I see her?'

He frowned. 'The midwife?'

'No. The baby. Can I see our little girl?'

'It was a boy, Luce. They've taken him away.'

A boy? I'd been so sure we were having a girl. The facts reassembled themselves in my head as I substituted pink with blue. The girlie shopping trips to the mall and the cute little dresses I'd imagined were replaced with images of us standing on the touchline at football matches and piles of smelly trainers. A little boy. We'd been having a little boy.

'But I want to see him,' I said, pulling myself up to a sitting position.

'Lucy, no, you can't,' Miles said, a look of panic crossing his face. He pointed to the bag of blood and the IV line in my arm I'd been too woozy to notice.

'How long before it's out?' I said, waving my other arm at the drip as I sank back into the pillows.

'They said it would take up to four hours. You lost a lot of blood.'

'While I was having him?'

He nodded. Squeezed my hand. Shifted in his seat.

'I lost our baby,' I gasped. 'Our little boy.'

Miles let go of my hand and leaned over to smooth the hair away from my face. 'What do you remember?'

I tried to think but I felt so lightheaded it was hard to pull the facts from the vivid dreams I'd been having.

I swallowed. 'Waking up at the bottom of the spiral staircase.'

He nodded, his expression grim. 'You tripped and fell down the stairs. It was an accident. You mustn't blame yourself.'

What did he mean, I mustn't blame myself? Why would I blame myself for tripping? A terrible thought struck me, but I was so frightened of the truth that seconds ticked by before I summoned up the courage to ask him.

'Had I... had I been drinking?'

He lowered his gaze. 'Don't torture yourself. It won't help.'

So, I had. The knowledge was almost too much to bear.

But try as I might, I couldn't remember much about that night beyond sitting down to eat.

I'd cooked Miles roast pork with all the trimmings because he was due back on the rig the following morning. The smell of roasting meat and sage and onion stuffing filled the apartment and a bottle of Merlot stood breathing on the worktop. Not for me. I'd been happy with water. But Miles had reached into the cupboard for a second wine flute and poured me half a glass, saying a little bit of what I fancied wouldn't hurt the baby.

The phone had rung then. It was Mum, FaceTiming from Portugal. She called every week for pregnancy updates.

Miles rolled his eyes. 'Impeccable timing,' he grumbled.

'You start,' I said. 'I'll tell her I'll call her back tomorrow.'

When I returned a few minutes later Miles was already halfway through his dinner. I sipped the wine and toyed with my food, which was already starting to congeal, while Miles prattled on about his plans for the nursery.

I wasn't surprised when the wine went straight to my head because I hadn't touched a drop for weeks, and when I began yawning Miles cleared the table and ordered me up to bed.

'Get some sleep. You've obviously been overdoing things,' he scolded, kissing me goodnight. A wave of dizziness hit me as I climbed the staircase to our mezzanine bedroom, and my legs felt like lead. Perhaps Miles was right and I was overdoing it. More likely I was coming down with the flu virus that had laid Tess up in bed for three days. But I didn't feel feverish, just so damn tired. And drunk. Even though I couldn't have been.

'I only had half a glass of wine,' I told Miles now.

'You had a placental abruption,' Miles said, ignoring me. 'It's where the placenta comes away from the uterus wall. The doctor said they're rare before twenty weeks. Not that it's much consolation.'

I gazed at my husband, taking in his red, puffy eyes, the six o'clock shadow, the creased shirt. He looked like he hadn't slept in days.

'When can I see him? When can I see our baby?'

'You can't. I told you. They've taken him away.'

'Away where?'

'I don't know. Wherever it is they take them. They said something about helping us arrange a cremation, but I wasn't really listening, to be honest, Lucy. I was more worried about you.'

'Did you take a picture?'

He pulled a face, as if I'd just waved a plate of rotting entrails under his nose. 'A picture? It was a foetus, for Christ's sake. Why would we want a picture of that?'

Shocked to the core, I snatched my hand away from him. I knew it must be different for men. An unborn child was an abstract concept for them. They didn't have the physical or emotional attachment a mother had with her baby. But his ice-cold response was breathtaking.

'There's something else you need to know,' he said, as I gaped at him. 'Something you're going to find hard to hear. Your doctor said I should wait until you're stronger before I told you, but I think it's best you know now. It'll stop you getting your hopes up. And we promised each other there would be no more secrets, didn't we?'

I stared, unseeing, at the wall behind him. Somewhere along the corridor a baby cried, and the sound pierced my heart. Whatever news Miles had, however bad it was, nothing could be worse than losing my son.

'What?' I said dully.

He took my hand again and I didn't have the energy to pull it back. 'After the birth, you haemorrhaged so badly they had to perform an emergency hysterectomy.'

It took a moment for his words to sink in. 'A hysterectomy?'

He nodded. 'They had no choice. You'd have bled out if they hadn't. The surgery saved your life.'

'So I can't ever have children?'

'I'm sorry, Lucy. I know how much you wanted to be a mum. But it obviously wasn't meant to be.'

'Go,' I said, turning my head to the wall.

'What?'

'Go. Go away. I want to be on my own.'

'But, Lucy—'

'Please, Miles. Just do as I ask for once in your life. Leave me alone.'

'I'm only trying to help you,' he said in an aggrieved voice, but I didn't have the energy or inclination to smooth his ruffled feathers. He had let them take our baby to God knows where and he hadn't even taken a photo first so I would have something to remember him by. At that moment I couldn't stand to be in the same room as him.

'Miles!' I cried.

'All right, I'm going,' he huffed. 'I'll come back when you've had time to calm down.'

A loud exhale of breath was followed by the scrape of a chair. The door clicked open and closed. I winced as I turned back round to check I was alone.

I tried to picture my tiny baby, so small he'd have fitted snugly in the palm of my hand. My perfect little wren. And I'd killed him. Because it was my fault he'd died. I must have drunk more than I remembered and fallen down the stairs, and the knowledge that I was to blame was like a hammer blow.

Fate had already meted out my punishment, taking away any chance I had of having another baby. And I had no one to blame but myself.

I cradled my head in my hands and wept for the baby I had lost, and the babies I would never have.

20

The full force of Miles's revelation slammed into me afresh as I rocked Theo in my arms in Sarah and Toby's beautiful home. Three years later, the injustice of it all still had the power to knock the wind from me. I'd have curled up in a ball in the corner of the room until the feeling had passed if I'd been on my own. But Sarah had left me *in loco parentis* and I had a responsibility towards Theo. I couldn't – I *wouldn't* – disintegrate into a sobbing heap while I was looking after him.

Theo's grizzles had quietened and his breathing had deepened as I'd paced his room reliving the past. I peered down at his face. He was asleep. His dark lashes traced the sweep of a crescent moon on his pale cheeks and every so often his mouth puckered as if he was dreaming about his next feed.

I considered placing him back in his cot, then told myself he'd only wake; he wasn't yet in a deep enough sleep. I'd hold him a little longer just to make sure. Then I remembered Sarah asking me to tell the boys their dinner was almost ready. I stepped onto the landing, following the sound of gunfire, and knocked on the door of the next bedroom along.

The oldest of the boys, Jude, was lounging in a gaming chair in front of a huge flat-screen TV. On the screen, a muscular tattooed man in army fatigues, and with what looked like a submachine gun in his hands, fired indiscriminately at anything that moved.

On the bed, the two younger boys – Henry and Freddie? – were gazing blankly at their Nintendo Switches, their thumbs flying over the control pads.

'Boys, your mum says tea's almost ready.'

'What?' Jude said, his eyes never leaving the screen.

'Your mum says you need to come down now.'

'I've just gotta finish this game,' Jude said, leaning forwards in his chair as his avatar took out a gruesome-looking alien. 'Bugger,' he said as another alien jumped out of a bush and shot at the avatar, which exploded into a million pieces. Jude flung his controller on the floor and scowled at me. 'That was your fault.'

'Why have you got Theo?' Freddie, the youngest, asked.

Without thinking, I kissed Theo's head again. He smelt delicious, of warm skin and baby shampoo.

'He was crying,' I said. 'Your mum asked me to settle him.'

'Bet she didn't ask you to kiss him. He's not yours,' the middle boy – Henry – said. With a puffed-out chest, fine, sandy-coloured hair and a cockiness bordering on arrogance, he was a dead ringer for Toby. Poor kid.

'Yeah, you could give him your germs,' Jude added, draining a can of Coke and pulling himself to his feet.

'Well, I don't have any germs,' I replied tartly, any patience I'd had waning fast. 'Downstairs, now,' I barked. 'And don't forget to wash your hands.'

The boys weaved sullenly past me and galumphed down the stairs. Theo was growing heavy in my arms and I headed back into the nursery. It was time to put him down.

'Your brothers are spoilt brats, aren't they?' I said to Theo, once I was sure they were out of earshot. 'There's no way I'd let a child of mine play those awful shooting games. Isn't there enough violence in the world without spending hours pretending to kill others for fun? Not that your mummy and daddy care one iota,' I added self-righteously.

I crossed the room to Theo's cot. 'You might have a nice house and everything,' I said, cradling his head in my hand and lowering him gently onto the mattress. 'But you'd be much happier with me. You'd be my best boy. Would you like that? Would you like to come and live with me and Miles? I would love to be your mummy.' I stroked his cheek and he turned towards me in his sleep and let out a small sigh of contentment.

'I had a baby once, Theo. But I killed him. I didn't mean to,' I said quickly, forcing down the lump that always appeared at the back of my throat when I thought about my lost baby. 'But I fell down the stairs and by the time I hit the bottom my poor little wren was gone. Thing is, Miles said I was drunk but I'd only had half a glass of wine, so how's that even possible?'

I laid Theo's fleecy blanket over him and tucked it into the sides of the cot.

'It's not really fair, is it? Your mummy and daddy have four boys – four! – and I don't have a single one,' I said, warming to my theme. 'In fact, it's the opposite of fair. It's a fucking travesty. Oops.' I clapped my hand over my mouth. 'Pardon my French, but you know what I mean.'

My head swam a little as I straightened my back and I gripped the bars of the cot to keep me steady. I was drunker than I thought.

'No more wine for Auntie Lucy today,' I slurred. 'Otherwise Uncle Miles will get very cross. Again. He's always cross, is Uncle Miles.' I sighed loudly. Talking to Theo was strangely cathartic and I could have happily stayed and chatted to him for the rest of the evening, but the others would be wondering where I was and, anyway, I was beginning to feel peckish.

'Goodbye, my darling boy,' I said, bending down to stroke Theo's forehead one last time. Tears pricked my eyes as I closed the door carefully behind me. I tramped along the landing looking for a bathroom, craving a few moments to myself before I rejoined the others.

The family bathroom was a couple of doors down from Jude's room. I let myself in, locked the door and sank down onto the closed toilet seat with my head in my hands. It really wasn't fair that one woman could have four babies, when another couldn't have a single one.

My eyes welled with tears of self-pity. I had never asked for much, never been one of those people who expected a bright, golden future handed to them on a plate. But I'd always assumed that if you went through life being fair and kind, life would be fair and kind to you. Not a bloody chance.

I pushed myself to my feet and staggered over to the sink. My mascara-smudged eyes were pink and puffy, and my lips were chapped. I looked a mess. I ran the cold tap and splashed my face with water, patting it dry on the hand towel under the sink. Then I grabbed the tube of kids' toothpaste on the side of the bath, squeezed a pea-sized amount onto my finger and rubbed it over my teeth. Finally, I dragged a hand through my hair, straightened my top and squared my shoulders. I couldn't hide upstairs forever. It was time to return to the others.

I knew something was wrong the minute I stepped out of the bifold doors. When I'd left, Miles, Sarah and Toby had been chatting like old friends, but now an awkward silence had befallen them. Even the boys, half-heartedly kicking a football into the net on the lawn, seemed subdued.

Toby was standing with his back to me, fussing over the barbecue, while Sarah fiddled with a napkin, folding it and unfolding it, her eyes firmly fixed on the ground. Miles's expression was thunderous. What on earth had happened?

Before I'd even reached the table Miles jumped to his feet, strode over and thrust my bag into my hands.

'We're going,' he said. 'But first you owe Sarah and Toby an apology.'

I grabbed my bag with one hand. The other fluttered to my throat. 'What are you talking about?'

Miles jerked his head towards the far end of the table. 'What d'you think?' he spat.

I followed his gaze, unsure what I was supposed to be looking at. The pretty earthenware bowl filled with salad? The bottles of ketchup and dressing? The pile of cutlery?

And then the blood drained from my face as my gaze fell on the baby monitor, and the entire contents of my stomach nosedived.

Shit.

This couldn't be happening. I forced myself to remember what I'd said as I'd put Theo down to sleep. How his brothers were spoilt brats. How Theo would be much happier with me. How I killed my own baby...

Shit, shit, *shit*.

'Lucy?' Miles growled. 'An apology?'

I blinked. Swallowed. Pawed roughly at the tear rolling down my cheek. I looked first at Toby and then at Sarah. 'I am sorry. So, so sorry. It was the drink talking, you know? I didn't mean it. Any of it.'

Sarah opened her mouth to speak, then closed it again. Toby gave the slightest nod, then turned back to his barbecue. You could cut the atmosphere with a knife.

'I'm sorry,' I said again, as Miles took my elbow and guided me along the length of the patio and out of a side gate.

We walked back to the car in silence. In fact, it wasn't until we were almost home that he turned to me and said, 'Have you any fucking idea how embarrassing that was for me?'

I didn't trust myself to speak because he had every right to be livid. I would have been too if the roles had been reversed.

'Did you not stop to think even for a second that we'd be

able to hear every word you said?' He put on a whiny voice, mimicking me talking to Theo. '"You'd be my best boy. I'd love to be your mummy. Of course, I killed my own baby. I didn't mean to, but I was drunk." *Again.*'

I recoiled at the blatant hatred in his voice, curling in on myself, my arms wrapped around my chest like a shield. But it couldn't deflect Miles's rage.

'I offered to drive so you could have a couple of drinks to loosen up, not so you could get pissed out of your head. I'm tired of it, Lucy.'

'I'm sorry.'

'Not good enough. I've had it up to here.' He jabbed the top of his head with his index finger, then glanced at me. His glacial expression sent a shiver down my spine and I hugged myself tighter. 'Look at the state of you. You're out of control. You make me sick.'

'It won't happen again,' I promised. 'I'll stop drinking.'

He shook his head. A muscle was pulsing in his jaw. 'I've heard it all before.'

'But this time I mean it. I managed it when I was pregnant. I didn't touch a drop.'

A bitter laugh escaped his lips. 'Until you did.'

His words stung, but even Miles couldn't heap more guilt on me for our baby's death than I'd already heaped on myself.

'I'll phone Sarah in the morning, apologise properly. I'll make everything right,' I said.

Miles swung into our driveway and slammed on the brakes, almost running over Percy, who had been stretched out on the gravel enjoying the sunshine. Miles yanked up the handbrake, switched off the ignition and balled the keys in his fist so tightly the colour bled from his knuckles.

'You don't get it, do you?' he said, banging his fist on the steering wheel. 'It's too late for apologies. Too fucking late.'

21

Two months may have passed, but the sting of shame I feel as I remember that awful day is as sharp as it was at the time. Sarah's distress. Toby's discomfiture. Miles's barely suppressed rage.

I kept my promise and phoned Sarah the very next day. When she didn't pick up, I left a long, grovelling apology on her voicemail, leaving my number and offering to buy her lunch to say sorry. I wasn't surprised when she didn't call back.

Miles gave me the silent treatment for days. It was as if I didn't exist. I was used to his sulks – I could tease him out of them if I put my mind to it – but this one lasted until the day he drove back up to Aberdeen. Usually I hated saying goodbye, but his anger had cast such a black cloud over the cottage that I felt only relief as he slammed the front door behind him.

The weird thing was, when he rang the next day, it was as if the whole episode had never happened. And I didn't question his change of heart. I knew I'd been in the wrong, and I was just pleased he appeared to have forgiven me.

Wren's fleecy blanket has worked itself loose and I tuck the ends carefully back under the mattress of the Moses basket. I'd forgotten Theo was a Valentine's Day baby, which would make him almost four months old, the same age as Wren, if I've guessed correctly. When the woman in the pharmacy asked Wren's age, I thought I'd plucked the fourteenth of February out of the air, but had I?

Could Wren be Theo?

I slide from the sofa to the floor and sit cross-legged on the rug, my chin resting in my hands and my elbows on my knees as I gaze at Wren and try to remember.

I picture myself walking up the wide staircase in Sarah and Toby's perfect house towards Theo's nursery, my hand trailing along the wall. Easing the door open to be met by the Milky Way projected onto the ceiling. Bending over the cot to see Theo's face all red and scrunched up. I rub my eyes and peer into the Moses basket at Wren. In repose, his face is smooth and untroubled, making it impossible to compare.

Was Theo's hair a shade or two lighter? It was too dark in the nursery to be sure. I exhale loudly, the puff of air catching Wren's cheek and he stirs in his sleep.

If Wren was Theo, surely I'd know it by now. If someone had taken him, Sarah would have been straight on to the police, pointing the finger at me.

'And I can tell you exactly who took him. This crazy woman I went to school with. We heard her tell Theo she wanted him to go and live with her. Yes, that's right, Officer. She actually told him she'd love to be his mummy.'

The police would have been knocking on my door within the hour. But twelve hours have passed since I found Wren in the living room and no one has called. I can't even be sure anyone has reported him missing.

I chew my bottom lip, mulling it over for a while, then have a brainwave. I pull out my phone and open Facebook. I'm not friends with Sarah, but I am friends with a girl who used to knock around with her at school. Tanya Cummings née Wentworth was even louder and posher than Sarah, and had tracked me down on Facebook when she'd been organising a school reunion a few years back. I'd accepted her friend request safe in the knowledge that living in Dubai gave me the perfect excuse not to go.

I find Tanya's profile page, click on 'See all friends' and scroll through the hundreds of results, amazed that anyone can know so many people. Finally, I find what I'm looking for: a photo of Sarah in ski gear on the top of a snow-covered mountain.

Hoping she's lax about privacy settings, I click onto her profile. I'm in luck. The most recent photo she's posted is of their second-youngest son, Freddie, sitting on a slide in a children's playground with Theo squashed between his legs. Both boys are laughing. It's such a lovely photo, spontaneous and joyous, that I find myself smiling too.

It takes less than a second for me to reassure myself the baby asleep in front of me is not Theo. Theo's brow is much higher than Wren's and the shape of his eyes is all wrong. Wren's ears stick out more and his cheeks dimple when he smiles. Theo's don't.

Even though I'm as convinced as I can be that these are two very different babies, I still read the caption with trepidation.

Happy boys waiting for their brothers to finish school. I check the date it was posted. June 9 at 2.55 p.m. This afternoon.

It's all the confirmation I need. Wren is not Theo, and Theo is with Sarah, where he belongs.

My head spins with relief. Or is it fear? I can't honestly be sure. Because I may have found the answer to one question, but I am no closer to discovering the truth.

I still have no idea whose baby I have taken.

22

I give Wren his last bottle of the day with half an eye on the *News at Ten* but the coverage is dominated by the latest political scandal at Westminster and there's nothing about a missing baby.

I blow raspberries onto Wren's belly as I change his nappy. Percy watches us from the doorway, a look of deep mistrust on his face. I call him over and eventually he caves in and stalks towards us, his tail erect.

'Percy, meet Wren. He's staying with us for a little while, so please play nice. Wren, this is Percy. He may give the appearance of being aloof, but he's a big softie at heart.'

I hold my hand out and Percy sniffs it cautiously. Seeing him, Wren pumps his arms and legs in excitement.

'You're a cat person, are you?' I lift Wren out of the Moses basket and hold him on my lap so he can get a better look at Percy. Giggling, he tries to grab Percy's tail but the cat wheels away and disappears through the door.

It occurs to me that it probably would have been sensible to have turned the lights off and fed Wren quietly in the dark instead of revving him up, but it's too late now – he is wide awake.

I lay him on the sofa and hand him the toy zebra I bought him. I snuggle up next to him, curling my body around his so he can't fall off, and stroke his head until, eventually, we both fall asleep.

A shaft of light is streaming through a gap in the curtains when I wake with a start, panicked that I might have rolled onto Wren in the night. Or, worse still, that I've fallen asleep curled around a cushion and Wren was nothing more than the product of a particularly realistic dream. But when I prise my gritty eyes open, relief surges through me. Wren is real, and he's still sleeping soundly beside me, his hands balled into fists above his head, the zebra by his side.

Once we're both washed, dressed and fed, I carry Wren back into the living room and do my usual checks of the news websites while Wren tries, with varying degrees of success, to grasp his toes. I've just opened the *BBC News* app when I hear the crunch of gravel outside.

It can only be the delivery driver with Miles's new phone, which means I won't have to wait in all day after all. Which also means I have no excuse not to take Wren to the police station this morning.

I pull myself to my feet. 'You stay here,' I tell him. 'I won't be a second.'

I'm halfway down the hallway when the door opens inwards and the sight that greets me is so unexpected, I let out a little yelp of surprise.

Miles is standing in the doorway, his keys in one hand and his holdall in the other.

'Miles!' I gasp.

'Now there's a guilty face if ever I saw one,' he says, dropping his keys in the wooden bowl on the sideboard. 'Anyone would think you've got something to hide.'

'What are you doing here?'

'I live here.' Miles's voice is jovial but a muscle is twitching in his jaw. 'Unless you'd forgotten.'

'I mean, you're supposed to be in Scotland,' I say, my eyes darting towards the living room door.

'I've quit. I told you yesterday.'

'Don't you have to work your notice?'

'I've been given gardening leave, so there didn't seem much point hanging around. I drove through the night to miss the traffic. Why, aren't you pleased to see me?'

'Of course I am,' I say. 'It's just that—'

'Just what?'

'Nothing.' I step forwards and take his bag. 'You must be exhausted. Come into the kitchen and I'll make you a cup of tea.'

Miles sits on a kitchen chair and bends down to pet Percy as I flick the kettle on and busy myself fetching mugs and teabags. My hands are trembling so badly the teaspoon slips through my fingers, clattering onto the floor. My mind is racing. Wren's going to start grizzling for his mid-morning feed any minute. What the hell am I going to do? Sneak him into the shed while Miles is upstairs having a shower? Pretend I'm looking after him for a friend? But there's no way I'm shutting him in the shed, and Miles knows the only friend I have is a seven-hour flight away in Dubai.

As I set the mug on the table, boiling tea sloshes over the rim, scalding my fingers.

'Dammit!'

Miles is on his feet in an instant, guiding me over to the sink and holding my hand under the cold tap until the pain eases.

'Are you all right?' he says, handing me a tea towel. 'You seem very tense.'

'I'm... I'm fine.' But I'm not. I'm all out of options. I'm going to have to tell him about Wren and face the consequences.

But first, I let him drink his tea. I watch him as he sips, his hands wrapped around the mug. There are bags under his eyes and his skin has a grey tinge of exhaustion. Not surprising if he's driven through the night to get here.

I lay a hand on his shoulder. 'You look shattered. Can I get you something to eat? Scrambled eggs?'

He nods and, grateful to buy myself a few extra minutes, I pop a couple of slices of bread in the toaster and break three eggs into a bowl.

'How did work take the news that you'd quit? I bet Jim was gutted.' Jim was Miles's boss on the rig, a straight-talking Glaswegian he'd worked with in Dubai until Jim and his wife Maeve made the move back to the UK a couple of years ago when their youngest daughter started university. When we moved back Jim pulled a few strings, finding Miles a job on his rig in the North Sea.

Miles makes a non-committal noise.

'He didn't try to talk you into staying?'

'Why would he? He knows it's been on the cards for a while.'

I slide the plate of scrambled eggs onto the table and pass Miles a knife and fork. He attacks the food as if he hasn't eaten for days, and when his plate is cleared accepts my offer of more toast.

'You won't miss Scotland?' I ask. Jack Quinn was born and raised in Inverness and although Miles didn't have a good word to say about his father, he was proud of his Scottish roots. He always said the only time he'd been happy growing up was when Jack had driven the family up to Scotland every July to spend their summer holidays in a remote crofter's cottage in the Cairngorms.

Miles would spend hours on his own, hiking through the

mountains, tracking herds of red deer and scouring the skies for golden eagles and osprey. When he hit his teens, he would take his tiny one-man tent and wild camp under the stars or in the shelter of the vast forests of Scots pines.

I loved it when he told me about those holidays. The tiny stone croft with a peat fire and views of the glen. Watching the sun set at ten o'clock at night, and staying up to see it rise again just a few hours later. The natural high from a swim in the freezing loch and the time he saw a family of otters playing on the shore. He made the Cairngorms sound magical, but every time I suggested we go, his face shut down. I suppose it stirred unhappy memories too, so I never pressed it.

'No,' he says shortly. 'I'm done with the place.'

He pushes his chair back and I know I have to tell him about Wren now, before he walks into the living room and discovers him for himself. I straighten my shoulders and take a deep breath.

'Miles, there's something I need to show you.'

'Can it wait until I've had a shower?'

'No, it can't. I'm sorry.' I attempt a smile, but it's a half-hearted affair, the corners of my mouth barely lifting. I squeeze his arm. 'In here,' I tell him and he follows me into the living room.

Anxiety flutters in my chest like a trapped bird. Wren is sleeping soundly in his Moses basket. I hold my breath and step aside so Miles can see him.

His eyebrows concertina. 'Lucy, why is there a baby in the house?'

23

Miles stares at me, unblinking.

I clear my throat. 'I... I found him.'

'What d'you mean, you found him? Where?'

'That's the thing. I don't know. I woke up yesterday morning, came downstairs, and he was here, fast asleep, in that.' I point to the drawer, which I still haven't returned to the bureau. 'Like the stork brought him.'

'The stork?' Miles scans the room, taking in the proliferation of baby paraphernalia that has accumulated in the short time Wren has been here. The nappies and sleepsuits, the baby carrier and car seat. The wipes and soft toys. I search Miles's face for clues, but his expression is closed. He's giving nothing away.

I perch on the edge of the sofa and pick at a loose thread. 'I'm being facetious. There is no stork, of course there isn't.'

'Then how the hell did he get here?'

I drop my head and mumble, 'I think I might have stolen him.'

'Stolen him? From where?' Miles slumps onto the sofa next

to me as my words sink in. He drags his hands down his face. 'Jesus, Lucy. What have you done?'

'I can't remember taking him,' I say quickly. 'But I'd had a bit to drink, so...'

'When?'

'The day before yesterday. I went into Canterbury to see the dentist, like I told you. After my appointment I had a sandwich in the Westgate Gardens and bumped into an old friend from school who suggested going for a drink.'

Well, it was almost the truth.

'What friend?'

Telling Miles I spent the evening with Pete, a guy I'd had a crush on when I was a teenager, is going to make an appalling situation much worse. One little white lie can't hurt.

'Anna. You don't know her.'

'Is it her baby?'

'No.'

'Jesus Christ.' He jumps to his feet and starts pacing the room, just as I had when I found Wren yesterday morning. It's impossible to believe it was only twenty-four hours ago. Wren is already as familiar to me as my own husband, if less unpredictable. I look from one to the other, trepidation gnawing my insides. Miles stops by the window, his hands thrust deep into his pockets, and stares out into the garden. 'Where was this drink?'

'In the ABode. We had a few. I must have caught a taxi back. I... I can't really remember.'

'You can't *remember*? For fuck's sake, Lucy.'

'I know. I'm sorry,' I say again. 'I found him, Wren, yesterday morning when I came downstairs. He was just there, asleep in the drawer like I said.'

'Wren?'

'It's what I've been calling him. Just while he's here. Because he's so small. He reminded me of... of... our little boy.'

Our eyes meet and a flush creeps up Miles's neck. He finds it hard to talk about the baby we lost.

'And you didn't think to tell me you'd found a baby?' he says.

'I was going to take him to the police station yesterday, but he needed a feed, so I didn't. And so I was going to take him this morning, but then you asked me to stay in for your phone, so I couldn't.'

'Don't you dare lay the blame for this on me. You could have rung them.'

'I know.' I hang my head. 'I just thought it would be easier to explain in person.'

'Is that right?' Miles's voice drips with sarcasm. 'It's not because you didn't want to hand him in at all?'

'No one's reported him missing, Miles. That's the thing. No one even cares he's gone. Perhaps he's better off with us.'

He stares at me in disbelief. 'Are you out of your mind? You genuinely think that if you don't tell anyone about him no one will know anything's wrong and you can keep him here forever?'

I'm trying to dredge up an answer when Wren cries out, and the sound is so surprising it's like a jump scare in the cinema and we both startle.

Miles turns on his heels and stalks back to the window as I scoop Wren out of the Moses basket and cuddle him close.

'I'll take him this afternoon,' I promise, because I know I have no choice. It's what I should have done the moment I found Wren yesterday morning. 'I don't suppose you'd come with me?'

Miles snorts. 'Not a fucking chance. I've cleaned up enough of your messes over the years. You're on your own this time, Lucy.'

The whole cottage shakes as Miles slams the front door.

Moments later, his Audi shoots out of the drive and Wren and I are alone again.

He reaches up and grabs my ear and I kiss his forehead, then press his face against mine, his skin smooth and warm against my cheek.

'Want some milk, angel?' I ask, blowing a raspberry into his neck to make him giggle. Normally, the sound is like a shot of pure joy straight into my veins, but this time the joy is tinged with sadness that my time with Wren is almost at an end.

Miles was incandescent, but what did I expect? I've stolen a baby. There's no other explanation, and the sooner I face up to the fact the better. Taking Wren to the police will be the hardest thing I've ever done, but I know in my heart he can't stay here. He's not mine to keep.

He plays with my hair as I warm the feed I made up earlier, squirting some on my wrist to make sure it's not too hot. I fix a bib over his sleepsuit and he slots comfortably into the crook of my arm to have his bottle.

For all I know, Miles might even be on his way to the police station right now. Would he turn me in? My self-righteous husband is happy to bend the law when it suits him, like the time he talked me into taking the rap for a speeding ticket because he'd have lost his licence for six months if he'd taken the three speeding points himself. But would he bend the law for me? I have no idea.

When Wren has finished his bottle, I change his nappy and put him in his car seat on the kitchen table so he can watch me wash up. I grab a wooden spoon from the jug on the worktop and check every millimetre for splinters before giving it to him. Soon, he's waving it like a conductor at the Royal Albert Hall, a beaming smile on his face. He's happy here. The thought is almost exquisitely painful. Whatever happens to me when the truth comes out, I know I would have made a good mother. I should take comfort from that.

I call Miles. When he doesn't pick up, I leave a message on his voicemail.

'Miles, it's me. I'm sorry. Really, really sorry. But I'm going to make this right. I'm taking Wren to the police station. I know your phone is supposed to be arriving, but I'll stick a note on the door telling them to take it next door. I'll give Arthur a ring and ask him to sign for it. I'll call you from the station once I know what's happening. I love you.'

Next, I phone Arthur. He's lived next door to Grandad for over forty years. They used to play golf together, switching to bowls when they hit their seventies and their knees started protesting too much.

'Of course, Lucy, love. How are you and Miles?'

'We're fine,' I say, feeling a prickle of guilt that I don't go round to see him more often. 'Miles is going to be home a lot more now, actually. He's left the rig.'

'Has he now?'

'Mmm.' Grandad never bothered to hide the fact that he thought I could have done a lot better than Miles, and I get the sense Arthur's not that impressed with my choice of husband either. But their generation thinks anyone who hasn't done national service is a waste of space. 'Listen, I'd better go. Thanks so much, Arthur. I really appreciate it.'

I scribble out a note to the delivery driver and stick it to the front door, then find a couple of shopping bags. It takes an age to gather all Wren's things. It's a metaphor, I think, as I rescue a bib from down the side of the sofa. His belongings have found their way into every corner of the house just as he's crept into every corner of my heart.

Life without him seems unthinkable, but the sadness I feel is mixed with relief, fuelled by the knowledge that by taking him to the police station I'm doing the right thing. He should be with his real mum, not me.

'Hey, buddy, we need to go,' I tell him as I lift the car seat off the table and carry it to the front door. I load all the bags into the boot first, then strap the car seat in, yanking the seat belt twice to check it's secure before tweaking Wren's nose. He dissolves into giggles, so I do it again. It's as addictive as alcohol.

Tonight, I will drink myself into oblivion.

The thought is in my head, just like that. And it calms me. Alcohol will be my reward for giving up the one thing I have wanted all my life: a baby. I will drink until I'm numb, and when I wake up, I'll do it all over again. Drink, sleep, repeat. And that is how I will get through this.

24

Just as I'm imagining taking the first velvety sip of a full-bodied Merlot, I remember with horror that I can't drink until I'm numb, because Miles is home. And Miles has no idea how much I drink when he's away. No idea at all.

Feeling doubly bereft, I check Wren's seat belt one last time, then clomp around to the driver's side, wrench open the door and collapse into the seat. I open Google Maps on my phone, tapping in the police station's address, even though I know exactly how to get there, then fiddle with the rear-view and side mirrors. Distraction techniques. I pull down the sun visor and check I haven't got anything stuck in my teeth. Finally, having run out of excuses, I switch on the ignition and ease the car into reverse.

I hear the other vehicle before I see it. A guttural growl as it roars down the lane. And then it flies into the drive, brakes squealing and gravel flying. I slam on my own brakes and the Mini jerks to a halt, inches from the bonnet of a silver Audi that has slewed to a stop, blocking the drive. Miles's car.

Miles jumps out and sprints to my door, wrenching it open.

He squats down so his face is level with mine. His expression is wretched.

'Don't go to the police, Lucy. I don't want you to go.'

He's not making sense. He's the one who said I couldn't keep Wren here forever. 'But you said I needed to sort it out. And that's what I'm doing. I'm putting it right.'

'No.' He leans across me and snatches the keys from the ignition. 'I don't want you to.'

'I don't understand.'

He runs a hand through his hair. I've never seen him so agitated.

'Come back into the house and I'll explain.'

Just the thought of being inside the cottage, with its low ceilings and tiny windows, makes me feel claustrophobic.

'Not the house. The garden.'

He nods, and before I have unclipped my seat belt he is around the other side of the car, lifting Wren's car seat out of the Mini. He leads me along the path to the back garden and puts the car seat on the wooden-slatted table by the rockery. I sit on the bench next to it, expecting Miles to sit beside me, but he stands stiffly, his hands thrust in his pockets. There is a pent-up energy about him, a simmering beneath the surface that hints he could explode at any minute. It's unnerving. I sit on my hands and wait for him to speak.

'I don't want you to go to the police. You'll be arrested for child abduction.' He pulls his phone from his back pocket and waves it at me. 'I've been looking. There was a woman who stole a baby from outside a hospital a while back and she was detained in a secure psychiatric unit indefinitely. Indefinitely, Luce. She can only be released with the approval of the Secretary of State for Justice. And this woman only got as far as the car park with the baby before she was caught. You've had this little one for almost two days.' He glances at Wren, who is playing with his feet, and something remarkable happens. His face softens. Then he turns back to me.

'What if they send you to prison? You could be away for years. And imagine how baby snatchers are treated in a women's prison. You'd be eaten alive.'

I hadn't thought much beyond arriving at the police station, if I'm honest. I suppose I'd assumed they'd take Wren with a polite, 'Thank you very much, Mrs Quinn,' as if I was handing in a wallet I'd found in the underpass. But I've been fooling myself. Taking a baby is about as serious an offence as you can get. I picture myself in handcuffs being led to the dock in a courtroom, a judge peering at me over half-moon spectacles as he sends me down for ten years. Even if I only served half my sentence, I'd be almost forty before I was released. Practically middle-aged.

I realise Miles is talking again.

'I've been thinking about what you said, about the fact that no one's reported the baby as missing. What if you took him from a family that really doesn't give a shit? What if someone gave him to you?'

'I don't think—' I begin, but Miles cuts across me.

'You don't know. You can't remember.' His lips curl slightly and I brace myself for a lecture on the evils of alcohol, but it doesn't come. Instead, Miles finally sits next to me and takes my hands in his.

'What if you're right? What if he could have a better life with us?'

'Don't you think he should be with his real mum?'

His hands grip mine tightly. 'What if it's karma, Luce? We lost a little boy, and now a little boy has found us.'

The possibility Wren has been gifted to us by the universe to replace our own baby is so seductive it's impossible to argue with him and I feel myself weaken. But what about Wren's mum? His family? I can't take him just because I want him. Life doesn't work like that.

'But you'd be complicit if anyone ever found out,' I reason. 'You'd go to prison too.'

He leans forwards and tucks a loose strand of hair behind my ear. 'Not if they can't find us.'

I stare at him open-mouthed. 'What d'you mean?'

'We could go to Scotland.'

'*Scotland*? I thought you said you'd had enough of the place.'

'Enough of the rigs, not enough of the Highlands. We could stay in the croft we used to visit when I was a kid. It's available to rent, I checked. And it's miles from anywhere. Think about it, Lucy. Up there, you could pretend the baby's yours. And if we ever did come back down to Kent, you could tell people you had him up there. Some women don't show until they're six or seven months pregnant, I've checked.'

There is so much to unpick in this that for a moment I'm speechless. Miles wants us to move to Scotland and bring Wren up as if he's our child? It's not just absurd, it's bat-shit crazy.

'What do you mean, if we ever came back to Kent?' I focus on this, because of all of Miles's suggestions, it's the easiest to address.

'Surely you can't want to live here forever?' He waves an arm at the cottage, at Grandad's shed, the fruit bushes still waiting for me to net them. 'It's suffocating. It's... it's like we've gone to bed one night in our thirties, and woken up the next day in our seventies. You'll be wanting me to join Arthur in a game of bowls next. It's sucking the life out of me, Lucy.'

I watch a robin drinking from the bird bath, its chest puffed out and its eyes beady.

'Scotland's so vast and wild. It makes me feel alive. You'd love it, Luce, I know you would. And Sonny Jim here,' he says, nodding at Wren, 'he'd love it too. All that freedom and space to explore.'

Miles was like this when he was trying to convince me to move to Dubai with him, extolling the merits of the city: the tax-free earnings, the amazing social life and fantastic apartment we'd have. All the trappings of an ex-pat life. And when I'd wavered, he pulled an engagement ring out of the bag and it was enough to convince me.

This time he's luring me with a baby.

25

'Well?' Miles looks at me expectantly, his face animated. 'What do you say?'

I shake my head. It's all too much to take in. 'I don't know,' I answer eventually. I look around. 'What would we do with this place?'

'Rent it? Sell it? We'd be able to afford a palace up there for the price of this hovel.' He sees me bristle. 'Come on, you can't seriously want to live here for the rest of your life?'

'I love it here.' I pick at a patch of lichen on the arm of the seat. What would Grandad think of this hare-brained scheme? Selling his beloved cottage and schlepping up to Scotland with someone else's baby? He'd think I'd lost my mind, that's what he'd think.

But I know from experience that Miles won't stop going on about it until he gets his own way, so I exhale slowly and meet his gaze.

'I'll think about it, all right?' He goes to speak but I hold up my hand to silence him. 'It's the best I can do.'

'Just remember I'm doing this for you, Lucy. If you take that baby to the police, they'll chuck you in prison and throw away the key. I'm offering you a way out. I am prepared to do this because I love you. But my offer won't last forever. I need to get back to the letting agent if we're going to take the croft. You have until the end of the week to decide what you're going to do.'

Miles is a model husband for the rest of the day. He always is when he wants something. He helps me net the fruit bushes while Wren watches from his car seat, then replaces the piece of broken glass in the greenhouse that I've been asking him to fix for weeks. At lunchtime, he finds an old tartan picnic rug in the boot of his car and lays it under the gnarled apple tree by the vegetable garden before assembling a picnic of cheese, bread and pickles.

'I'll pop to the supermarket this afternoon,' he says. 'There's not much in the fridge.'

'Sorry. I was going to go on my way back from the police station.'

'Is there anything Sonny Jim needs?'

Wren is lying on the picnic rug beside me, arms and legs pumping as he stares up at the kaleidoscope of leaves as they flutter in the breeze.

'We could probably do with some more milk and nappies. I'll write you a list.'

I breathe a sigh of relief when the Audi pulls out of the drive. Miles has barely left my side since he's been home, and his constant presence is beginning to overwhelm me. He'll back off if I agree to go to Scotland with him, but until then he'll be overly attentive, as if subconsciously he's showing me what I'll be missing out on if I say no.

I put Wren down for his nap and spend the next hour pottering in the kitchen, sweeping the floor, wiping down surfaces and cleaning the windows and oven. I wash Wren's bottles and place them in the steriliser, then remember the bag of his clothes I'd left in the Mini. Once I've checked he's still dead to the world in his Moses basket in the living room, I poke through the bowl of odds and sods on the sideboard in the hallway, looking for the Mini Cooper key ring Miles gave me when we bought the car.

There are coppers and old batteries and a tape measure in the bowl and – randomly – a packet of dental floss, but no keys. I check the coffee table in the living room, my handbag and Wren's changing bag but they're not there either.

I call Miles. He answers immediately.

'Lamb steaks or pork loin? What d'you fancy? Apart from me, of course.' He laughs.

'Have you seen my car keys?'

'Car keys? Why would you need them?'

'Because I left a bag of Wren's clothes in the Mini.'

'Oh, right. Hold on a sec.' There's a muffled noise as if he's placed the phone between his head and shoulder, and then he's back. 'Sorry, Luce, they're in my pocket. I must have picked them up by accident.'

'Right.'

'I'll be home in half an hour. It can wait till then, can't it?'

'Of course.'

'Love you,' he says.

'Love you too,' I reply, and he is gone.

It is only when I am giving Wren his bottle later that it crosses my mind that Miles might have taken the keys deliberately, rendering me carless so I couldn't drive to the police station and hand myself in.

Miles is still in an uncharacteristically chipper mood when he arrives home from the supermarket, laden with bags of shopping.

'You didn't say which you preferred, so I bought lamb steaks. We'll have them with new potatoes and tenderstem broccoli. I'll cook,' he says, handing me a carton of milk, which I put in the fridge.

'Sounds delicious.'

'And that Rioja you like was on offer. I bought a couple of bottles. That should last you tonight.' He guffaws, then sees my face and holds his hands up in supplication. 'Only joking.'

We finish unpacking the shopping in silence, then Miles says, 'Oh, I almost forgot. I've left something in the car. I thought it might come in useful. It's on the back seat if you want to get it.' He dangles his keys from his finger and I swipe them from him, lips pursed.

On the back seat is a pearly-white baby bath. I pull it out. Inside the bath is everything you could possibly need for a baby's bath time. Baby sponges and nappy cream. Johnson's baby shampoo and a bubble bath specially formulated for babies' sensitive skin. A pack of blue sleepsuits and three yellow rubber ducks. A baby bath book. There's even a fluffy hooded towel and wash mitt set. Miles has thought of everything, and something thaws inside me.

I hoist the bath onto my hip and head back into the house. Miles is in the living room, hunched over the Moses basket. He looks over his shoulder as I come into the room.

'He's waking up,' he whispers. 'Does he need a feed?'

I check the time. 'He had eight ounces a couple of hours ago,' I whisper back. 'He's not really due another feed till bedtime. We'll leave him for a bit. He might settle himself.'

We creep out of the room, and I pull the door to behind me.

'Thank you,' I say, gesturing to the bath. 'This was really thoughtful. We made do with the washing-up bowl last night.'

'Only the best for my boy,' Miles says, taking the bath from me and carrying it into the kitchen. And even though I know Wren's not really our boy, pleasure sweeps through me.

Later, while Miles lays the table and prepares our tea, I fill the bath with warm water, swirling a generous squirt of baby bath until I can't see the water for bubbles.

Wren laughs out loud when he sees the bath, his arms and legs pumping in excitement. Miles stops scrubbing potatoes and kneels down beside me. He scoops a handful of bubbles up and dabs them on his nose.

Wren squeals with laughter. It's infectious, and I find myself laughing too, especially when Miles gives himself a white moustache and beard to complete the look.

'You're a natural,' I tell him, wetting the wash mitt and running it across Wren's face and down his chubby arms.

'That's what comes of having a sister so much younger than you.'

'I didn't know you helped out with Justine when she was a baby.'

'There's a lot about me you don't know.' He winks and I roll my eyes, and Wren gurgles with happiness and if I could bottle this moment, preserve it forever, I would, because it is all I have ever wanted. A perfect little family.

The water's growing cold, so I hold out my hand and Miles squeezes a thimbleful of baby shampoo into my palm. I lather it into Wren's hair, then use the mitt to rinse it off, careful not to let the water run into his eyes.

Miles holds Wren's new towel ready and I lift him out of the bath and wrap him in it. With his apple cheeks and rosebud mouth, he looks ridiculously cute in the little hood. How is it possible no one is missing him?

If he were mine, I wouldn't let him out of my sight, not even for a second.

And then I remember that Wren can be mine. I can have my perfect little family. Me, Miles and Wren. All I have to do is tell Miles I will come to Scotland with him. All I have to do is say yes.

26

We eat at the kitchen table, Wren in his car seat by our feet, playing with the bath book Miles bought him. The lamb is delicious, pink and tender, and the potatoes are slathered in butter and mint from the garden. It's the first decent meal I've had in days, and I eat greedily, accepting a second helping of potatoes when Miles offers them, not caring about the calories.

He pours me a large glass of wine without asking if I actually want one, and when I protest, he cocks his head and asks what's wrong.

'Nothing.' I try to hide the irritation in my voice. Miles always does this and it drives me insane. Encouraging me to drink then having a go at me when I – inevitably – drink too much. He did it all the time in Dubai. He did it when we went to Sarah and Toby's. He even encouraged me to drink when I was pregnant. And the consequences of that were catastrophic. It's not his fault. I should have stopped at half a glass that night. I just wish he wouldn't undermine my flimsy resolve not to drink. Every. Bloody. Time.

I push the glass across the table towards him. 'I want to make sure I hear Wren if he wakes in the night.'

'Suit yourself. All the more for me,' Miles says. He takes a sip and smacks his lips together. 'God, this is good. You don't know what you're missing.'

That's where he's wrong. I know exactly what I'm missing. A longing to take a deep slug of the smooth, oaky Rioja has pushed all other thoughts from my mind. To feel its soft tannins sliding down my throat and into my bloodstream. And there's nothing to stop me having a glass. Just one. It would be the perfect accompaniment to Miles's beautifully cooked lamb. My right hand, resting on the table, tingles with the urge to grab the glass back. My fingers are literally trembling. I snatch my hand away before Miles notices. I can't have one glass, because one will lead to two… three… five. I'm just the girl who can't say no.

And I can't do that to Wren.

Miles disappears while I clear the table and I hear him clumping above me in the small box room I used to stay in when I was a kid. He reappears with a stack of books in his hands. I recognise them at once. *The House at Pooh Corner*, *The Water-Babies*, *Alice in Wonderland* and *Through the Looking-Glass*. The books of my childhood.

'Oh!' I exclaim. 'Grandad used to read those to me when I was little.'

'I remember you telling me. You said they're what made you want to be a children's author.' He scratches his chin. 'I know they're too old for Sonny Jim but I remember when Justine was born Mum said it was never too early to establish a bedtime routine.'

'You never call him Wren.'

Miles pulls a face. 'It's a wussy name for a boy. His name could be George or Leo for all you know.'

Miles is right, of course. I have no idea what his real name is. But I had to call him something.

126 A J MCDINE

'Or Archie or Max,' Miles continues, warming to his theme. He pretends to take off a helmet and deepens his voice. '"My name is Maximus Decimus Meridius, and I will have my vengeance in this life or the next."' His impression of Russell Crowe is surprisingly good, and I can't help but chuckle. 'Max is a better name than Wren,' he says in his normal voice.

'I know, but Wren suits him, don't you think?'

'Actually, I don't. Why would you name him after a tiny bird when you could name him after a shit-hot gladiator? He'll have the piss ripped out of him at school.'

I gape at Miles. 'You're thinking about school already?'

'Sure, why not? There's a village school a twenty-minute drive from the croft. He'll go there.'

I fold my arms across my chest. 'I haven't decided we're coming yet. And, anyway, don't you think you're getting a bit ahead of yourself? I mean, the police could turn up on the doorstep at any moment.'

He frowns, his grip on the stem of his wine glass tightening. 'And why would they do that?'

'I don't know. Maybe someone became suspicious and reported me to the police. Like the woman in the baby shop. Or Claudie.'

'Who the fuck is Claudie?'

'The woman who used to run the post office. She saw me with Wren yesterday. I had to pretend I was looking after him for Tess and Charlie while they went to a wedding.'

'But Tess and Charlie live in Dubai. They don't even have a baby.'

'I know that, but I had to tell her something, didn't I? And anyway, they are having a baby. Tess is four months pregnant. She's due in November.'

Tess's momentous news is evidently of no interest to Miles, who leans back in his chair and clasps his hands behind his head. 'You're being paranoid as usual. No one has called the police because no one cares.'

'Or they can't call the police because something has happened to them.'

'What d'you mean?'

'What if his mum's been hurt, you know, in some kind of domestic incident or stranger attack? What if I happened to stumble upon him while she lay dying in the bushes just out of sight?'

Miles's chair thwacks back down on the floor with a thud. 'Now you're being ridiculous. Are you going to read his story, or am I?'

'We could do it together, all snuggled up in bed,' I suggest, hoping to appease him. 'And when we've put Wren down you can find us a film to watch.'

'Sure. Have you made up a bottle?'

'In the fridge. I usually heat it up in a bowl of boiling water.'

Miles fills the kettle and flicks it on while I find the Pyrex bowl I use to warm Wren's milk. While the kettle's boiling, Miles crouches down in front of Wren and shows him the books, one by one.

'Which one d'you want, Maximus? Winnie the Pooh, Alice or some swimming babies?' Wren tries to grab the dog-eared copy of *The House at Pooh Corner*.

'Good choice. That was always my favourite too,' I tell him.

Miles disappears into the living room to find the Moses basket while I fetch a clean bib and Wren's blanket.

Miles is taking his new role as surrogate father very seriously, but this is of no surprise to me.

Ever since I've known him, he has jumped from hobby to hobby as his interest waxes and wanes. It goes something like this: Miles discovers a new activity. It's usually something one of his workmates on the rig tells him about. Over the last decade this list has included, but is not limited to: boxing, scuba diving, rock climbing, kite flying, fell running, playing the guitar, golf and photography.

The interest becomes an obsession, and Miles spends hours researching everything there is to know about the new activity. Next, he kits himself out with all the gear he could possibly need, with little thought to the cost. I call it the Shiny New Thing Syndrome, although I'd never say it to his face. But, seriously, we could open a shop with all the abandoned equipment he's bought over the years. Wetsuits and regulators, climbing shoes and harnesses, power kites and camera lenses. You name it, we have it.

Miles throws himself into his new hobby with the fervour of a zealot, hungry for the dopamine hit his new passion will provide. Conversations revolve around aretes and belays (rock climbing), BCDs and shot lines (scuba diving), and downswings and double bogeys (golf).

This phase can last from a couple of weeks to several months. And then boredom sets in. Miles realises his new obsession is actually a bit harder than he envisaged. He catches on to the fact that he could spend a lifetime learning to play the acoustic guitar and he'll never be as good as Eric Clapton. It takes months of training to be able to hold his own against people who have been fell running for years. Mastering photography takes time and patience. Patience he doesn't have.

His enthusiasm withers and dies, and he moves on to the next shiny new thing.

It's a constant surprise he hasn't substituted me for a shiny new wife, to be honest.

I wonder how long Miles's laser-like interest in Wren will last. Probably until Wren's first bout of vomiting and diarrhoea, or when he wakes Miles in the night once too often. Then there's a very real possibility that he'll be cast aside to make way for the next shiny new thing. But that's OK, because Wren will always have me. And I'm going nowhere.

27

The next few days are without doubt the happiest of my life. Wren, Miles and I are cocooned in a little bubble, safe from the outside world. We spend the long summer days in the garden under the shade of the apple tree, lying either side of Wren as he kicks and plays on the picnic rug. When Wren naps, Miles takes my hand and leads me upstairs to bed and we make love silently, urgently, my legs wrapped around his back, his hands tangled in my hair.

Every evening at six on the dot, we give Wren his bath, and every time Miles dabs bubbles on his face he dissolves into peals of laughter. This joke never grows old. We give him his bottle cuddled up together on our bed, Miles and I taking it in turns to read *The House at Pooh Corner* while Wren sucks his thumb and his eyelids grow heavy.

Miles cooks dinner while I tidy Wren's things and tackle the small mountain of washing he generates every day.

If it sounds like domestic bliss, it is. Miles is loving and attentive, not just to me but to Wren too. The nickname Maximus has stuck, although Miles shortens it to Max more often than not. And I can see now that Miles is probably right, that while the name I chose might be great for a four-month-old baby, it wouldn't necessarily suit a fourteen-year-old boy. And so I find myself calling him Max in front of Miles, although he will always be Wren to me.

Our little gladiator goes to sleep like an angel, waking like clockwork at three every morning, and I stumble out of bed half-asleep to warm his bottle before his cries rouse Miles. I feed him in the old armchair by the window, in silence and with no eye contact, because Miles has read it's better not to overstimulate babies in the middle of the night, which makes perfect sense when you think about it.

Miles has read so many parenting websites he's a walking encyclopedia on babies. The man who claimed he never wanted kids has already looked up the latest Ofsted report for the little village school in the Highlands he wants Wren to attend. He has researched the best baby backpack to buy, and he is fully genned up on practices for baby-led weaning.

I try to recall if he was like this when I was pregnant, but my memories of that time are hazy. Even the few things I do remember feel like they happened to someone else. When I confided this to Tess one night before we left Dubai, my tongue loosened by one too many vodka tonics, she told me she suspected I had dissociated myself from the whole sorry episode.

'What d'you mean?' I asked her.

'Your brain has blocked the memory of the miscarriage in an attempt to protect itself. I suppose you could say it's a form of escapism,' Tess explained.

'But I remember every bloody detail about the hospital, the midwives, the birth. They play on a loop in my brain. What I can't remember is what happened before. Getting drunk. Falling down the stairs. Killing the baby,' I added quietly.

Tess took my hand and gave it a squeeze. 'It was an accident. It wasn't your fault.'

'You don't know that. You weren't there. I was drunk, Tess. I was pissed out of my head as per fucking normal.' I pushed my empty glass away.

'So Miles says,' she said eventually.

I sat up in my chair. 'What's that supposed to mean?'

'You can't remember. It's only natural you believe his version of events.'

'But you don't?'

'I didn't say that. Something might trigger a memory one day. Just because what happened is locked in your brain doesn't mean it's not there.'

'How d'you know all about this stuff, anyway?'

'My dad was in the military. He was sent to deliver humanitarian aid to the Kurds after the First Gulf War. He came back with a Tabasco bottle of desert sand and PTSD.' Tess shrugged. 'He dissociated to forget the things he'd seen. It took years of Mum's nagging, but he finally went to see a psychiatrist who diagnosed him with dissociative amnesia. His brain had responded to a trauma he couldn't control by creating gaps in his memory.'

'I suppose it makes sense,' I said. 'It's like compartmentalising bad memories, shutting them in a box and chucking away the key.'

'That's the perfect analogy,' Tess agreed.

'And your dad? Is he better now?'

Her gaze flickered to the ceiling. 'He blew his brains out a week before my twenty-first birthday.'

I'd pushed back my chair and gone round to hug her, and we never spoke of dissociation again but, three years later, I find myself thinking about what Tess insinuated that night. How I had been naive to believe Miles's version of events. But why wouldn't I? There's no question I was drunk. I remember the wine going straight to my head, the wave of dizziness hitting me as I climbed the stairs. And then nothing until I regained consciousness at the bottom of the stairs, bar an excruciating pain in my abdomen and the awful realisation that something terrible had happened and it was all my fault.

'Penny for them,' Miles says, prodding my foot with his big toe.

We are sprawled out on the picnic blanket again, Wren sandwiched between us. He is chewing his zebra, a look of intense concentration on his face.

'I was just thinking we should buy Wren – sorry, Max – some teething rattles.'

'I'll add them to the list.' Miles has been putting together an Amazon order for the things we'll need in Scotland, even though I still haven't agreed to go.

I prop myself up on an elbow and take the zebra away. Wren's face crumples so I give it back to him.

'You think he's teething?' Miles asks, sitting up.

'I don't know, but it would make sense.'

'They normally don't get their first teeth until about five months. I was reading about it yesterday,' Miles says. 'Trust the little man to be one step ahead of the competition.'

This makes me think of all the milestones Wren's mum is going to miss. Not just his first tooth but the first time he sits up on his own, the first time he crawls. His first steps, the day he masters riding a bike, his first day at school. All those major life events she won't be there for, and the knowledge pricks my bubble of domestic bliss and it bursts around me, just like that.

'What's wrong?' Miles says, watching me closely.

'Have we lost our minds? We can't keep him,' I say, jumping to my feet. 'We need to call the police right now and tell them everything. Wren – Max – needs to be with his real mum where he belongs.'

Miles frowns. 'What's brought this on? You've been quite happy to keep him until now.' His face clears. 'You're worried because his mum's not going to see his first tooth?'

'Aren't you? We're not his parents, Miles!'

'All right, don't get hysterical.' Miles stands too and takes a step towards me, a calming hand outstretched as if he's stopping traffic, but I bat it away. It's like a mist has lifted and I'm seeing things clearly for the first time in days.

'I have done something terrible and I need to put it right. All this,' I say, sweeping my arm over the picnic rug, Wren's toys, Wren himself. 'It isn't real life. We're living a lie, can't you see?'

'We've been through this,' Miles says. 'They'll throw the book at you if you hand yourself in.'

'So what? I deserve everything I get and more. I stole a baby, Miles. And yes, it is about his mum not seeing his first tooth, his first steps and his first day at school. I can't steal those from her too. I just can't.'

'Don't lose sleep over that bitch,' Miles spits, and I stare at him, my jaw dropping. He shrugs. 'What kind of mother doesn't report her baby as missing? And before you ask, I checked all the news websites an hour ago. There's nothing on them. She doesn't give a shit, I'm telling you.'

'Maybe she doesn't, but what we've done, what we're doing, it's still wrong. Surely you can see that?'

Miles sinks onto his haunches and strokes Wren's cheek. Wren turns to look at him, gurgling with delight.

'What exactly are you proposing to do?' he asks.

'Call the police and tell them everything. It's OK, I'll say you were in Scotland and had nothing to do with any of it. But I have to, Miles. I don't have a choice.'

'Everyone has a choice,' he says roughly. 'Clearly, you're choosing your conscience over me and the baby.'

'That's not fair, I—'

'Do me one thing,' he says roughly. 'Wait until tomorrow before you call them. Let us have one last night together. You owe me that.'

Will one more night make a difference? I suppose not.

'OK,' I say. 'One more night.'

Miles gives a curt nod, turns on his heels and stomps back to the house, shoulders hunched and his hands balled into fists at his side.

'Miles,' I call after him. 'I'm sorry.'

I know he hears me because he shakes his head. But he doesn't stop.

28

We go through the motions at bath time, playing the parts of a happy family, but when Miles gives himself a bubble beard even Wren's laughter seems forced. The atmosphere in the cottage is thick and heavy, as though a storm is brewing, and I suppose it is of sorts. A shitstorm.

I try not to think about what's going to happen in the morning, instead imprinting everything I can about Wren on my memory. The softness of his peachy skin against mine; the contented sigh he makes when he sees his bottle; the way his cheeks dimple when he smiles. I drink him in, I inhale him, because I know that soon all I will have are memories.

When Wren snuggles up in the crook of my arm to have his bottle I have to hand *The House at Pooh Corner* to Miles to read, because my eyes are blurry with tears.

'You don't have to do this,' Miles says quietly, as he flicks through the pages to find where we left off last night, when I was still kidding myself we could be a family.

'I do.' I attempt to swallow the lump that's wedged at the back of my throat, but it's going nowhere.

Wren is asleep in minutes but I don't follow Miles downstairs straight away. Instead, I busy myself sorting laundry and tidying the clutter on my dressing table while I get my tears in check. Crying won't soften Miles, the mood he's in. I might want him to hold me, wipe my tears away and tell me everything is going to be all right, but he finds it hard to deal with emotions at the best of times. Stiff upper lip is the way to go.

In the bathroom, I wash my face and blow my nose, then head downstairs where Miles is making chilli. I lay the table and fix us both a glass of water.

'I hope it's not too hot for you. The lid fell off the chilli powder when I was tipping it in,' Miles says when we eventually sit down to eat.

I take a mouthful and try not to wince. I'm not a fan of spicy food and the heat in the chilli scorches the back of my throat. I take a sip of water, my eyes streaming. 'Lovely,' I say.

He raises an eyebrow and carries on eating. I try to make conversation, but it's like talking to a wall, and halfway through the meal I give up altogether and we finish the chilli in silence.

I yawn as I clear the plates and stack them in the ancient dishwasher. The interrupted nights must be catching up with me. I'm knackered. Bone-tired. I chuck a dishwasher tablet in the bottom of the machine because the door of the detergent compartment fell off years ago. As I straighten, I'm hit by a wave of dizziness and have to grab hold of the worktop until the room stops spinning.

It takes an inordinate amount of time to wipe the surfaces down and empty the bin. My movements feel slow and deliberate, like I'm operating at half-speed or wading through water.

I shuffle into the living room. Miles is lounging on the sofa, his feet on the coffee table, channel-hopping. He doesn't look up.

I clutch the doorframe to stop myself from swaying.

'I'm going to have an early night. I'm bushed,' I say, but the words come out as one long jumble. *Imgonnahaveanearlynight-Imbushed.*

Christ, I must be really shattered.

Miles finally looks at me and smiles.

'Sleep tight,' he says.

Sunlight is streaming through the curtains when I wake. As I lift my head to check the time on the clock radio – it's just after nine, a couple of hours later than I usually wake up – the room swims in and out of focus. There's a pounding behind my temples and my tongue is thick and furry.

I feel like death. I must be ill. When I had the flu last summer I was laid low for a week. Exhaustion, coupled with a thumping headache, swollen glands and a hacking cough, left me as spaced out as a zombie. I felt so poorly I could barely lift my head off the pillow. Perhaps Miles brought something back from the rig.

I move my head infinitesimally slowly to check his side of the bed but it's empty.

'Miles?' I croak, but there's no answer. He must be with Wren.

Wren! I drag myself to a sitting position, even though the movement causes an explosion of pain in my head.

Did Wren wake in the night? I scrabble through my memories of the previous evening like a bargain hunter tearing through racks of clothes in the January sales, but I have absolutely no recollection of anything after loading the dishwasher.

I throw the duvet off and slowly swing my feet out of bed. When I had the flu, I had terrible brain fog, but this doesn't feel like that. It feels more like a... like a hangover.

But it can't be. I only drank water last night. I haven't had a drop of alcohol since the day I found Wren in the living room. *The day of your last hangover*, the voice in my head taunts. I drag my hands down my face and stare at the floor, and that's when I see it. The neck of a bottle poking out from under the bed. I curl my right foot around it and kick it out. It spins on the wooden floorboards like a bottle on a Ouija board.

I groan out loud and bury my face in my hands, shame blooming in my stomach. Not again. Please, not again.

I peek through my fingers at the bottle, which has come to a rest, the neck pointing straight at me like an accusatory finger. It's my favourite brand of Absolut Blue Vodka. My go-to tipple when I'm seeking oblivion. Forty per cent proof and smooth enough to drink neat, although I have never, ever drunk it straight from the bottle.

Just like the night I brought Wren home, my memory has vanished, as if it has been sucked into a black hole. I remember Wren's bath time, the too-spicy chilli, telling Miles I was having an early night. And then... nothing.

29

Suddenly my phone springs into life, dancing on the bedside table next to me. I grab it gratefully. Anything to distract me from the well of self-pity I'm in danger of falling into.

'Hey, babe,' Tess says. 'Just checking everything's cool.'

I swallow, but it does nothing to lubricate my parched throat. 'Hi, Tess.'

'Ker-rist, are you ill? You sound terrible, mate.'

'Not ill, no,' I say, licking my lips. 'Had a bit of a sesh last night, if the empty vodka bottle by the side of the bed is anything to go by.' I laugh, as if getting hammered is all a bit of a jape and not the car crash it really is.

'Ah, while the cat's away...'

'Actually,' I say, looking over my shoulder to check Miles isn't standing in the doorway, listening in. He isn't. 'The cat's back. He's left the rig. He handed in his notice on Friday.'

'Bloody Nora, what brought that on?'

'He says he's had a gutful. It's been on the cards for a while.'

'What'll you live on, fresh air?'

I give a hollow laugh. 'He thinks I'm the next bestselling

author and publishers will be staging a bidding war over my debut novel.'

'Bugger me.' Tess is the only person in the world who knows I'm barely halfway through the first draft of my first book.

'Yes, it sucks. But that's not the half of it.'

'What d'you mean?'

The urge to tell Tess everything that's happened since I woke up with a hangover on Friday morning is almost too much to contain, and I'm about to offload when I check myself. It's not fair to saddle her with my mess just to ease my own guilt. Instead, I sigh. 'Miles wants us to move to Scotland.'

'Scotland? I thought you loved your grandad's little cottage.'

'I do. But Miles has become a bit fixated about it. You know what he's like.'

I try not to read too much into Tess's silence.

'Anyway, what did you mean, you wanted to check everything was cool?' I ask.

'Ah, you know. About the baby and everything.'

'Oh, Tess, don't be silly. I'm thrilled for you. Really.' I hope I sound as sincere as I feel, because I really am over the moon for her. 'How're you feeling?'

'Human again, thank goodness. Although I'm still getting up at least three times a night to pee. Hey, you know how you always found it funny the way the medics used food as a way of measuring babies? This little fella's as big as a pomegranate and weighs as much as a ball of mozzarella already, can you believe it?'

'Wait till it's the size of a melon,' I tease, and Tess yelps.

'Rub it in, why dontcha?'

'Sorry, couldn't resist.'

We giggle and, clearly relieved I'm not as fragile as she feared, Tess says she has to dash because she's running late for her aquanatal class.

We say goodbye and I flick through my phone aimlessly,

putting off the moment when I have to go downstairs and face Miles. I automatically check the *BBC* website, then scroll through the top stories on *Kent Online*. Finally, I open Facebook and check the handful of Canterbury residents' groups I found the other day. There's nothing about a missing baby.

I'm just about to click away when I spot a message request on Messenger. I open it, curious to see who it might be from as I rarely post anything these days.

> Hello Lucy, I hope you don't mind me contacting you like this, but I need to talk to you. Call me, please?

There's a mobile number at the end of the message and a name. Shona MacDonald. Frowning, I click on the woman's profile. The privacy settings mean I can only see her profile picture, which, rather unhelpfully, is of a waterfall on a misty day. I dredge through my memory but her name doesn't ring a single bell. That doesn't mean I haven't met her, of course. The ex-pat community in Dubai was huge and people came and went all the time. It was impossible to keep track of them all.

Whether or not I've met this woman before, her imperious tone rankles. 'Call me, please,' indeed. If she thinks I'm going to phone her straight back she can think again. She probably assumes I'm still in Dubai, has heard I used to work in publishing and wants me to give a talk at her book club or something. Not a chance.

I close Messenger, not caring that she'll see I have opened, read and ignored her message. My head is still thumping and my need for a cup of tea is greater than my fear of the inevitable dressing down I'm going to get from Miles.

It's only then I realise how quiet the cottage is. Too quiet. By now Wren is normally sitting in his car seat on the kitchen table, babbling away to himself as I clear the breakfast things, the radio on in the background. Miles would be back from his morning run, sweaty but smiling as he scoops Wren out of his car seat and waltzes around the room with him in his arms.

Perhaps they're in the garden. I push myself off the bed and shuffle to the window that overlooks the back garden, but there's no sign of them there. I edge out of the room and head downstairs, trying to ignore the stab of pain behind my eyes every time I take a step.

They're not in the kitchen, nor are they in the living room or the dining room. I ease the front door open. My Mini is where I left it, but Miles's car has gone. Flashes of our argument last night pierce the fog in my brain. *Don't lose sleep over that bitch... she doesn't give a shit... you're choosing your conscience over me and the baby.*

Did Miles have a wake-up call last night and realise I was right, that we couldn't keep Wren forever? Has he taken him to the police station to spare me? A sob rises from my gut at the thought that I might never see my baby boy again.

But he was never mine, and I was a fool to think he ever could be.

I crumple onto the doorstep and let the tears come, hard and fast, until my throat is raw and my eyes are swollen slits.

30

I have no idea how long I sit on the doorstep, hugging my knees and wishing I could turn the clock back to yesterday afternoon when life was perfect, before I ruined everything. But at some point, the crunch of wheels on gravel penetrates my misery and I look up to see Miles's Audi pull into the drive.

It's only as I drag myself to my feet that I realise I'm still in the shorts and T-shirt I was wearing yesterday. I sniff my armpits and grimace at the faint trace of stale sweat, smooth down the T-shirt and hover by the front door.

Miles jumps out of the car. My heart plummets when he doesn't immediately reach for Wren's car seat but instead pings open the boot and pulls out a couple of shopping bags. It can only mean one thing. Wren's gone.

I try a smile and hold out my hands for the shopping as Miles stomps towards me, but he pushes past, his mouth in a disapproving moue.

'Where's Wren?' I burst.

His face darkens. 'Max. Where's *Max*? And why the fuck do you care, anyway? You'd rather be drinking yourself into a stupor than looking after our baby. Where were you when he woke in the night, crying his poor little heart out? Comatose in bed, snoring your head off, pissed, that's where. Don't pretend to give a damn when it suits you.'

'Come on, Miles, don't be like that. Of course I care.' My gaze darts nervously to the Audi. 'Where is he? What have you done with him?'

He jerks his head towards the car. 'He's sleeping.'

Thank God. Relief makes me light-headed and my grip on the doorframe loosens. 'I'll fetch him.'

'Leave him where he is,' Miles growls. 'You've done enough damage for one day.'

His words sting like whiplash and I flinch, but Miles hasn't finished. 'Look at the state of you,' he sneers. 'You're a fucking mess.'

'I know, and I'm sorry. I don't know how it happened. I can't even remember having a drink last night. I can't remember anything.'

My chin sinks to my chest and I grab a handful of my hair and give it a vicious tug, as if I could pull the memories from my ossified brain if I used enough force.

Miles continues to watch me with distaste. 'That's the trouble, isn't it? You never can.'

31

There's a wail from the car. I don't care what Miles says. I'm not leaving Wren in there on his own. I scuttle over, wincing as the gravel cuts into my bare feet, and yank open the rear door. Wren's face is working, his eyes glassy with tears. I cover my face with my hands, then open them as if they're a pair of patio doors and say, 'Boo!'

He is so taken aback that his eyes widen and his mouth forms a perfect circle. I do it again, and this time he can't stop himself letting out a garbled noise halfway between a wail and a gurgle of laughter. By the third time the tears are forgotten and he is in fits of giggles. I look up at the cottage, but Miles has already disappeared inside. I plant a kiss on Wren's head and carry the car seat towards the front door, relieved that he at least has forgiven me.

I find Miles in the kitchen unpacking packets of baby formula into a cupboard.

'I'm sorry,' I say again, pushing a bag to one side to make room for Wren's car seat.

He runs a hand across his face. 'Just forget it, OK?'

I nod, pick up a pouch of organic puréed sweet potatoes that's fallen out of the bag and pretend to study the ingredients.

'I thought you'd taken him to the police station,' I say after a while.

'And why would I do that? I told you, he's better off with us.'

Wren's eyes are tracking from Miles to me and back again as if, even at the tender age of four months, he knows his future lies in our hands.

'Perhaps you're right.' I hand Miles the pouch and he slots it into the cupboard. 'I won't go to the police. I'm probably over the limit anyway.'

Miles finally smiles and it's as if the sun has come out from behind a dark storm cloud, and its warm rays are a balm to my skin.

After lunch, Miles straps Wren into the baby carrier and we go for a walk up onto the North Downs. I'm content to listen as Miles outlines his plans for the croft.

'The garden's south-facing and there are raised beds and a small polytunnel where we can grow all our own veg. We'll need to be organised, because the nearest supermarket is miles away, so we can't just pop to the shops for the paper or a pint of milk. But there's a big chest freezer in the lean-to, and a fish and chip van comes to the village every Thursday. It's a bit of an event, as you can imagine.'

'How d'you know it still comes? You haven't been for almost twenty years.'

'Oh ye of little faith. I checked the village's Facebook page.'

I stop to catch my breath. 'That reminds me. You don't remember a woman called Shona MacDonald, do you?'

He's still striding up the hill, so I have to run a few paces to catch him up.

'Don't think so. Why?'

'She sent me a message on Facebook.'

'Saying what?'

'Asking me to call her. She didn't say what it was about. I must have met her in Dubai.'

'She'll be after something, you know what those women are like. She'll be wanting you to join some committee or other. She probably thinks we're still out there.'

'That's what I thought.' We reach a kissing gate and I stand back to let Miles and Wren go through first.

'I'd ignore her if I were you,' Miles continues, as he holds the gate open for me. He pulls me towards him and kisses me lightly on the lips. A dart of lust fizzes through me and I kiss him back.

'We'll be happy in Scotland, Luce,' he says when he finally pulls away.

'I know,' I say, and in that moment I believe him absolutely.

As we walk back to the cottage we pass the pub. People are sitting at the picnic tables outside, sipping pints and enjoying the sunshine.

'Why don't we pop in for a quick drink?' Miles suggests.

The thought of alcohol turns my stomach. 'I'm bushed. But you go. I'll take Max and make a start on tea.'

Miles unclips Wren's baby carrier and I hitch it on and do up the straps. I stand on my tiptoes and give Miles a peck on the cheek. 'Have fun.'

Back at the cottage, I lay a sleepy Wren in his Moses basket and scan the contents of the fridge. There are a couple of salmon fillets that need using up. We can have them with new potatoes and mange tout from the garden.

My phone rings just as I'm letting myself out of the back door. It's Tess.

'I know you've probably got mumnesia, but even you must remember you phoned me already today,' I say, laughing.

'I know that,' Tess says steadily. 'Is Miles there?'

'No, he's at the pub. Why?'

'I just wanted to check I heard you right. You said he gave in his notice at work, right? On Friday?'

'That's right,' I say, mystified.

'Only I mentioned it to Charlie when he got home and he went really quiet and I knew something was up, so I told him if he didn't tell me what was wrong, I'd put his original Lego Millennium Falcon on eBay when he was at work, and you know how much he loves that thing, more than he loves me, probably. So he told me.'

'Told you what?'

'Miles didn't give in his notice. He was sacked, Luce.'

'That's not true. Charlie must have misunderstood.'

'Miles didn't turn up for the helicopter one day and it had to leave for the rig without him. When his manager tried to contact him, his phone was turned off and he wasn't replying to emails. Charlie says an unauthorised absence isn't usually a sackable offence, and sometimes employees will be given retrospective permission for a leave of absence, say if a family member suddenly fell ill or they had last-minute childcare issues. And even if they couldn't offer a reasonable explanation for the absence, they would receive a written warning the first time it happened.'

Tess is speaking quickly and the line isn't great, so it takes a moment for her words to sink in. But it still doesn't make sense.

'Even if all that is true,' I say eventually. 'Why did they sack him?'

Tess sucks in air. 'Ah, well, Charlie says it wasn't the first time it had happened. Miles was on a final warning, apparently. That's why they gave him the boot.'

When I don't reply, Tess says, 'I'm so sorry. I'm only telling you because I love you and I think you ought to know that Miles has been lying to you.'

'I'm sure he would have told me in his own time. Things have been a bit crazy here.'

Of course Miles hasn't found the right time to sit me down and tell me. Our focus has been on Wren since he's been home.

'That's the thing, Luce. It didn't happen last week. Charlie says Miles's last unauthorised absence was in February. That's when he was sacked. Four months ago.'

32

Tess's call has sent me reeling. I sit at the kitchen table with my head in my hands, replaying the conversation, telling myself she must have got the wrong end of the stick. But, hard as it is to believe, Tess has no reason to make it up. What would she gain from it? Nothing.

She might give the impression of being a pleasure-seeking party girl, but beneath the surface she is one of the kindest, most empathetic people I have ever met. She was there for me after I lost the baby. Miles had grown tired of my tears by the time he flew back to the rig. But Tess came over to the apartment every day so I wasn't on my own. For three weeks she held my hand and listened to me weep. She bought me maternity pads and stroked my brow and then listened to me weep some more. I have no reason to doubt her.

Even so, something is nagging at me. Something that doesn't add up. It's only when my gaze falls on the empty shopping bags hanging on the back of the door that I realise what it is. We've been fine for money these last few months. Miles hasn't said anything about tightening our belts, at any rate. I've been buying petrol and food as normal. I paid the garage over five hundred quid for the Mini's service and MOT. I even ordered some new patio furniture for the garden, and not once has my debit card been rejected.

There's no way we could have covered the bills for the last four months with no money coming in. I just need to check our statements to confirm Miles is still being paid.

Miles handles our finances and has the banking apps on his phone. But he has yet to go completely paperless and keeps the statements in a set of files in a bookcase in the dining room.

I'm about to check when the back door bursts open and he appears, his cheeks flushed and his eyes ever so slightly glazed.

'Did you have a nice time?' I ask, flicking on the kettle.

He shrugs. 'Made a change. And it's not fair if you're the only one who gets to go out and get pissed, is it?'

I let this go and make two mugs of tea.

'Where's Max?' Miles asks.

'In the living room having a nap. He crashed out the minute he finished his bottle. Must be all the fresh air.'

I hand Miles his tea and sit opposite him.

'How are we for money this month?' I ask.

'Why?'

'I wondered if there was enough in the current account for a buggy for Wren... I mean Max.'

'Depends how much they are.'

I open Amazon on my phone and scroll through a couple of pages of buggies. 'Anything from fifty upwards.'

'Do they have any running ones?'

I change the search parameters and keep scrolling. 'This one has good reviews.' I hand Miles my phone.

He glances at the picture. 'Order it.'

'Are you sure? It's over three hundred pounds. And now you're not going to be working...'

'I told you, I'm still getting paid while I'm on gardening leave,' Miles says belligerently. 'We're fine for money. Order it.'

'OK.' I add the buggy to the basket and the payment goes through without a hitch. I sip my tea and reflect. If Tess is right and Miles hasn't been paid for four months, where's all this money coming from?

33

Miles sticks to my side like glue for the rest of the afternoon and I don't get a chance to check the bank statements. When he stifles a yawn as we're bathing Wren I seize the opportunity, reaching out to touch his arm.

'You look shattered, love. Why don't Max and I sleep in the spare bedroom tonight so we don't wake you?'

Miles never so much as stirs when Wren wakes for a feed, but I'm counting on the fact that he can't resist being made a fuss of. He lifts Wren out of the bath and lays him on a towel and I pat him dry and slather him with baby cream.

'Actually, I am feeling a bit drained, now you come to mention it. I think I might be coming down with something.'

'You poor thing.' I feel his forehead. 'Gosh, you do feel a bit hot. What you need is an early night. Would you like me to make you a Lemsip?'

'Yes, please,' he says feebly. 'Can I have a bit of honey in it?'

'Of course you can. Come on, Maximus, let's get you dressed and we'll go and make Daddy a Lemsip.'

It's a gamble, calling the man who never wanted children

Daddy, but as I glance at Miles he is watching me fix the poppers on Wren's sleepsuit with a goofy smile on his face.

I wait until eleven o'clock before I creep out of the spare room and hover outside our bedroom door. Miles is snoring softly, his breathing deep and regular. He's always been able to sleep anywhere. He says it's a legacy of shift work where you have to grab a nap when you can.

Satisfied he's fast asleep, I tiptoe down the stairs and across the hallway to the dining room. I sit cross-legged in front of the bookcase and pull out the first black lever arch file. I flick furtively through the bank statements using the torch on my phone for light. I don't know why it feels so underhand given they're all joint accounts. I suppose it's because Miles has always looked after our financial affairs. He's financially literate. I'm not sure I even know what an ISA is.

The first file is for the NatWest account we use for all our household outgoings, from the extortionate heating oil bill to our council tax and water rates. I remember Miles telling me he'd set up a standing order to transfer a thousand pounds into this account from our main current account on the first of every month. We call it the budget account and any money left over at the end of the month sits there as our rainy-day fund. I check the balance on the most recent statement. It's £1,423.69, which sounds about right.

I pull out the next file. This is for our instant access savings account. Miles calls this one our Maldives fund. Looking at the statements, we transfer £250 from our current account into this once a month. The balance stands at just over five grand.

So far, everything is just as it should be, and I wonder yet again if Tess got her wires crossed.

The third file is for our current account and I scan the income and outgoings on the most recent statement. Miles gets paid on the 28th of every month. As an experienced offshore drilling worker, he earns a pretty decent salary which, after tax, is £2,655 a month. I run a finger down the column of figures and there it is: a credit of £2,655 on 28 May. I flick through the previous three statements, and the payment appears like clockwork on 28 April, March and February.

I sit back on my haunches. Miles told me he was on gardening leave, in which case he would still be getting paid. A publishing executive at the imprint I used to work for was given three months' gardening leave when she joined a competitor, so she didn't poach authors or share any sensitive information with her new company. I can't imagine a situation where it would be necessary for an oil rig worker to go on gardening leave, but that doesn't mean it's not possible.

I keep flicking absently through older statements when something catches my eye. Miles's January salary came from the oil company, as you'd expect. I flick back to the March statement. That month the £2,655 came from another NatWest bank account. I feel a prickling of unease.

The only other bank account we have is a NatWest online savings account, which has a higher rate of interest and is where we've been keeping Grandad's inheritance while we decide what to do with it. I want a conservatory and to put the rest in premium bonds. Miles wants to upgrade his seventeen-year-old Audi A4. The money's been sitting in the account until we reach a compromise.

I can't remember the account number, so I pick up the fourth and last file, which is for the online account. The first thing I notice is the balance. There's just over £40,000 in there. Grandad left me a little over £50,000. Ten thousand pounds unaccounted for. My chest tightens. I run my index finger down the line of figures, hoping for the best, expecting the worst. And there they are. Four withdrawals of £2,655 over the last four months. The money has been transferred from this account to our current account on the 28th of every month since February.

Miles has been using Grandad's money to pay himself a salary for the past four months. Tess was right. He hasn't worked on the rigs since February. That nonsense about being on gardening leave is a crock of shit.

I have proof Miles has been lying to me. The question is, why?

34

I sit at the kitchen table, my hands clasped around a mug of tea, my thoughts spiralling. Going to bed is pointless. There's no way I'll ever sleep now I know Miles has been lying to me for the past four months.

Why didn't he just tell me he'd been given the sack? I'd have understood. And I'd have gladly used Grandad's money to live on while he looked for another job. He only had to ask.

Charlie told Tess that Miles had been dismissed for unauthorised absences, which doesn't make sense. Of the two of us, Miles is the punctual one, the one who plans his day almost by the hour. He hates flaky people, in fact he views unreliability as only marginally less offensive than dishonesty.

Possible reasons for his going AWOL march through my head like a line of soldiers on parade. The most likely explanation is that he was ill, but if that was the case, surely he'd have let his line manager know? Perhaps the car broke down on the long journey up to Aberdeen. But, again, there would be no reason not to inform his boss.

Other scenarios force their way into my head. He was drunk. Drugged. His drink was spiked at a lap dancing club and staff cloned his bank cards and stole his car keys. I know it happens. There was a story in the *Daily Mail* a while back about a man who lost thousands when he was slipped a date rape drug while visiting a lap dancing club in Soho. I remember thinking at the time it served him right. Miles has never visited a strip club as far as I know, but there's a first time for everything.

Perhaps he has a secret gambling addiction or he's developed a prescription drug habit. Maybe he'd fallen into a depression, unable to drag himself out of bed.

Each time a reason for his absence from work pops into my head I dismiss it immediately, because Miles is not a drunk or a drug addict. He is not depressed, and I've never known him go to a lap dancing club.

Which leaves only one possibility.

There is another woman...

And all at once, I'm transported back to Dubai and the real reason we fled back to the UK.

I was at the beach club the day the news broke that a man had disappeared from Miles's rig. John Westfield, a thirty-year-old father of one from North Wales, was a roustabout, one of the unskilled labourers who look after the drilling equipment on the rig. He was reported missing after he failed to turn up for his shift one morning. When it was discovered his bed hadn't been slept in, a search was launched. Local coastguards found his body in the sea the following day.

John Westfield's medical records revealed he had once been treated for depression by his GP, and the general consensus among the Emirati police and the oil company's own staff was that he had jumped to his death.

I remember feeling a twinge of sympathy for the poor man's family back in Colwyn Bay, mixed with relief that my own husband was safe.

About a week after Westfield's body was found a rumour started to circulate that he'd been overheard having an altercation with a fellow rigger the night he disappeared.

'Is it true?' I asked Miles, during one of his brief calls home.

'Of course it's not,' Miles had scoffed. 'It's just the usual gossip mill going into overdrive. The stupid fucker jumped off the rig.'

And that would have been that, but then I started getting sympathetic looks from other women at the beach club and hushed conversations would fall away whenever I walked into the bar.

'Something's going on,' I told Tess as we shared a bottle of rosé at hers one evening. 'Everyone's giving me these really weird looks, like I've grown two heads or something. And I swear they're talking about me behind my back.'

When Tess avoided eye contact I knew I hadn't been mistaken. I groaned. 'Oh, God, I knew it. I made a tit of myself at Jo and Peter's barbecue, didn't I? I knew I should never have touched that rum punch.'

'It's not that.' Tess took a sip of her wine, then looked sidelong at me. 'Promise you won't shoot the messenger?'

I'd felt a flicker of disquiet. 'Promise.'

'You know people have been saying John Westfield had an argument with someone the night he fell off the rig?'

I nodded, the muscles in my neck tensing.

'Charlie used to work with the rig's manager, and he says Miles was the man Westfield argued with.'

I'd laughed then. 'What a load of rubbish. Of course it wasn't Miles. He would've told me.'

'John Westfield wasn't the saint everyone's painting him to be,' Tess said. 'Far from it. Two of the women on the rig had made formal complaints about him for inappropriate behaviour. He's what the tabloids would call a sex pest, Luce. A bit handsy, you know?' She scratched at a mosquito bite on her ankle.

'Apparently, he was a whisker away from being sent home on the next chopper and NRB'd.'

When a rig manager tells a worker they're Not Required Back they've basically been blacklisted, not just from the rig they were working on, but all rigs in the area. It's the worst thing that can happen to a rigger.

'No wonder he was suicidal,' I said.

Tess made a non-committal noise. I frowned. 'What aren't you telling me?'

'One of the women who complained about Westfield was a newly qualified chemical engineer who'd only been on the rig for a few months. She confided in Miles after Westfield sexually assaulted her. It seems she and Miles were... close.'

'What's that supposed to mean?'

'Westfield claimed they were having an affair.'

'That's ridiculous. Miles wouldn't do that to me.'

'I know.' Tess reached for my hand and gave it a squeeze. 'It was probably sour grapes, but you wanted to know why people were being a bit weird around you.'

'Everyone knows?' I asked, horrified.

'You know what rigs are like, as leaky as a colander. And rumours spread like wildfire.'

'Jesus.'

'Don't lose sleep over it, Luce. Miles was probably just doing the chivalrous thing and sticking up for this girl and Westfield misunderstood. And once he realised the deep shit he was in he jumped ship, so to speak.'

Tess was right. There was no doubt in my mind that John Westfield killed himself rather than face the music. 'So what do I do about the gossips? Should I say anything?' I asked her.

She shook her head. 'You'll only fan the flames. Ignore them. They'll have moved on to a new scandal by next week.'

A week later Miles rang to tell me he was being transferred

to a rig in the North Sea and to start packing up the apartment because we were leaving Dubai.

I never asked him about the argument he'd had with John Westfield the night he died. I never asked him why he was suddenly being transferred, nor about the young chemical engineer, either. The whole incident was overshadowed by a phone call from my dad the very next day to tell me my beloved grandad had suffered a fatal stroke in his sleep.

I flew straight home and spent the next couple of weeks helping my parents organise the funeral and clearing out the cottage in Chilham. By the time Miles had tied up all the loose ends in Dubai I had already buried Grandad along with the questions I'd had about John Westfield and the young chemical engineer Miles had apparently been so keen to protect.

35

A faint cry from the spare bedroom is a welcome release from my thoughts, and I warm up a bottle and trudge upstairs. Wren coos when he sees me and the sound lifts my heart.

I flick on the bedside lamp and gaze at him as he feeds. Sod Miles's no eye contact rule. Wren's eyes lock onto mine and I'm moved beyond measure at the trust mirrored back at me. At this moment, I don't care what Miles has or hasn't done. Wren is what matters.

When he's finished his bottle, I change his nappy. He wriggles like an eel and gurgles with laughter when I blow raspberries on his little pot belly. Once I've wrangled his sleepsuit back on, I pick him up and bury my face in his neck. He giggles again, his hot breath tickling my ears.

This, I think. This is happiness.

Wren takes over an hour to get back to sleep, by which time I'm prickly-eyed with exhaustion. But when I climb back into bed and close my eyes, my mind is still galloping. I remember the sleep app on my phone. A bit of guided meditation might halt the racing thoughts.

The phone powers on but before I click on the sleep app icon I have a compulsion to check the news websites. *BBC*, then local news, and finally Facebook.

There's another message from Shona MacDonald.

Lucy, I know you probably think I'm a scammer or some creepy stalker, but I really need to talk to you. Please call me. Shona.

To my surprise it was sent less than half an hour ago. Three o'clock in the morning seems a strange time to be sending messages to someone you've never met.

Whoever this Shona woman is, she's right. I am worried she's a nutter or a criminal. It's hard to spend any time online these days without someone trying to trick you into parting with your life's savings. One of Miles's favourite pastimes is to string cold callers along for as long as possible. His current record is a twenty-seven-minute conversation with a guy offering to help him claim compensation for a mis-sold payment protection insurance policy. When Miles eventually said, 'Oh, you mean PPI. I thought we were talking about PPE. You know, helmets and goggles and shit,' the caller had told him he was a fucking twat before hanging up. Miles had been in stitches.

I suppose I should give this Shona woman the benefit of the doubt. But if she tells me I've won an iPad, sends me a link to click on, or asks me to help with the medical bills for her sick kid, I'll block her immediately. I rub my face, then tap out a message.

What do you want?

A reply appears almost instantly.

It would be easier to explain on the phone.

Sorry, I type, it's Messenger or nothing. Why have you contacted me?

Is your husband Miles Quinn?

The question takes me by surprise and I pause before I reply. Miles doesn't have an online presence. He hates social media with a passion, says it's toxic and inane, a complete waste of time. So this Shona woman hasn't stumbled on my profile by chance; she must know I'm his wife. Another message pops up on the screen before I have a chance to reply.

If I'm right, your husband used to work on the oil rigs in Dubai but now works on a rig in the North Sea.

Not any more he doesn't, I think. My curiosity is fully aroused now, and I quickly tap out a reply.

I am Miles's wife. How did you find me?

This time a photograph appears on the screen. I recognise it at once. It was taken at a fundraising charity ball at the beach club a couple of years ago. Tess and I were tasked with running the raffle and we roped in Miles and Charlie to help. A photographer from the *Gulf News* was at the event and the photo he took of the four of us appeared in the paper's online edition. Perhaps Shona does know me from Dubai. Perhaps she's an aspiring author and wants tips on publishing from someone who used to be in the business. Another message pops up.

Your names are in the caption.

You still haven't told me why you're contacting me?

This time there's a delay before she answers, as if she's taking a moment to compose a response, although it could just be our terrible internet connection. Eventually a message appears.

I think you or your husband might know my sister, Rae MacDonald.

I frown as I type.

I'm sorry, I think you must have mistaken me for someone else after all. I have never met or even heard of a Rae MacDonald.

Rae worked for an oil company in Dubai until just over a year ago. I believe she worked on the same offshore rig as Miles.

Was she part of the catering crew? I type, although I have a horrible feeling I know the answer. My fears are confirmed when Shona's answer pings back.

No, she's a chemical engineer.

I creep downstairs, my phone in my hand and my heart in my mouth, and head for the kitchen, closing the door quietly behind me. I have dialled Shona's number before I can talk myself out of it.

'Thank you,' she says, and the relief in her voice is unmistakable.

'For what?'

'For not dismissing me as a nutter.'

'Actually, I'm reserving judgement.'

She laughs softly. 'Touché.'

'You're Scottish,' I say.

'Edinburgh born and bred. Rae left after she finished university. I'm still here.'

'So it's nearly four in the morning for you too?'

'I couldn't sleep.' She pauses. 'I'm sorry, I shouldn't have been messaging you in the middle of the night.'

I sigh. 'It's all right, I couldn't sleep either. We might as well talk now.' And get this nonsense over and done with, I think silently.

'My sister, Rae, is ten years younger than me. My parents thought they couldn't have another baby, and then she came along. Do you have children?'

The question takes me by surprise. How am I supposed to answer *that*? 'No,' I say eventually.

'Me neither. I've never seen the appeal. But I loved Rae, and I took my role as big sister very seriously. We were very close until I left for university.'

'I don't really see—'

'The relevance?' Shona guesses. 'You will. Stick with it. Please.'

She must see my silence as affirmation, because she resumes her story. 'Rae was eleven when I graduated. That's the day she told me she wanted to be an engineer like our father when she grew up. He worked on the oil rigs, you see. I told her I couldn't imagine anything worse than living in the middle of the North Sea for weeks at a time, but she was adamant. She was a bit of a daddy's girl.'

Rae, Shona said, had studied chemical engineering at the University of Aberdeen, spending her year in industry working for one of the big six oil companies. Her managers rated her so highly they offered her a job when she graduated.

'And it wasn't to tick a diversity box. She was a brilliant engineer – analytical and creative. They were lucky to have her.

Her first job was onshore in a lab, but her ambition was always to work on a rig and eighteen months ago she transferred to the UAE.'

'Dubai?' I guess.

'Yes. And that's where it all went wrong. She'd spent years in a predominantly male environment, both at university and in her first job, but working on the rig was a culture shock. The oil companies might claim to be inclusive, but that doesn't always filter down to the workers. Not all of them anyway. There was one in particular who set Rae in his sights, the sexist bastard. It started with the odd inappropriate comment, but when he realised how much it was upsetting her, he stepped it up until she was facing harassment on an almost daily basis.'

I think back to that evening at Tess's, when she'd told me about the newly qualified chemical engineer who'd been touched up by John Westfield.

'Was it that guy who fell from the rig?'

'You knew John Westfield?' she asks sharply.

'No, only of him. His death was the talk of the ex-pat community for a while. Men don't jump off oil rigs very often.'

'Or for no good reason,' she says. 'Yes, it was John Westfield. And, according to the coroner's report into Westfield's death, your husband was the last person to see him alive.'

36

'What exactly are you suggesting?' I say hotly.

Shona sighs. 'Nothing.'

'So why are you calling me?'

'Because Rae's missing. Nobody's heard from her for almost a year. And I think there's a chance your husband might know where she is.'

As I digest this bombshell, I become aware of a door creaking upstairs and the unmistakable sound of footsteps crossing the landing.

'I need to go,' I whisper into the phone. 'I'll call you back when I can.'

When Miles lets himself into the kitchen moments later I'm playing Candy Crush on my phone, a look of intense concentration on my face.

'What are you doing down here?' he asks.

'Couldn't sleep, and I didn't want to wake Wren.'

'Max,' he says irritably. He runs a hand through his hair. 'I thought I heard voices.'

'I was watching Netflix on my phone for a bit. *Friends*,' I add. 'It was the one where Ross and Rachel take a break.' Miles hates *Friends*. 'Couldn't you sleep either?'

'Obviously not. Are there any more Lemsips? My throat's like razors.'

I push back my chair. 'I'll make you one and bring it up if you like.' I rootle around in the medicine drawer and find a flu-strength Lemsip, then reach into the cupboard for the honey. Miles sneezes and I peer at him. There is a pallor about him that suggests this is more than just a bout of man flu.

'You look like death warmed up,' I say, taking his arm. 'Come on, let's get you back to bed.'

For once he does as he's told, and once he's safely tucked up, I head back downstairs to make his drink. Dawn is already breaking and a wave of exhaustion sweeps over me. Sometimes, Wren doesn't wake till seven. If I'm lucky I can still grab a couple of hours' sleep. I take Miles his Lemsip, then pad across the landing to the spare room, slip under the duvet and, within seconds, I'm asleep.

It's gone half seven when Wren wakes. I'm still shattered but my head is clear.

After I've given Wren his bottle and changed and dressed him, I leave him on the rug in the living room and check on Miles.

The curtains are still drawn in our bedroom and the air is close, almost fetid. Miles stirs as I pick up the empty mug from his bedside table.

'How're you feeling?' I ask.

'Terrible,' he croaks, pulling the duvet under his chin. 'It's freezing in here.'

I'd been about to pull the curtains and open the window. Instead, I perch on the side of the bed and feel his forehead.

'You're burning up. Would you like a cup of tea and some toast?'

He shakes his head. 'Can't face it.'

'I'll make you another Lemsip. You need to keep your fluids up. Can I get you anything else?'

He shakes his head. At the door, I hesitate. I want to ask him about his job, about Rae MacDonald and the night John Westfield died. But he has already burrowed back under the duvet. The questions can wait.

There are only a couple of sachets left in the pack of Lemsips and we're almost out of paracetamol. When I check the fridge I realise we're running low on milk too.

'I need to pop to the supermarket,' I tell Miles when I take his Lemsip and a glass of water up. 'Will you be all right on your own?'

'You're taking Max?'

'You're hardly in a fit state to look after him,' I say crisply. 'We won't be long. Don't worry, I won't hand myself in at the police station. Do you still have my loyalty card?' Miles had taken it the last time he went shopping.

'In my wallet,' he mumbles.

'Where's that?'

'Jeans pocket.'

I pick the jeans up from where they've been discarded on the floor, thinking Miles must be ill – he's normally pathologically tidy – and feel in the pockets.

'It's not in here.'

'Try my jacket.'

'Will do. We won't be long. I'll pick up some chicken soup. Ring me if there's anything else you think of.'

Miles's jacket is hanging on a hook in the cupboard under the stairs. The wallet's in the inside pocket. I find the loyalty card then check in the little coin pocket for a one-pound coin for the trolley.

That's when I see it. A folded piece of paper, tucked right at the bottom of the coin pocket. Curious, I pull it out and unfold it, shocked to the core when I realise what I'm looking at.

It's an ultrasound scan. Our baby's twelve-week dating scan, to be precise. I haven't seen it since we left Dubai. I'd kept it in a small wooden box along with the pair of booties and tiny sleep-suit I'd bought before the miscarriage. Without a photo of him, they were all I had to remember him by. I was devastated when the box was lost during the move back to the UK. But here, somehow, is the scan. Miles must have taken it from the box and slipped it into his wallet before the removal firm packed up our stuff.

As I study the ghostly image, memories of the day it was taken come flooding back. Miles was offshore when the appointment came through, so Tess came with me for moral support. I'd been terrified as the sonographer squirted gel over my stomach and ran the ultrasound probe over it.

'What if there's nothing there?' I asked Tess in a panic.

'You're telling me you're not pregnant, it's just a bad case of wind?' she said.

The sonographer had chuckled. 'You don't need to worry, Mrs Quinn. There's definitely a baby in there.'

As one, our heads had swivelled round to the blurry black and white picture on the ultrasound machine, and Tess had gripped my hand tightly as the baby bounced around in its sac of amniotic fluid.

'Fuck me, it's a lively little bugger,' she said, breaking the tension, and the sonographer had watched indulgently while we burst into relieved laughter.

When I showed Miles the scan photo he'd joked that the baby looked like a skull atop a kidney bean, and I'd secretly been hurt that he could be so flippant about something so important. Now I realise I was doing him an injustice. He did care. He'd kept the photo all this time, hadn't he?

I take the photo into the kitchen and smooth it out on the table. I won't tell Miles I've found it. It would only embarrass him. He hates all forms of sentimentality. But I want a copy for myself.

It's as I'm taking a picture of the scan with my phone that something jars. It's the date in the top right corner. The 10th of August 2022. I fell pregnant in the summer of 2019 and my twelve-week scan was that November.

I stare at the date until the numbers start to dance and my vision goes blurry. I close my eyes for a moment, then look again, hoping I'm mistaken.

But the date is the same. The 10th of August 2022. Last year, not four years ago.

37

I shove the scan picture back into Miles's wallet with trembling fingers and grab the changing bag from the worktop.

Wren is babbling away to Percy in the living room. When he sees me he holds out his arms and I scoop him up, cradle him against me and try to slow my racing heart.

You don't need a degree in maths to do the sums. Wren is around four months old. To have been born this February he must have been conceived last May.

Which means... which means his twelve-week scan would have been due last August.

Upstairs in his sickbed, Miles has all the answers, but speaking to him is out of the question. I can't even bear to be in the same house as him, let alone the same room. I need to get out. Now.

I strap Wren into his car seat and carry him out to the Mini, a cold ball of fury growing inside me. Gravel scatters as I accelerate out of the drive and up the lane towards the village. Things are slotting into place. The way Miles is so natural around Wren. The lengths he went to, to stop me going to the police. He even took my car keys with him so I was stuck in the house, for God's sake.

I remember the way Wren's face lit up the first time he saw Miles. I'd been touched beyond measure, kidding myself there'd been an instant connection between them. Now I wonder if it was simply because Wren recognised Miles.

I'm so wrapped up in my thoughts that I don't see the motorcyclist bearing down on me until I'm pulling out onto the main road. I slam on my brakes and the motorbike wobbles precariously for a moment before the rider regains control. He turns his head and raises a fist as he zooms off.

'Fuck!' I close my eyes and rest my head against the steering wheel, a rush of adrenaline making my heart crash in my chest. I was a beat away from killing someone. I need to get a grip.

Behind me, a horn blares. Without looking in my rear-view mirror, I check left and right three times, then pull out, sticking resolutely to the speed limit as I head towards the supermarket.

By the time I turn into the car park my breathing's under control again, but the anger is still there, brewing in the pit of my stomach. I check Wren, glad to see he's fast asleep, and call the one person who might be able to make sense of all this.

Shona answers on the second ring.

'I'm sorry about earlier,' I say without preamble. 'Miles walked in.'

'No problem.'

'You said no one's heard from Rae since she left the rig. When was that?'

'A week after John Westfield died.'

'Last May?' I check.

'Aye. I tried calling her, obviously, but her phone was disconnected. I called everyone I could think of. The few friends she'd made in Dubai, her immediate boss, the company's HR department. They all said the same, that she'd handed in her notice and flown home. Other than the fact that they were a little surprised she'd decided to leave, they didn't seem to think there was a problem.'

'But she didn't contact you?'

'No.'

'And that was out of character?'

'Totally. She used to text or email every few days to check on Mum. She's in a nursing home. Dementia,' Shona explained.

'I'm sorry to hear that,' I say automatically.

'It is what it is. Which is pretty bloody shitty, actually.' Shona sighs. 'Mum was diagnosed the week before Rae was due to start the Dubai job. She wanted to pull out, or at least ask if she could delay for a couple of months, but I talked her into going. It was too good an opportunity to miss.'

'Hard on you though.'

'Ah, it wasn't so bad. Rae would FaceTime when she could so Mum could see her. And d'you know the funny thing? I visit three times a week and Mum doesn't know me from Adam. Rae used to FaceTime from Dubai a couple of times a month, but Mum always knew exactly who she was. Strange how the mind works.' Shona says this without a trace of resentment and I find myself warming to this mysterious Scottish woman with her soft Edinburgh accent and her lost sister.

'Did you report Rae missing to the police?'

'Of course. I contacted them both in Dubai and here in Edinburgh. The Emirati police were very helpful and checked the manifests of all the flights from Dubai to the UK. Rae was a passenger on a BA flight to Edinburgh on the twenty-fifth of May.'

I inhale sharply. 'She came home to Scotland?'

'She did,' Shona agrees.

'But she didn't tell you?'

'No.'

'Was she definitely on the flight?'

'Passport control confirmed she'd landed. The police here

classed her as a low-risk missing person, which is common if you're an adult with no history of mental illness and no vulnerabilities. It's not against the law to walk out of your life and never come back, you see.'

'That's what you think she did?'

'That's what the police think.'

'And you?' I ask.

'Ah, well, I'm not so sure.'

She breaks off and I watch a woman dripping in gold jewellery load half a dozen brand-new carrier bags into the boot of her immaculate Porsche Cayenne. I tut to myself. She might as well have *Sod the Planet* tattooed across her Botoxed forehead.

Shona has started talking again.

'Sorry, I didn't catch that,' I say, dragging my attention back to her.

'I think Rae might have told Miles where she was going.'

'Why Miles?'

'Because they seemed... close.'

My ears prick up. 'What d'you mean?'

'She mentioned him in her emails home a few times in the months before she disappeared. Reading between the lines I think she had a bit of a crush on him.'

'A crush?'

'I'm not saying it was reciprocated,' Shona says quickly. 'I just got the feeling Rae would have turned to Miles if she'd been in trouble.'

'You're saying that, for whatever reason, he helped her disappear?'

'I suppose I am.'

Twenty-four hours ago, I would have told this stranger she was deluded, that I knew my husband inside out and if he had helped a young woman walk out of her life I would have known, no question. Twenty-four hours ago, I had no idea he's been lying to me for months.

'Even if that's the case, you haven't heard from Rae for over a year. Why are you asking this now?'

'Oh, but I did ask Miles at the time. Like everyone else I spoke to, he said he was surprised she'd left, and assumed she must have been more homesick than he realised.'

'There you go then,' I say. 'He can't help you, and neither can I.'

'I think he was covering for her. I think Miles knows exactly where Rae went and I need you to ask him for me.'

Behind me, there are little sighs and whimpers as Wren starts to stir. I need to end the call.

'Look, Shona, you sound like a lovely person and I'm sorry your sister's missing, I really am, but I don't think Miles or I can help you.'

I hold my breath as Wren cries out, and swivel in my seat so I can stroke his cheek.

'I thought you said you didn't have children?' Shona says, her voice sharp as a tack.

'I... I'm looking after him for a friend. I have to go. He needs a feed. I'm sorry I can't help,' I say again, and before Shona can react, I end the call.

38

I push the trolley up and down the supermarket aisles in a daze, picking apart everything I know and trying to make sense of it all. Rae had a crush on Miles. John Westfield was making Rae's life a misery. Miles was overheard arguing with Westfield the night he fell from the rig. Within days of Westfield's death, Rae had flown back to Scotland never to be seen again, and Miles had been transferred to a rig off Aberdeen.

The fact that this all happened last May, the same month Wren must have been conceived, has to be significant, but I'm almost too scared to join the dots.

I find myself in the medicine aisle, staring blankly at the cold and flu remedies. Giving my head a little shake, I pick up a packet of Lemsip and a bottle of Night Nurse. As I pass the display of pregnancy tests something occurs to me. Did Westfield's abuse escalate during his last days on the rig? Could he have *raped* Rae? As horrifying as the thought is, the more I consider it, the more likely it seems. Tess said two women had reported him for inappropriate behaviour. I try to remember her exact words.

He's what the tabloids would call a sex pest.

The facts begin to assemble themselves in my mind. West-field raped Rae, and she discovered she was pregnant. She confided in Miles, which would explain the argument between the two men the night Westfield died. Maybe the showdown helped Westfield see the error of his ways and, full of remorse, he plunged from the rig into the warm waters of the Persian Gulf.

With her attacker dead, there was little point Rae reporting the rape to the police. It's not like he didn't pay for his crime. And then, wanting to shield her sister and mum from the whole sorry business, she walked away from her life so they would never know what happened to her in Dubai.

I can see Miles offering to help Rae start over. He loves to play the hero; would never pass up the chance to help a damsel in distress. I remember the night we met, the way he came to my rescue, saving me from the arsehole with the tattoos at that club in Hackney. Miles, fearlessly defending my honour. My very own Prince Charming.

I feel a prickle of jealousy as I picture him doing the same for Rae. Stepping in, keeping her secret, protecting her. But any jealousy I feel pales into comparison when I consider the conundrum that remains unresolved.

I may have the answers when it comes to Rae, but there's one question I can't even begin to get my head around. Where the hell does Wren figure in all this?

I'm standing in the queue for the checkout when my phone buzzes in my pocket. My heart misses a beat when Miles's name flashes up on the screen.

I step to one side, letting a man in a high-vis jacket clutching a Pepsi Max and a Ginsters Cornish pasty take my place.

'Hi,' I say, a little breathlessly.

'Can you get some Strepsils?' Miles croaks down the phone.

'Er, sure. Anything else?'

'No.' He sneezes, then says, 'How long are you going to be?'

'Half an hour? I need to pay and fill the car up.'

'Don't be any longer. I'm dying here,' he says, then hangs up.

I pick up three packets of Strepsils and am about to head back to the checkout when I change my mind. I retrace my steps to the baby aisle instead and pile enough formula, nappies and wipes to last a couple of weeks into the trolley, in case I go down with the flu too.

That's what I tell myself, anyway.

39

Wren begins to grizzle five minutes from home. I check the time, dismayed that I've been so preoccupied with Shona and Rae that I've completely forgotten to give him his lunchtime bottle.

'Sorry, angel,' I say, glancing in the rear-view mirror and pulling into the garden centre on the outskirts of the village. I'll feed him in the cafe. It'll give me the headspace to work out what I'm going to say to Miles once we're home.

It's busy in the cafe but I find a free table in the corner and ask the waitress for a pot of tea for me and a jug of water so I can heat Wren's bottle. While we're waiting I bounce him on my knee and blow raspberries into his neck, which takes his mind off his hunger pangs and has the elderly couple at the next table in raptures.

'Remember when our William was that age, Joe?' the woman says, nudging her husband's hand, then smiling at me. 'Our youngest's just had his first grandchild,' she tells me, shaking her head in disbelief. 'Make the most of him,' she adds, dipping her head at Wren, who is trying to grab fistfuls of my hair. 'He'll be a grandad before you know it!'

'Is it your first great-grandchild?' I ask.

The old woman laughs. 'Our seventh. The oldest is nine. What's your little one called?'

We chat about babies until the waitress brings the hot water and I pop Wren's bottle in the jug, then dig about in the changing bag for a clean bib.

I've just squirted a dribble of milk on the inside of my wrist when the waitress reappears, carrying two plates laden with food. As she heads our way I catch a whiff of sage and onion stuffing and my head spins.

Like the flip of a switch, I'm transported to our apartment in Dubai, watching myself from the ceiling as I carve a shoulder of pork while roast potatoes and parsnips brown in the oven. The air is fragrant with the smell of sage and onion. I always make my stuffing from scratch with fresh breadcrumbs, fresh sage and a hint of garlic. Miles says it's the best he's ever eaten.

I'm wearing my grey jersey dress, not just because it's Miles's favourite but because it's one of the few things in my wardrobe I can still fit into. I look radiant. Curvy. The soft jersey clings to the swell of my belly. My breasts are full, my complexion glowing. I am in the second trimester and loving every minute of it.

Miles appears, his hair still damp from the shower, and reaches across me to pinch a piece of crackling.

'Oi,' I say, batting his hand away. 'Make yourself useful and lay the table. Have you finished packing?'

'I have.' He finds mats and cutlery while I strain the tender-stem broccoli and green beans.

'I wish you were here for the scan,' I say. I was already starting to feel anxious about the twenty-week scan, which was due in a couple of weeks. It was the biggie, the one where they looked at foetal abnormalities like heart defects, spina bifida and cleft lip. Miles had promised to move heaven and earth to be there after missing the first scan, but they were short on riggers and his leave request had been turned down.

'I know. But Tess'll be with you, won't she?' Miles says, pouring himself a glass of Merlot and giving an appreciative murmur as he takes a sip. 'You should try this. It's delicious.' He reaches into the cupboard for a second wine flute.

'I'm not drinking,' I remind him, my hand creeping protectively over my belly.

'A little bit of what you fancy won't hurt,' he says, pouring me half a glass. I take a sip, then carry the vegetables over to the table.

My mobile rings. It's Mum, phoning for her weekly update on the baby. I take the phone into the hallway so Miles can eat his dinner in peace. Yes, everything's fine. Yes, I can still feel the baby moving. No, the heartburn's not too bad. And yes, I'll make sure I put my feet up while I still can.

'Are you all right?' a voice says. 'Only I think someone wants his lunch.'

It takes me a moment to refocus. I look around, trying to centre myself. I'm not watching our apartment from a vantage point on the ceiling, I am sitting at the back of a fuggy cafe attached to a garden centre on the outskirts of Chilham. The old lady at the next table is staring at me with a concerned expression on her face. In my arms, Wren is whimpering plaintively.

'Sorry, I was miles away.' I shift Wren into the crook of my arm and offer him the bottle. He takes it greedily, his eyes seeking mine as he guzzles.

I breathe deeply, allowing my subconscious to take me back to the apartment. I can't shift the feeling that something important happened that night, something I need to remember.

I close my eyes briefly and there I am, saying goodbye to Mum and heading back to the dining table. Miles has filled my glass almost to the brim – I hadn't remembered him doing that –

but I don't say anything because he'll view it as criticism. He just wants to enjoy his last night onshore before he heads back to the rig. It's fair enough.

I push my lukewarm dinner unenthusiastically around my plate and sip my wine while Miles reveals his plans for the nursery. He has seen a set of white-painted furniture online that would be perfect. There's a cot bed and a chest of drawers that doubles up as a changing table. It's expensive, but money's no object where his baby is concerned.

I leave my wine half-finished and rest my chin in my hands as Miles talks. Every so often my eyelids flutter closed. It's funny, because I don't remember feeling tired while I was cooking. When I stand to clear the plates, I sway like a sapling in the breeze.

'Steady,' Miles says, jumping up to catch my elbow, and as I watch myself gripping onto him, I can almost feel his taut, muscular body under the brushed cotton of his T-shirt.

Miles pulls away first and I yawn, my hand fluttering to my mouth.

'I feel strange,' I mumble. 'Like my legs don't work.'

'Get some sleep. You've obviously been overdoing things,' Miles says. He pecks my cheek and sends me towards the spiral staircase with a pat on the bum. I stagger up the stairs, hands clutching the rail. I look like I'm at the wrong end of an all-day bender, yet I could only have had half a glass of wine.

Miles clears the table and stacks the dishes into the dishwasher. His movements are jerky, almost robotic, and a muscle jumps in his jaw. Every so often he glances up the spiral staircase to the mezzanine. I zoom in on our bedroom where I'm lurching from bed to dressing table and back again as I attempt to undress and pull on a nightshirt. I stumble over to the glass balustrade and call down, 'Can you bring me a glass of water, please?' Only it comes out as an almost indecipherable garble, as if I'm speaking with my mouth full of marbles.

Miles turns from wiping down the worktops and looks up at me, irritation scoring his handsome features, making them ugly. He yanks open a cupboard, pulls out a glass and fills it from the tap, even though we always used to drink bottled water in Dubai.

My heart's in my mouth as I watch him cross the room to the bottom of the staircase. I will myself to stand back from the balustrade, to sit on the bed where I'll be safe. Where the baby will be safe. But I don't. Instead, I grip the stainless-steel handrail and wait for my husband to join me.

Fear squeezes my heart as I watch myself watching Miles. I want to turn away, but I know I can't. I have to see what happens next. Miles reaches the top step, shakes his head.

'Look at the state of you,' he spits.

My eyes widen and I take a step back, colliding with the corner of the dressing table. I reach out a hand to steady myself, knocking over a lamp. Miles steps towards me, raises the glass and throws the water in my face.

'Drunk bitch.' His face is blank, like he's checked out. He holds me by my shoulders and turns me towards the top of the spiral staircase. 'You really shouldn't drink in your condition,' he continues, pushing me forwards. 'It's not good for the baby.'

I teeter on the top step for an agonising moment, then he jabs me in the back with the heel of his hand, and I am falling, falling, as limp as a rag doll.

40

Wren wriggles in my arms, pulling me back to the present, and I run a finger along his cheek, hoping the warmth of his skin will ground me.

Tess told me my brain had likely blocked my memories of the miscarriage to protect itself, just as her dad had dissociated to forget the traumatic scenes he'd witnessed in the Gulf.

I must have buried the events of that night so deeply I couldn't retrieve them at will. It took a trigger, as Tess said it might, to release them to my conscious mind. And that trigger happened to be sage and onion stuffing, of all things.

For three years the memories have been there on a spool in my brain, just waiting to be replayed.

The scene in our apartment was so real, so vivid, I know I didn't imagine it. If I was in any doubt, it's the closed expression on Miles's face that convinces me. It's an expression I've seen countless times before, usually when Miles doesn't get his way. The charming smile disappears to be replaced by a set jaw and a coldness in his eyes that could freeze water.

I saw the same emotionless look on his face when I told him I was pregnant. With a shiver I remember his barely suppressed anger as he accused me of being careless. The flash of revulsion as he described our baby as nothing more than a mass of dividing cells. When he finally smiled, I'd assumed he'd come round to the idea and was picturing himself as a dad. Was he planning how to get rid of our baby even then?

The thought is so horrific, so Machiavellian, that I dismiss it at once. No more secrets, that's what he said. But the doubts refuse to go away. This, after all, is the man who is steadily working his way through my inheritance because he can't – or won't – tell me he's been given the sack. No more secrets? What a joke.

The Miles I know hates to lose above all else. If he had even the smallest suspicion that I'd tricked him into having a baby he'd have retaliated, I have no doubt.

He must have congratulated himself on a job well done when my placenta broke away from my uterus, the resulting hysterectomy leaving me unable to bear any more children.

I take a sip of tea, turning my head away from Wren so he can't grab the cup. I've left it stewing in the pot too long, but it's warm and wet and comforting.

Miles must have spiked my drink the night I miscarried because there's no way I could have been that drunk on half a glass, even if I hadn't touched a drop in weeks. Dubai is notoriously intolerant of drug abuse, but I bet it's easy enough to get your hands on roofies or GHB if you know where to look. He must have dropped a pill into my wine while I was on the phone to Mum. If she hadn't called he'd have created another diversion. Miles is nothing if not resourceful.

My husband has shown he'll stop at nothing to get his own way.

But where does that leave me? I can't let on that I know what he's done. If he gets an inkling I've remembered what happened that night I could be in danger. Our relationship has always worked because I've been happy for him to take the lead,

I see that now. I am weak and easily manipulated and he has taken full advantage of that.

I'll go home and pretend nothing's happened while I work out what to do. It's not much of a plan, but it's the only one I have.

Wren's fidgeting for England now, so I drain the last of my tea, strap him into his car seat and begin to gather our things.

'Don't worry, love, it won't last forever,' the old woman at the next table says as I haul myself to my feet. 'The sleepless nights,' she adds, seeing the quizzical look on my face.

'Oh, right, yes. Thanks.' I smile ruefully. 'Is it that obvious?'

'Well, you do look a bit washed out. Try to sleep when the baby sleeps, although I know it's easier said than done.' She glances at her husband, who's at the counter paying for their lunch. 'I expect Joe'll tell me off for interfering, but you need to remember to put your own oxygen mask on first.' She nods at Wren, who beams at her. 'You take care of yourself and your gorgeous little boy.'

To my horror my eyes fill with tears, and her eyebrows draw together.

'Is everything all right?' she asks. 'If you need to talk, I'm a good listener.'

What would this kind old lady say if I told her the truth: that Wren isn't mine, that I have, for all intents and purposes, stolen him. That three years ago my husband drugged me and pushed me down the stairs, killing our own baby. That for most of my adult life I've used alcohol to fill the empty void inside me. That drinking has left my self-worth in tatters. That I don't deserve to be a mum.

She'd be horrified.

So I do what I always do: muster a smile and tell her I'm fine, everything is fine, but I'll do as she says and rest when I can. Reassured, she strokes Wren under the chin, lays a hand briefly on my arm, and gives me a smile before fetching her handbag and shuffling over to join her husband.

My phone buzzes in my back pocket as I'm buckling the car seat into the Mini. When I see Miles's name on the screen my pulse quickens, but I take a deep breath and answer it.

'Where are you?' he demands.

'In the cafe at the garden centre.'

'You said you were coming straight home.'

'I know, but Wren needed a feed.'

'I'm sure *Max* could have waited until you got home.'

'He probably could, but I needed a change of scenery. I've been going stir crazy cooped up in the house. We're just leaving. We'll be home in ten minutes.'

Miles starts to say something, but I cut across him. 'Sorry, I can't hear you. You keep breaking up.' And I hang up.

It's a tiny act of defiance, but it gives me courage. And God knows I'm going to need every ounce of courage I have.

I unload the shopping, leaving the extra nappies and formula I bought in the boot of the Mini. I warm a bowl of chicken soup in the microwave and set it on a tray with a packet of Strepsils, the bottle of Night Nurse and a glass of water. As I trudge up the stairs my heart rate quickens. I am scared, I realise. Scared of my husband, of what he's capable of.

'Lucy, is that you?' he rasps.

I push the door open with my foot and lick my lips. 'I brought you soup.'

'I don't want soup.'

'Come on,' I say, balancing the tray on his bedside table. 'You need to eat something.'

The curtains are closed and there's a tang of stale sweat in the air. Miles pulls himself onto his elbows and looks at me blearily.

'Where's Max?'

'Asleep downstairs.' I place the tray on the bedside table. Miles looks terrible. His face is grey and there's a patch of flaky skin around his nose. I tentatively reach across and feel his forehead. He's burning up.

'If you won't have soup, at least have a drink of water and some Night Nurse. It'll bring your temperature down.'

He gives an imperceptible nod, and I measure out a generous dose and hold it to his lips, as if he's six, not thirty-six. He swallows obediently, and I hand him the glass of water. He hitches himself further up the bed, wincing at the effort. I could rush around plumping his pillows. I could hold the soup bowl for him while he eats. I could go to the bathroom, wet a flannel with cold water and dab his fevered brow. Yesterday I would have done all this and more. Not today. Today I watch the man I thought I loved and feel nothing but hatred.

41

Back in the kitchen, I find the baby carrier and slip Wren into it. I need to work off some of the nervous energy zipping through me. Wren is only too happy to go for a walk and his legs pump with excitement as I pick up my phone and scribble a note to Miles on the back of an old shopping list. *Gone for a walk. Be back before dinner.* I don't suppose he'll even see it, but at least he can't accuse me of not letting him know where I've gone.

I've barely reached the end of the lane when my phone buzzes. It's bound to be Miles. I used to think the constant calls and texts to see where I was and what I was doing were because he cared, but everything has shifted in my mind since I remembered what really happened the night I miscarried. Miles doesn't care about me. He has been controlling me since the day we met, and I can't believe it's taken me this long to see it.

I pull my phone out of my pocket with a sigh, my brow wrinkling when I see Shona's name on the screen. Which bit of 'I can't help' didn't she understand?

'Hello, Shona.'

'Lucy.' Her lilting voice is a little breathless. 'I'm with Mum at the nursing home. I don't usually visit her on a Sunday, but I was missing Rae and just wanted to talk about her to someone, you know?'

I don't know what to say to this, so I keep quiet.

'I thought it would be nice to look through a couple of our old family photo albums together,' Shona continues. 'On a good day Mum remembers quite a bit, even if she can't remember what she had for breakfast. Anyway, I was flicking through the pages of one album and a photo fell out. I thought it was Mum at first, but the clothes were all wrong. When I looked closer, I realised it was Rae. Everyone always said she was the image of Mum, whereas I looked more like Dad. Anyway, she's standing in front of a little house in the middle of nowhere.'

And? I'm thinking, because I'm not sure finding a picture of her sister in a photo album warrants a call to me, a virtual stranger. But her next sentence makes my mouth fall open.

'There's a baby in the photo, Lucy. Rae is holding a baby.'

I glance at Wren. He's chewing the top of the baby carrier, drool dribbling down his chin. 'Send it to me,' I whisper.

Moments later my phone pings with a text and I open it with trembling fingers. A woman with long red hair the colour of burnt sienna is standing outside a white-rendered cottage. A mountain, dark and foreboding, looms behind the single-storey building. The woman is wearing a thick fleece, jeans, wellies and a woolly hat, and in her arms she is holding a baby. He's bundled up in a navy snowsuit with the hood up so you can't see his face. But I don't need to. I know who he is.

Before I can say anything, Shona is speaking again. 'I asked Mum where the photo came from, but of course she didn't know, so I asked a couple of her carers. One said she was pretty sure it arrived a month or so ago. Mum never gets any post, which is why she remembered. Why the hell she didn't think to mention it to me at the time I'll never know, but she's new. Perhaps she didn't know Rae's missing.'

'Was there a note with it?'

'Not that I could find, and I've searched high and low. You know what this means?'

'I—'

'It's Rae's way of letting Mum know she's safe. Not just safe, but that she's had a *baby*! I can't believe it!'

'What are you going to do?'

'Find her, of course.'

I stop walking and take a deep breath. 'Shona, there's something you need to know.'

Shona listens in silence as I describe how I woke up a week ago to find a baby in my living room. How I thought I must have stolen him because there was no other explanation.

'But you can't remember taking him? You can't remember *anything*?'

I'm glad she can't see my cheeks burning. 'Sometimes I, um... sometimes I black out when I've... when I've drunk too much,' I mumble.

'Jesus.'

'I haven't touched a drop since he's been here,' I say quickly.

'And you didn't think you should perhaps have reported this to the police?'

'I was going to, but then Miles arrived home early, and he talked me out of it. He said Wren's mum couldn't have cared about him because she hadn't reported him missing.'

'Wren?'

'It's what I've called him.'

'You think he's Rae's baby?'

'He has to be, doesn't he?'

'Then how the hell did he end up with you in— Where is it you live again?'

'Kent.'

'How the hell did he end up in Kent?'

'Perhaps Rae couldn't cope but didn't want to hand him over to social services. Miles must have told her I couldn't have children. Maybe she thought he would be better off with me?'

'Look at her face. Does she look like she doesn't want him?' Shona says roughly.

I zoom in on Rae's face as she stares at Wren. She is smiling, a wide, uncomplicated smile that crinkles her eyes and dimples her cheeks. Her gaze is so tender a sob catches in my throat. Shona is right. This is not a woman who is indifferent to her baby. Her love is plain for all to see.

And if that's the case there is only one alternative. That Miles took Wren from Rae and brought him to our house. I have no idea why he would do that, but I do know one thing for sure. Wren should be with his mum. I need to take him home.

42

By the time I return to the cottage I have a plan. It's not foolproof, but it's the best I have. I pack in silence. I can't tell Miles where I'm going. There's no way he'll let us leave.

I raid the washing line and the ironing pile because I can't risk him catching me taking clothes from the chest of drawers in our bedroom, even though he was fast asleep when I poked my head around the door. As an extra precaution, I bundle the clothes into black plastic refuse sacks so I can tell him I'm going to the tip if he sees me loading them into the car.

Shona has texted me her address. It's in Craigleith. 'Not the island in the Firth of Forth,' she said. 'Only puffins live there. You need the other one, north-west of the city centre.'

Google Maps says the journey will take eight-and-a-quarter hours. I've never driven that far before. Miles prefers to drive when we're together. I have studied the route, memorised it, because I will turn my phone off when I leave so Miles can't track me on Find My iPhone.

Once I reach the outskirts of Edinburgh, the directions to Shona's bungalow are too complicated to remember. I'll just have to take a chance and turn on my phone, but at least by then I'll have an eight-hour head start.

I warm up another bowl of soup and carry it upstairs. Miles is asleep, the sheets tangled between his legs, the soup I brought him at lunchtime untouched on his bedside table.

I watch him for a moment, trying to equate this sweat-soaked stranger with the man who swept me off my feet all those years ago. Because when Miles rescued me from that sleazeball in the nightclub I truly believed I'd fallen head first into a fairy tale.

But the bouquets of roses he bombarded me with, the declarations of love, the marriage proposal in the middle of a busy restaurant, weren't the romantic gestures I'd thought they were. They were the actions of a controlling man who had set me in his sights. I wasn't a person to Miles. I was a prize to be won. And Miles always wins.

'Miles,' I say, shaking his shoulder. 'Wake up.'

He groans, opens one eye and squints at me. 'What is it?'

'I've brought you some more soup. And you need to take your medicine.' I'm already pouring another generous measure of Night Nurse into the little plastic measuring cup. It was Shona's idea. It turns out she's a theatre nurse at the Royal Edinburgh Hospital.

'One of the active ingredients in Night Nurse is promethazine,' she said when I told her Miles was in bed with the flu. 'It's a sedating antihistamine. If you give him a couple of doses he'll sleep like a baby.'

I'm planning on giving him three to be on the safe side.

'I've had some already,' Miles mumbles.

I frown. 'That was yesterday.' I tap his shoulder and he reluctantly pulls himself to a sitting position. 'Come on, it'll bring your temperature down and help with the shivers.'

His skin was pale earlier, but now there are two high points of colour on his cheeks. I gaze at him dispassionately as he slurps down the noxious-looking green liquid.

'I'll sleep in the spare bedroom with Wren again tonight. I can't risk him catching this,' I say.

Miles nods. I hold out the soup, but he turns his head away like a sulky toddler who's just been offered a bowl of cabbage.

'I feel terrible,' he whines. 'Do you think I need to see the doctor?'

'It's the flu, Miles. You need rest and fluids. I'm sure you'll be feeling better in a couple of days.' I pick up the other bowl of soup. 'I'm going to give Wren his bath. I'll pop up later, OK?'

I'm halfway through the door when he bleats, 'His name's Max.'

Once Wren's safely tucked up in his Moses basket I make myself a big plate of beans on toast. I've decided to wait until it's dark before I leave, and sunset's not till a quarter past nine at this time of year, so I still have a couple of hours to kill.

After I've cleared away my plate and tidied up the kitchen, I make up a couple of spare bottles of milk for Wren then find a piece of paper and a pen and write the note I've already composed in my head.

M,

    I have taken Wren/Max to the police station. I know it's against your wishes, and I'm sorry for that, but I can't live with the knowledge I have stolen another woman's baby.

    If I'm not back by morning, it means I've been arrested and am being held in custody. I will phone you as soon as I can.

    I love you.

    L

The last three words stick in my craw but better that than

raise Miles's suspicions. And sending him on a wild goose chase to the police station will buy me a little more time if he does wake in the night and discover Wren and I have gone.

I prop the note against the kettle and check my watch. It's just gone half eight. Time for Miles's last dose of Night Nurse.

This time he's still half-asleep when I hold the plastic measuring cup to his lips and he drinks it without a murmur. I stand by the side of the bed waiting until his breathing deepens, then head downstairs.

Every sound makes me start as I carry our stuff to the car, and when Percy jumps out from behind a rose bush and weaves around my legs I have to clamp my hand over my mouth to stifle a shriek.

Shit, I'd forgotten about Percy. Miles won't remember to feed him and although he can probably fend for himself for a couple of days if I leave enough dry food down, I have no idea how long I'm going to be.

I dart inside, grab a bag of dry food and two boxes of Whiskas from the cupboard, and scurry next door to Arthur's.

He pulls open the door, a smile on his face.

'Hello, Lucy. To what do I owe this pleasure?'

Immediately I feel awash with guilt that I haven't been round for ages.

'I'm sorry to bother you so late, but I have a favour to ask.' I grimace. 'Mum's summoned me over to Portugal for Dad's sixtieth birthday and I'm sure Miles will remember to feed Perce, but, well, I thought I'd leave you some food just in case he forgets.'

'Of course. Can't let the old boy go hungry now, can we? How long are you away?'

'I'm not sure at the moment.' I bite my lip. 'It depends how long the birthday shenanigans last.'

'Want me to water the tomatoes?'

'Yes, please, Arthur.' I couldn't care less about the bloody tomatoes, but I need to keep up the pretence that I do.

Arthur's smile never wavers as he takes the cat food from me, and as I turn to go, he catches my arm.

'Is everything all right, Lucy, love? Only you know where I am if you ever need anything, don't you?'

His eyes are full of sympathy and I wonder if I'm the only person in the world who hasn't seen my husband for what he really is. No, because Mum and Dad fell for his charm. It's just they haven't spent long enough in his company to realise he's anything other than the perfect son-in-law.

'Everything's fine, Arthur, I promise. And thank you.' I hug him fiercely. His frailty and old man smell remind me painfully of Grandad and I have to concentrate really hard to stop myself from bursting into noisy sobs.

Eventually, I pull away. 'Better go. My flight's at silly o'clock and I haven't finished packing. Thanks so much for feeding Percy. He won't appreciate it – you know what cats are like – but I do.'

To my relief, Wren doesn't stir when I lift him gently from the Moses basket into his car seat. Before I leave the house, I creep up the stairs one last time. Miles is lying on his back snoring loudly.

I allow myself a small smile, tiptoe back downstairs, pick up Wren's car seat and leave the cottage.

43

Radio 4 is my soundtrack as the Mini eats up the miles on the long drive north. I listen to the calm, measured voices of the presenters, glad to have something to distract me from my thoughts, even if it is the day's events in parliament. The shipping forecast is playing when I pull into a service station for a loo break in Rugby just before one o'clock. By the time I reach Carlisle *Farming Today* is on and the sun is peeping over the horizon to the west.

Wren sleeps so soundly in the back of the car he doesn't even wake for his three o'clock feed, and we're approaching the outskirts of Edinburgh when he finally starts to grizzle. I pull into a quiet residential street to feed him. The milk's cold, but he's so hungry he drinks it anyway. I change his nappy on the back seat of the car, and am about to switch on my phone when I hesitate.

I'd always intended to look up the directions to Shona's house once I was in Edinburgh because I'd told myself that even if Miles did check the Find My iPhone app, I'd have an eight-hour head start on him. But, as I stare at the blank screen, misgivings start to surface.

What if he's woken from his Night Nurse-induced slumber earlier than I'd planned and has realised Wren and I have gone? If he's read my note, there's a chance he's already contacted Kent Police and discovered I haven't handed myself in at all. I put myself in his shoes. What's the first thing he'd do? It's obvious. He'd check his phone and see I'm in Scotland, and I can't risk him coming after me.

I gaze around the street in desperation and give a start when I see a figure dressed in black advancing along the pavement towards me. But it's just a runner: a tall, slim guy with dark hair tied in a topknot, wearing wraparound shades, Nike track pants and a matching T-shirt. I can just make out the tinny sound of a bass guitar emanating from his earphones.

'Excuse me?' I say, taking a hesitant step towards him. But he doesn't even shorten his stride as he pounds past. It's as if I'm completely invisible.

'Thanks, then,' I mutter, shaking my head at his retreating back. I hand Wren his rattle, which he bangs against the bottom of the seat while I gather up his bottle, bib and dirty sleepsuit and drop them into his changing bag.

How the hell am I going to find Shona's house without my phone? I force myself to think, but the long drive through the night has left me poleaxed with exhaustion and I'm all out of ideas. All I want to do is curl up on the back seat next to Wren and sleep for a month of Sundays. But I can't. I told Shona I would be with her by ten at the latest and it's already a quarter past eight and I have no idea how long it'll take me to reach Craigleith.

Before I do anything, I need to get rid of Wren's nappy, which stinks to high heaven. I hook the handle of the nappy sack on my little finger, blip the car lock and jog towards the bin I clocked when I turned into the street.

I'm dropping the nappy into the bin when there's a snap of

a letterbox behind me. I spin round to see a postman walking down a garden path, a clutch of envelopes in his hand.

His cheery 'Morning,' is accompanied by a wide smile and my shoulders slump in relief. If anyone can give me directions to Shona's house, it's a postie.

'Hello,' I say, smiling back. 'I wonder if you can help.'

'Sure,' he says. 'What's up?'

'I'm a bit lost.' I smile again, apologetically this time. 'And my phone it's... it's run out of charge. I'm trying to get to Craigleith.'

He sucks in his cheeks. 'You're in Swanston. You've still a way to go.'

'Is there a garage nearby where I could buy a street map?'

'I can do better than that. Got a pen and paper?'

I nod, open the passenger door and burrow through the glove box in search of the notepad and pencil I keep in there in case I'm ever hit with an idea for a book.

I give the postman Shona's address, and he scratches his chin, then reels off a set of complicated instructions, which I copy down verbatim, wondering if a street map might have been easier.

'It shouldn't take much more than twenty-five minutes,' he says, patting the bonnet of the Mini. 'Safe journey.'

I thank him and head back towards the bypass, following signs for Edinburgh West and Heriot-Watt University, as he'd told me to do. After five miles I turn off onto the A71. We pass through streets of post-war housing, past a large park and under a railway bridge. As we approach Murrayfield the houses increase in size, and when we reach Ravelston they become grander still.

From there it's not far to Craigleith, and soon I'm turning into Shona's street. I check the clock on the dash. It's almost ten to nine.

Shona lives in a traditional Scottish sandstone bungalow

hiding behind a tall beech hedge. The bungalow is pleasingly symmetrical, with bay windows flanking the vermilion front door and tall chimneys at either end of the slate roof. A gravel path lined with white lavender splits the immaculate lawn in two.

I park behind a cream Fiat 500 and twist in my seat to check on Wren, glad to see he's fast asleep. With his thumb in his mouth and a kiss-curl of hair stuck to his forehead, he looks utterly angelic.

I grab my handbag, unclip the car seat and make my way up the path to the front door, suddenly shy. What will Shona make of me, never mind the nephew she knew nothing about until yesterday?

I set the car seat down on the doorstep, take a deep breath and ring the bell.

44

I've barely had time to run a hand through my dishevelled hair when the door opens.

'Lucy?' says a tall woman with cropped black hair and intelligent blue eyes that gaze at me keenly behind black-framed glasses. She is wearing denim dungarees over a white T-shirt and a red scarf is tied jauntily around her neck. Her eyes flicker down to Wren, asleep in the car seat. 'You must be exhausted. Come in.'

I follow her into the bungalow, my head swivelling this way and that as I take everything in. The hallway is a sun-baked orange and the front room a dramatic Aubusson blue. There are houseplants everywhere: in huge terracotta pots on the floor, hanging from the ceiling, and lining every window ledge. The walls are covered with paintings – bold daubs of colour in mismatched frames. The effect is both chaotic and mesmerising.

'Your house is beautiful,' I say, setting the car seat down on a burnt-orange rug.

'Thank you.' She is still staring at Wren as if she's worried he might disappear in a puff of smoke if she looks away. 'Is this Rae's baby?' she asks.

'I think so. I mean, he must be, don't you think?'

She nods, then finally drags her gaze away. 'Have you eaten?'

'I grabbed a sandwich in Rugby.'

'Then you must be famished. I'll make some toast.'

I'm about to protest but my stomach rumbles loudly. 'That would be great, thank you.'

I follow Shona into the kitchen at the back of the house. It's another explosion of colour. You'd think the vibrant turquoise units would clash with the lime-green walls, but the bright jewel-like colours complement each other perfectly.

'Coffee?'

'Yes, please.' I place the car seat on the floor by the French doors, which look out on to a patio that is ringed by terracotta pots of hostas and dark red geraniums.

Shona pours coffee from a jug and hands me a carton of skimmed milk. She cuts two slices of bread and pops them in the toaster and my stomach clenches in anticipation.

'Honey, marmalade or Marmite?' she asks, placing a stone butter dish on the small kitchen table.

'Honey, please.' I pour a dash of milk into the coffee and take a sip. It's so strong you could stand a spoon in it and although I know it'll make me even more jittery than I am already, I drink it gratefully.

'Did the Night Nurse do the trick?' Shona asks.

I nod. 'Miles was dead to the world when I left last night.'

'And he has no idea you're here?'

'I left him a note saying I was taking Wren to the police station back in Kent.'

'Why didn't you?' Shona says, handing me the plate of toast.

I glance at her, surprised at her bluntness, but her voice is gentle.

'I'm curious, Lucy. It seems to me that the obvious course of action when you found the baby in your house was to call the police.'

'I was going to, but Miles talked me out of it.'

'And why would he do that?'

'Your guess is as good as mine.' I shrug, and start buttering the toast. I'm so hungry I've started to salivate. 'Because he didn't want social services involved?'

Shona hmms. 'You think?'

'To be honest, I don't know what to think. It's all such a mess. Either Rae left Wren with Miles because she couldn't cope, or Miles took Wren from Rae. But why would he do that?'

I drizzle honey over both slices of toast and take a bite, closing my eyes briefly as the sweetness dissolves on my tongue.

'And if that's the case, where's Rae?' Shona asks.

I meet her eye briefly and swallow, but the toast sticks in my throat, and I have to take another sip of coffee to help it down. Because that's the question at the centre of everything, isn't it?

Where *is* Rae?

45

After I've finished eating, Shona hands me the photograph of Rae and Wren she found in her mother's room at the nursing home. Even though I spent ages zooming in on every single detail on my phone yesterday, I pretend to study it anew.

'You don't recognise the cottage?' I ask.

She shakes her head.

'What about the mountain?'

'There are two hundred and eighty-two Munros in Scotland.' She sees my quizzical look and explains, 'Munros are mountains over three thousand feet. Never mind all the smaller summits.'

'What about a reverse image search?'

'I tried, but nothing came up.'

I stare at the photo. A stubby hawthorn tree to the right of the cottage is covered in creamy-white blossom, yet there's still snow on the top of the mountain. The lower slopes are covered in heather. The croft is shabby but the scenery is stunning. Magical, even.

I can't escape the feeling that I know this place. But it's impossible. This is the first time I've ever been to Scotland.

Perhaps it's because the mountain reminds me of our annual pilgrimages to North Wales when I was a kid. The craggy peaks of Snowdonia loomed over the caravan park we used to stay in just as this mountain towers over the little white cottage.

But I don't have a chance to dwell on it further because Wren wakes up demanding a feed. As I lift him out of the car seat, I realise I've left the changing bag with the ready-made cartons of milk in the car.

Shona looks flustered when I give him to her, and when I let myself back into the house she's holding him awkwardly, a faint grimace on her face.

'Would you like to feed him?' I offer; she is his auntie, after all.

'You're all right, thanks. I don't really do babies.' She gives an apologetic shrug. 'I prefer dogs.'

I hold out my arms and Shona hands Wren back with undisguised relief before pulling out a chair and watching her nephew glugging his milk from the other side of the table.

'Has Rae ever done anything like this before?' I ask.

'Had a baby and not told us? No!' she scoffs.

'That's not what I meant. Has she ever gone missing?'

Shona stands so abruptly the chair rocks back, hitting the wall. She stalks across the kitchen to the sink, runs a cloth under the tap and starts wiping the already spotless worktops.

'Shona?'

She stops, glances at me and sighs. 'Once, when she was at university. She'd been dumped by her boyfriend and took off halfway through the summer term of her second year. The first we knew of it was when the university's welfare officer phoned to ask if she'd come home. We were on the verge of contacting the police when she called.'

'Where was she?'

'She'd taken herself wild camping in the mountains. She said she needed space to clear her head. She was phoning because she'd run out of food. Dad drove up to the Cairngorms to pick her up and that was that.' Shona shrugged. 'She never did it again.'

That's where Shona could be wrong, I think. Perhaps Rae did run away again, this time to escape the suffocation, the mind-numbing drudgery, of new motherhood. She wouldn't be the first woman to walk out on her baby, and I don't suppose she'd be the last. It happens. Maybe she did literally run for the hills. The Cairngorms. I reach across the table for the photo of Rae and Wren. The feeling that I know this place is there again, only this time I understand why. I make a little noise of surprise and Shona's head jerks up.

'What is it?'

'I can't believe I didn't see it before,' I say, jabbing at the photo with my finger. 'I know where this is.'

46

Shona's thick black eyebrows knit together as she looks from me to the photo and back again.

'What do you mean, you know where it is?'

'It's the cottage in the Cairngorms Miles used to go to when he was a boy. His family used to stay there every summer.'

'Are you sure?'

'Absolutely.'

Shona produces a phone from the pocket of her dungarees and looks at me expectantly. 'What's the address?'

'Um. Well, I don't know the actual address.'

Her frown deepens. 'Are you saying you do know where this is, or you don't?'

Wren has finished his feed and I set the bottle on the table and lean him forwards so I can burp him.

'I'm saying I know it's the place where Miles and his family used to stay. It's obvious when I think about it. There was a mountain just behind the cottage which he used to climb. I bet there's a loch nearby, too. He told me the cottage was available for a long-term let.' I look sidelong at her. 'He wanted us to move there with Wren. He said no one would bother us and we could pretend Wren was ours.'

Shona's eyes widen. 'Let's get this straight. He wanted you to move into the house Rae was living in and play happy families with her baby while she was Christ knows where? Jesus.'

I don't blame Shona for being shocked. I would be, too, in her shoes. 'I know it doesn't sound great but Miles has this way of talking you into things you'd never normally consider. It's one of his superpowers, like lying through his teeth and self-aggrandising.' As jokes go, it's pretty lame and I'm not surprised when Shona doesn't smile. I shift Wren onto my shoulder and pat his back gently as I try to recall everything Miles told me about the cottage.

'The village has its own Facebook page and a fish and chip van comes every Thursday. Oh, and there's a primary school nearby too.'

'Can you remember the name of the school?' Shona asks.

'Something Scottish.' I try to picture the screen of Miles's phone as he waved the Ofsted report under my nose. 'Kin-something. Kinkirk, that was it.'

Shona types furiously into her phone. 'There's a village called Kinkirk just south of Aviemore.'

'Does it have a school?'

She nods and keeps typing. 'And a Facebook page.'

'How far is it from here?'

'Over two hours away.' Shona starts flinging things into a canvas bag. Two water bottles from the fridge, apples and bananas from the fruit bowl on the table, a cardigan from the back of the door.

'You want to leave now?' Despite the coffee, I'm on my knees with exhaustion. I don't think I could muster the energy to drive to the corner shop, let alone navigate the two-hour drive to the Cairngorms. And we might have identified the nearest village, but we have no idea where the croft itself is.

But Shona is already grabbing a set of keys from the work-top. 'The sooner the better. We'll take my car. You can sleep on the way.'

Half an hour later we are driving across the Firth of Forth in Shona's tiny Fiat 500. The Queensferry Crossing, she tells me, took six years to build and is over a mile-and-a-half long. I pretend to be interested but the truth is I'm struggling to keep my eyes open.

I turn in my seat to check on Wren. He's babbling away to himself in the back seat, taking the latest chapter in this crazy adventure in his stride.

Shona glances at me as I stifle a yawn. 'There's a travel cushion under the seat. I'll wake you when we reach Kinkirk.'

I fish the cushion out and tuck it between my head and shoulder. Classic FM is playing on the radio. Shona taps the steering wheel in time to the music and I let the rich notes wash over me as the Fiat trundles along in the slow lane.

When I close my eyes I see Rae standing in front of the croft, her slender arms wrapped protectively around Wren.

If she's there when we arrive I will have to give him back, and the possibility is so painful it leaves me breathless. My marriage is over, that much is clear. And with Miles out of the picture, Wren is all I have left.

I force down the lumpen mass that seems permanently lodged at the back of my throat and deepen my breathing, hoping sleep will rescue me from my spiralling thoughts. Oblivion, when it finally comes, is a blessed relief.

'Lucy, we're here.' Shona's soft Scottish accent drags me from a dreamless sleep. I rub my eyes and stretch, wincing at the crick in my neck.

'What's the time?' I ask groggily.

'Just after three.'

I unclip my seat belt to check on Wren. His eyes light up when he sees me.

'He's been as good as gold,' Shona says. 'I haven't heard a peep from him the whole way here.'

'Good.' I look around. We're in a small car park next to a stone building with a red awning. There are tables and chairs outside, and a sign on the side of the building says The Old Post Office Tea Rooms.

'I'm going to ask here if anyone recognises either Rae or the croft,' Shona says, unclipping her seat belt.

'I'll come with you.'

I slip Wren into his carrier and follow Shona into the tea room. It's busy with ramblers slurping tea and sharing hiking stories. Shona's about to march straight up to the counter but I touch her arm and point to a table in the corner. 'Let's have something to eat while we're here.'

She shakes my arm away. 'There isn't time.'

'Half an hour won't make a difference,' I say firmly. Huffing, she pulls out a chair.

We've barely sat down before a girl aged about fifteen appears with a couple of menus. Shona whips the photo of Rae from her bag and asks if she recognises the woman or the croft.

The girl takes a quick look and shakes her head. 'Sorry, I don't. But I'm sure Julia will.'

'Julia?'

'The owner. She's lived in Kinkirk all her life. She knows literally everyone. I'll ask her to pop out when she has a moment.'

'Thank you.' I hand the girl my menu. 'I'll have a cream tea, please. Shona?'

'Yes, whatever,' Shona says.

I smile at the girl. 'Make that two cream teas. Thank you.

And I don't suppose I could have a jug of hot water?' Wren's not due a feed for another hour or so, but it makes sense to give him a bottle now.

Moments later a white-haired woman arrives with a Pyrex jug of water.

'Are you the lady who wanted to know if I recognised someone?' she asks, setting the jug on the table out of Wren's reach. He gazes at her, wide-eyed. She smiles and chucks him under the chin. Shona slides the photo across the table to her. The woman's eyes widen a fraction. She knows, I think, my heart quickening.

'This is my sister, Rae,' Shona tells her. 'We've lost touch these last few months, but we think she might be living nearby.'

'I don't recognise the lassie, but that looks like Patrick Ryan's holiday place to me. The Nook, he calls it.'

Shona appears to have lost the power of speech, so I step in. 'How far is it from here?'

'Four or five miles as the crow flies, but about twenty minutes in the car.' She reels off directions, which I do my best to remember, trying to ignore the fluttering in the pit of my stomach.

When our cream teas arrive a few minutes later I find I have completely lost my appetite.

47

We follow Julia's directions to the letter, along narrow lanes, over bridges and past lochs, the only constant the wild beauty of the mountains in the distance.

We almost miss the single-track lane for the cottage, hidden as it is by walls of acid-green bracken. The Fiat complains bitterly at the potholes, lurching from side to side like a ship in a storm, Shona swearing under her breath when the little car hits a particularly deep hole and bottoms out.

After half a mile the bracken gives way to springy grass. And there it is: the tiny white croft in Shona's photo, with its slate roof, single chimney and a porch over the weathered front door.

The track widens out to an area of compacted hardcore that slopes sharply down to the cottage, and when Shona pulls up under a rowan tree at the top of the slope, I glance at her.

'How good's your handbrake?'

'OK, I think.' She pulls it up another notch and kills the engine. 'But I'll leave it in gear too. Better safe than sorry.'

A memory breaks loose in my mind. Miles and I had driven over to Hythe for the day not long after we'd moved back to the

UK. I'd parked the Mini on a hill behind the high street, then we'd headed through the town to the beach, walking all the way along the sea wall to Sandgate to have lunch at a pub. Miles, who'd offered to drive home, had ordered me a bottle of house red, and I was feeling pleasantly tipsy when we arrived back at the car. But the afternoon went pear-shaped when we realised the Mini had rolled down the hill, colliding with a low garden wall. The wall was fine but one of the Mini's headlights was cracked and the number plate had smashed. Miles had, predictably, been furious.

'For Christ's sake, Lucy, you can't have pulled up the hand-brake properly.'

'I'm sure I did—' I began.

'Then how did your car end up hitting a fricking wall? I hope you're feeling flush because this is going to cost an arm and a leg to fix.'

'I'm sorry,' I said, guilt slaying my happiness. It was weird, because I could have sworn I left the car in gear. I always did when I parked on even the gentlest of inclines. It was a habit my dad had drilled into me from the day I started driving. How on earth had I managed to forget?

'Not good enough,' Miles had muttered as he'd snatched the keys from me and yanked open the driver's door.

And that was the problem, I realise now, as Shona steps on the clutch and eases the Fiat into reverse. Nothing I did was ever good enough for Miles.

I clamber out and stretch my back, then peer through the rear side window. Wren's asleep again.

'Don't wake him. He'll be safe in the car,' Shona says. She's jiggling her keys in one hand and clutching her phone in the other, impatient to find Rae.

She's right; Wren probably would be perfectly safe in the

car if I wind down the window to let some air in, and it's silly to disturb him. But I can't bring myself to leave him on his own. I take the baby carrier from the boot of the car and bend down to kiss his cheek as I unclip him from the car seat and slip him into the carrier.

'Sorry, angel,' I whisper, as he whimpers in his sleep. I glance at Shona, who rolls her eyes then marches down the slope to the cottage.

She raps her knuckles on the front door. The sound is almost obscenely loud in the quiet of the glen. There's no answer, but did we really think there would be?

I walk around the cottage looking for clues, but the curtains in every window are tightly drawn. The place is keeping its secrets close to its chest. At the back of the cottage is the poly-tunnel Miles told me about. I pull open the sliding door and step inside. My mouth drops open. There are neat rows of peas, carrots and tomatoes, broad beans, onions and garlic. But every-thing is withered, the leaves scorched, the plants dead. Someone – and it must have been Rae, because who else could it have been? – has clearly spent hours painstakingly digging, planting and nurturing a whole polytunnel of vegetables only to let them perish by not watering them. It doesn't make sense. Then I remember that this is the woman who may have walked out on her son.

I leave the polytunnel to go in search of Shona, yelping in shock as I trip over something half-hidden in the long grass. I manage to stop myself from falling flat on my face by flinging my arms out just in time.

'Bloody hell,' I mutter, peering at the cast-iron manhole cover at my feet. I stroke Wren's head, appalled at just how close I was to landing on him, but he doesn't even stir.

On the way back to the croft we pass a flower border. The colourful muddle of cornflowers and blue poppies, lupins and campion seem out of place against the dramatic backdrop of the

Cairngorms. The idea that anyone could improve on the stunning setting is almost ludicrous. And, just as it was in the polytunnel, the neglect is evident. Bindweed and nettles are staking their claim, taking over, choking the life out of the delicate flowers.

Shona's still by the front door, peering through the letterbox.

'No luck?' I ask.

She turns around and shakes her head. 'I wondered if there was a spare key but I've checked in all the usual places and can't find one.'

'Let me have a look.' I turn side on to the door, slip my hand into the letterbox and feel around. When my fingers close around a piece of string, I can't help but grin.

'What is it?' Shona asks.

I show her the key on the end of the string. 'It's where we always leave our spare key. Miles's idea,' I explain, slotting it into the lock. It turns smoothly and I push open the door. Shona hovers beside me.

'What's up?'

'Won't we be breaking the law?' she asks.

I laugh mirthlessly. 'I've stolen a baby and drugged my husband. Being arrested for breaking into a house is the least of my worries.'

48

A musty smell hits me the moment I step into the narrow hallway. The stale whiff of air that hasn't been disturbed in a long while. There are a couple of envelopes on the doormat and Shona stoops to pick them up. She glances at them, then hands them to me wordlessly. They are addressed to Mr P. J. Ryan and look like bills. I remember Julia, the woman from the cafe, saying The Nook was Patrick Ryan's holiday place.

I follow Shona through a door to the right into a living room. She yanks open the curtains, disturbing a cloud of dust that tickles my nostrils. The sparsely furnished room is a throwback to the seventies, with a teak G Plan sideboard and matching coffee table, a cracked brown leather three-piece suite and a garish floral carpet.

But there are cosy touches: a collection of church candles in the fire grate; soft throws over the arms of the sofa; cutesy cushions featuring stags and Highland cattle; a sheepskin rug in front of the hearth.

We continue our exploration of the cottage. The furniture in the main bedroom is pure eighties pine. Pine wardrobe, pine dressing table, pine chest of drawers, pine bed. There's even pine cladding on the ceiling, but there are pretty shades on the bedside lamps and a string of fairy lights over the dressing table mirror. I pull open the top drawer of the chest of drawers, unsure what I'm going to find, but there's nothing in it. I try the rest. They're all empty.

The tiny bathroom is next to the kitchen at the back of the house. The cast-iron bath is stained a reddish-brown and I shoot a worried look at Shona.

'It's the peat,' she says. 'There'll be no mains drainage out here. The cottage probably gets its water supply from a spring or a well, and there'll be a cesspit or septic tank for the waste-water.' She turns on the cold tap and a gush of water the colour of weak tea gurgles out.

'I almost tripped over the manhole cover for the cesspit earlier,' I say, looking in the mirrored cabinet above the sink. 'Where are all Rae's things? She can't have taken everything with her.'

'I don't know.' There's a sag to Shona's shoulders that wasn't there earlier. She'd been full of purpose when we'd left Edinburgh. I suppose she thought there was a chance we would find Rae at the house, or at least come across a clue as to where she's gone. But her hopes must be ebbing away as we trudge from room to room finding nothing.

I touch her arm and give it a gentle squeeze. 'Come on, let's check the kitchen.'

Unlike in the rest of the house, there's a faint chemical smell in the narrow galley kitchen. I wrinkle my nose, surprised. Chlorine? No, bleach, I think. I look around. The dark oak-effect units fell out of fashion decades ago but the floor and worktops are all squeaky clean. Whether Shona has noticed the smell is hard to tell. She's taken a seat at the small round table at the far end of the kitchen and is slumped forwards with her head in her hands.

I check the cupboard under the old butler sink. There's a

bottle of supermarket own-brand thick bleach. Wren tries to grab it but I whisk it out of his reach and he lets out a frustrated cry.

'It's dangerous, sweetheart.' I give the bottle a shake. It's almost empty. Something about this gives me a prickle of unease. The rest of the house is tidy enough, but there's a layer of dust on every surface and the carpet doesn't look as though it's been near a vacuum in weeks. There's a ring of grime around the bath and toothpaste marks on the taps in the sink. Yet the kitchen is spotless. So why did Rae decide to give the kitchen a deep clean before she left and not bother with the rest of the house? I tell myself not to let my imagination run away with me. She probably ran out of time or inclination, nothing more sinister than that.

I flick open a few more cupboards but it's clear Rae hasn't left any essentials behind. There's a set of bland white crockery, the type that's ubiquitous in holiday lets the world over. Plain glasses, a glass measuring jug, some serving dishes and saucepans and frying pans. A stainless-steel cruet set and a wooden block of cheap kitchen knives.

Next to the toaster are coffee, tea and sugar jars. I open the lid of the coffee jar. The granules inside have clumped together so thoroughly that when I give the pot a shake, they don't move a millimetre.

I'm about to offer Shona a black tea when I spy a familiar-looking bottle right at the back of the cupboard. I don't need to read the label to know what it is. Absolut Vodka. My stomach lurches and I feel a flutter in my chest. Anxiety? Terror? Long-ing? I glance at Shona. Her head is still buried in her hands. How easy it would be to pour half a tumbler right now and down it in one. I can almost feel the scorch of the alcohol at the back of my throat, the sweet moment when it hits my blood-stream, the gloriously freeing sense of couldn't-give-a-fuckness as the vodka dulls my senses and insulates me from my fears. It would be so easy.

I take the bottle from the cupboard and weigh it in my hands. Just one drink to get me through this. It's not like I'm driving or anything. Vodka doesn't smell on your breath so Shona wouldn't even notice. I'm unscrewing the lid when Wren's tiny fingers reach for the neck of the bottle and I freeze. What am I thinking? I can't drink, not while I'm looking after him. My cheeks burn with shame and I drop the lid in my haste to screw it back on. It clatters onto the worktop and Shona looks up in surprise.

'What was that?'

'Nothing.' I angle my body so she can't see the vodka bottle. 'Have you tried the back door?'

'Why would I do that?'

'To see if it's locked.'

She hauls herself to her feet and when her back is turned I pick up the lid, screw it on and push the vodka back into the corner of the cupboard.

'It is,' she says dully.

I join her by the door. After a moment she holds out a hand to Wren and he grasps her finger. She widens her eyes in mock horror and purses her lips in a perfect circle. He chuckles. A smile creeps across her face. It's the first time she's properly engaged with him since we arrived.

'I might put Wren in his car seat for a bit. He gets heavy after a while. Could you hold him for a second while I fetch it?' I don't give Shona the chance to refuse, lifting Wren out of the carrier and handing him to her.

'How should I hold him?'

'Preferably not at arm's length,' I tell her, and she gives me a rueful smile. 'Like this, look.' I demonstrate, and she rests him against her side, facing outwards. He immediately turns and tries to grab the red scarf around her neck.

I bring the car seat and changing bag in from the Fiat and Shona watches as I change Wren on the sheepskin rug in front of the fire in the living room.

'I'll try putting him down for a nap in here. I don't suppose he'll sleep, but you never know.' I strap him into his car seat, tuck his fleece blanket around him and pull the curtains. 'Night-night, angel,' I murmur, even though he doesn't look very sleepy. But he is happy sucking his thumb and watching the beam of light rippling through the gap I've left in the curtains, so I drop a kiss on his little snub nose and head back to the kitchen.

There's a vase of dead flowers on the table. Rae must have forgotten to throw them away when she blitzed the kitchen. Once again, I am struck by the ways in which she tried to inject a bit of her personality into the croft, futile as it seems when viewed through a stranger's eyes. But the flower border in the garden, the candles and throws, the cushions and fairy lights barely scratch the surface, because in reality the place needs completely gutting and starting again.

Despite that, Rae did her best to make this shabby, damp cottage into a home, and her faith that she could do so breaks my heart.

49

I open the cupboard with the crockery in, trying not to look at the vodka as I reach for two mugs.

'Tea?' I call to Shona, who has stayed in the living room to keep Wren company. 'It'll have to be black, I'm afraid.'

'Yes, please. But there are some of those little pots of UHT milk in one of the drawers,' Shona calls back. 'The one by the toaster, I think.'

I fill the kettle and switch it on, then try the drawer. It's full of cutlery, so I try the next one down, which contains tablemats, coasters and a red and white checked tablecloth. I find what I'm looking for in the third drawer: next to a spare box of teabags and a jar of coffee there's an old ice-cream tub filled with plastic pots of long-life milk. I scoop a couple out and go to push the drawer closed, but it won't shut. Something is jammed at the back.

It's a white envelope with a first-class stamp in the top right-hand corner and a name and address written in neat hand-writing on the front.

Shona's name and address.

The tea forgotten, I jog back into the living room. Shona is kneeling in front of Wren playing peek-a-boo. He is chortling with glee.

'Shona,' I say urgently.

'What's up?' she asks, without turning around.

'I found a letter at the back of one of the drawers. It's addressed to you.'

This grabs her attention, and she whips around. 'Me?'

I pass her the envelope. She studies it for a moment, her face paling, then stares at me. 'It's Rae's writing.'

I give a tiny nod. I'd thought as much.

'Do you think I should open it?' she says, her index finger lightly tracing her name.

'Of course. It's addressed to you, isn't it?'

'But Rae didn't post it. Maybe she wrote it, then changed her mind about me reading it.' She glances at me again and must notice my raised eyebrows because she sighs. 'You're right, I should open it.' But she still doesn't move.

'Would you like me to read it first?' I ask her gently.

She gives a quick nod. 'I'll finish making the tea. Sugar?'

'One, please.' I wait until she's gone, then tear open the envelope and pull out the dozen or so handwritten sheets of paper inside, and as sunlight streams through the gap in the curtains and Rae's baby gurgles in his car seat by my feet, I begin to read.

Dear Shona,

I hope you never get to read these words, because if you do it means that things have not panned out as I'd hoped. If you're wondering what I mean, stick with it, kid. I'll get there.

[It's what you used to say to me when we were growing up, d'you remember? It used to drive me insane!]

I want to start this letter with an apology. I know you must have been out of your mind with worry this last year. I wanted to contact you so many times, believe me, and I hope that by the time you have finished reading this letter you'll understand why I didn't.

Remember when I first decided I wanted to be an engineer? I was still at primary school...

50

RAE

I was still at primary school when I decided I wanted to be an engineer. Ten, maybe eleven. I wasn't interested in make-up or dancing or singing like everyone else. I wanted to take things apart and see if I could put them back together again. Things like Dad's watch and the old transistor radio he and Mum threw out when they got their posh new digital one. And Mum's precious George Foreman Grill, although that didn't go so well.

But I always enjoyed figuring out how things worked and solving problems. Give me a puzzle and I'd sit there for as long as it took to crack it.

Mum always used to say the apple never fell far from the tree and according to Dad, I was my father's daughter. When my sister, Shona, left for university Dad and I would spend hours in his shed fixing everything from knackered old bikes to ancient lawnmowers. And while we dismantled and rebuilt the stuff other people would have taken to the tip, he told me stories of his life on the rig.

Like the time he rescued an exhausted barn owl that had crash-landed on the platform after being blown out to sea. He looked after the poor thing until it was strong enough to be flown back – by helicopter, no less! – to a rescue centre on the mainland. The pods of dolphins and minke whales he used to see. Sharks too, on occasion. And storms more ferocious than any we ever saw on land.

Oil rigs seemed impossibly romantic to me then: iron islands in the North Sea. Super-structures. Mighty fortresses.

I remember telling Shona I wanted to work on a rig. She thought I was joking, even though I'd never been more serious about anything in my life. But she was so proud when I graduated with a first in chemical engineering. And you should have seen Dad's face at my graduation ceremony. 'That's my girl,' he whispered in my ear as we posed for photos afterwards.

My first job onshore was all well and good, but I yearned to be on a rig with the tang of saltwater on my lips. The tragedy is that cancer had taken Dad from us by the time I got my first job offshore.

At first, working on the rig was everything I'd ever dreamt of and more. The camaraderie, the problem-solving, the satisfaction of a job well done. Our rig in the middle of the Persian Gulf was like a little village; the roustabouts, roughnecks and drillers my new family.

I was fulfilled. Happy.

The day I saw a blurry grey shape floating in the sea beneath the rig is the day everything went to shit.

I thought the grey shape was a dolphin at first, and had pulled out my phone from the pocket of my coveralls to take a picture when a voice remarked, 'A dugong. That's not something you see every day.'

I turned to see a heavy-lidded man with a sandy beard and ruddy cheeks standing beside me. I'd seen him around but had never spoken to him.

I smiled at him. 'What the heck is a dugong?'

'They're related to the manatee. They're also called sea cows.' He leaned on the rails, peering over at the dugong, which was meandering slowly through the water. 'They're known as the ocean's gentle giants. They're pretty rare.'

'So we're lucky to see it?'

'We are. They're said to have inspired the ancient tales of mermaids and sirens.' He produced his phone, tapped away for a moment, and showed me a photo of a strange-looking creature with black, soulful eyes, a large snout and a dolphin-like tail.

I laughed. 'I'd hope your average mermaid was a bit better-looking.'

He smiled at me, stepped forwards and held out a hand.

'John Westfield,' he said.

I slipped my phone back in my pocket. 'Rae MacDonald.'

'That's a funny name for a pretty girl.'

It seemed an inappropriate thing for him to say, and I know Shona would have torn him to shreds, but I let it go. 'It's R-A-E. I'm Scottish,' I explained, as if he wouldn't have been able to tell from my accent.

'And I'm Welsh. So we are both Celts. Something else we have in common. Apart from the dugong,' he added, seeing my perplexed expression. 'Nice to meet you, Rae.'

He was still holding my hand in his and I pulled away, suddenly uncomfortable. I didn't like the way his eyes roved over my coveralls, as if he could see right through them. I muttered something about an equipment check I needed to carry out and beat a hasty retreat.

And that is the day John Westfield decided I was fair game.

At first, I thought it was a coincidence that he was always standing behind me in the queue for the canteen, or working out in the rig's tiny gym at the same time as me. He would make small talk, asking me how my day was going or if I'd seen the pod of bottlenose dolphins that had been spotted north of the rig that morning and I would reply, of course I would, because he was just being friendly, wasn't he?

But my skin felt prickly after every encounter and I always made sure I had an excuse up my sleeve so I could make my escape.

Things escalated the day we found ourselves alone in the gym. I was stretching after a stint on the running machine, my back to the door, my T-shirt damp with sweat, when someone came up behind me and groped me.

'What the fuck!' I yelled, spinning around and twisting myself away. It was John Westfield. Of course it was. 'Get your fucking hands off me, you arsehole!'

'Just being friendly,' he said, pulling a face. 'No need to throw a hissy fit.'

My patience snapped and I squared up to him, my hands on my hips. 'Don't ever touch me again, you creep. Do you understand?'

He sneered at me. 'A girl like you should be grateful to get it where you can.'

'How dare you—!'

'Is everything all right?'

We both turned to see a tall, dark-haired man striding into the gym.

John Westfield seemed to deflate in front of my eyes. 'I was just going,' he said. 'It's not my fault some people can't take a compliment.'

He scurried out of the door and the man went to touch my arm, then obviously thought better of it.

'He wasn't giving you any grief, was he?' the man asked.

'Nothing I can't handle,' I said, and then, to my intense shame, I burst into tears.

He handed me a clean handkerchief, guided me to one of the weight benches and sat me down. Once the tears finally dried up, he asked if I wanted to talk about it.

I'd told Shona about Westfield's creepy behaviour in emails home but she was thousands of miles away, and the urge to unburden myself to a friendly face was too much. I found myself telling this kind man how every time I seemed to turn, Westfield was in my eyeline, watching me. How I'd written it off as a coincidence at first, but as the weeks had gone by, I'd found his constant presence downright disturbing.

'Why haven't you reported him?' he asked. It was a perfectly reasonable question, and I sighed.

'Although he's always around, he hasn't actually done anything wrong. I didn't think anyone would believe me. And it could just be a coincidence; there's not exactly much space on an oil rig.'

We shared a look of understanding then, because life on a rig is a noisy, cramped existence and the notion of personal space is just that, a notion.

'But something changed today?' the man guessed.

Just when I thought I'd cried myself dry, my eyes welled with tears again. 'He touched me up.'

'He did what?' the man growled. But I knew his anger was directed at Westfield, not me.

'He grabbed me from behind and tried to hug me. I told him to fuck off, and that's when you walked in. Thank God you did.'

'Listen, Rae – it is Rae, isn't it?'

I nodded. Most people knew my name. I was one of only a handful of women on the rig.

'You should report him. That kind of behaviour is not acceptable. I can come with you, if you like?'

'That's very kind.' I sniffed and ran the back of my hand across my tear-streaked cheeks. 'Let me think about it, OK?'

'OK,' the man said. 'But if he steps out of line again – and I mean even an inch – you come to me and I'll deal with him, all right?'

I nodded. 'Thank you.'

'I mean it. I've got your back.' He grinned. 'Although you did a pretty good job of handling him yourself, from what I saw.'

I gave him the glimmer of a smile. 'Sorry if the air was a bit blue.'

'No need to apologise. That jerk deserved everything he got.' He held out a hand. 'I'm Miles, by the way. Miles Quinn.'

RAE

Things were better for a while. John Westfield was a classic bully who, once confronted, slunk away to lick his wounds, and although I remained hyper-aware of his presence, he seemed to give me a wide berth.

It helped that Miles was on the same shift pattern as me, and made sure he was around in communal areas like the canteen and TV room when I was. I almost bit his hand off when he suggested we started training together in the gym. I hadn't been there since Westfield groped me and I missed the buzz of an intense workout like crazy.

Miles may have been twelve years older than me, but we just clicked. He was half-Scottish and had spent his summers in the Highlands when he was growing up. He loved fell running and rock climbing as much as I did and we shared the same sense of humour. It was good to have a real friend on the rig.

Shona would have probably said I had a crush on him, and perhaps I did. But Miles never made a secret of the fact that he was married, and he never once made a move on me. He was the perfect gentleman.

Life on the rig was good again, until the day I bumped into John Westfield in the engine room. He did his best to disguise his animosity, but I could see it in his clenched jaw and the subtle flare of his nostrils.

'Hello, stranger,' he said with a smile that made no attempt to reach his eyes. 'I haven't seen you around for a while. Anyone would think you're avoiding me.'

What was I supposed to say to that? *Of course I'm avoiding you, you pervy prick?* Instead I bit my lip and said nothing.

'Too busy fawning around Miles Quinn, I expect. You do know he's married, don't you?'

Heat coloured my cheeks. Hating my body for betraying me, I said, 'Of course I do. I've met Lucy. She's lovely.'

This, I'm ashamed to say, was a lie. Miles occasionally mentioned his wife, but he'd never suggested we all meet up while we were onshore. Nevertheless, it seemed to knock some of the wind out of Westfield's sails and his brawny shoulders slumped.

Sensing I had the upper hand, I said, 'Talking of wives, how's Siân? And little Dylan, of course?' Miles had told me Westfield had a wife and four-year-old son waiting for him at home in Colwyn Bay. Can you believe the actual fuckwittery of the man? 'It must be hard for her, keeping the home fires burning while you're away,' I said.

His lips compressed, as if he was biting back a reply.

'Anyway, I must dash. I should have been in the control room five minutes ago,' I added breezily, though my heart was going nineteen to the dozen at the sheer proximity of this creepy man.

He muttered something under his breath as I turned towards the door. I looked over my shoulder and said, 'I'm sorry, what did you say?'

'I said you're a fucking bitch,' he hissed. 'And you're gonna get what's coming to you, just you wait and see.'

Miles was incandescent when I told him and was all for marching straight to the rig manager and reporting Westfield for sexual assault.

'Miles, don't,' I pleaded, grabbing his arm. 'It was just words. He didn't touch me.'

My voice wobbled, and a tear slid down my cheek. Miles held out his arms.

'Come here,' he said softly. I sank into his embrace, revelling in the feel of his strong arms around me, breathing in the lemony scent of his aftershave. Lucky Lucy, I caught myself thinking, then pushed the thought firmly from my mind. Miles was my friend, that was all.

Perhaps he never found a chance to speak to Westfield. Perhaps he did, and his attempt to warn the sleazebag off backfired spectacularly.

All I know is that that night the unthinkable happened. The thing we fear every time we walk along an unlit street or pull on a tight-fitting top. The thing we fear above all else.

That night Westfield came into my room and raped me.

On the morning of my fourteenth birthday, I broke Mum's make-up mirror. I accidentally knocked it off the bathroom windowsill while I was putting on suntan cream before a family picnic at Portobello Beach, and it shattered into a hundred pieces.

I was terrified about the seven years' bad luck. Mum was more worried I would stand on a shard of glass and cut my foot to smithereens. I remember helping her sweep up the tiny pieces, which had scattered across the entire bathroom floor like seed pods on the wind, just waiting for a barefooted victim to troop into the room to clean their teeth or pee.

My memories of the night I was raped are like that shattered mirror. I can only recollect fragments. Tiny shards of memory that pierce my skin like broken glass when I least expect it.

I finished my shift at six and, after a quick shower, had dinner in the canteen. I can remember what I ate: chicken biryani and bread and butter pudding. Miles joined me as I was finishing and offered to fetch me a cup of decaf tea.

He asked if I wanted to watch a film with him in the TV room, but I was hit by a wave of exhaustion and could barely keep my eyes open, so I took myself off to bed, even though it wasn't even eight o'clock in the evening. My cabin mate, Shelley, was on the opposite shift, so I had the place to myself.

Assuming I was coming down with the flu-like bug that was doing the rounds, I didn't even bother to undress. I just went straight to bed. That shard of memory is still intact. I pulled the covers up under my chin and plunged into the deepest sleep, not realising I'd forgotten to lock the door. After that it's all tiny pieces of smashed memory. A pitch-black room... The sound of shallow breathing... Fingers sliding between my thighs... Hot breath in my face... A body pressing down on me...

And then nothing until I woke, dry-mouthed and anxious, the next morning, wondering if it was all a dream. Scratch that. A nightmare.

But deep down, I knew it wasn't and when I hobbled to the bathroom, the bruises, the blood and the torn skin just confirmed it.

John Westfield had slunk into my room when I was asleep, and he had raped me. And I had done nothing to stop him. I had neither screamed nor fought nor run away. I had been paralysed, trapped in a body that had lost its ability to do anything at all. I had frozen.

I don't know how I functioned in the days that followed. Miles saved me. He came to find me when I didn't turn up for the morning safety briefing, knocking softly on the door, his eyes widening with shock when he saw my tear-stained face.

He coaxed the truth out of me with kindness and compassion, respecting my decision not to report the incident, at least while we were still offshore. He told the rig manager I was sick, arranged for Shelley to bunk up with someone else, and made sure I ate.

'Why are you doing this?' I asked him, gesturing towards the tea and toast he brought me one morning.

'You say it like it's a chore. I like looking after you,' he said, perching on Shelley's bed and smiling. 'I care about you, Rae.'

A warmth spread through me then. Miles was the only person in the world who knew what had happened. I hadn't even told my own sister. Looking back, I'm not really sure why I hadn't.

But Miles was happy to listen as I wept and raged. He handed me tissues and calmed me down. And when I finally emerged from my room, pale and drawn, he was by my side.

When the day came for us to return to shore I was filled with relief. Everything had changed for me. I no longer saw the rig as an iron island rising from the ocean. It was now a prison, and the thought of being locked up with the man who had attacked me was too much for me to bear. I couldn't wait to be back in my tiny studio apartment in Dubai, looking out over landscaped gardens, not the endless blue of the Persian Gulf.

I was late turning up for the helicopter shuttle back to shore, and only when I had fixed my harness did I look up and straight into the eyes of John Westfield.

My fear was visceral, my scalp prickling and my stomach swooping as if the helicopter had just hit an unexpected patch of turbulence even though we hadn't actually left the landing pad.

I spent the journey staring out of the window at the turquoise sea below, trying to calm my breathing and wishing Miles was beside me.

Looking back, I think that was the moment I realised I could never go back to the rig.

Two weeks later I found out I was pregnant.

52

RAE

The stupid thing is, it had never even occurred to me that I might have been pregnant, perhaps because my memories of that night were still so fragmented. There were times I even wondered if the rape had happened at all.

My recall might have been hazy, but there was nothing ambiguous about the two blue lines on the pregnancy test.

I couldn't tell Shona. I couldn't bear to hear the shock and disappointment in her voice. I couldn't tell Mum. Dementia had stolen her from us. I had no friends in Dubai, not really. And so I called the one person I knew had my back: Miles.

He was on the doorstep within an hour, a pink box in his hands.

'Bubble bath, chocolate, a book, some cosy socks and a candle,' he said. 'The woman in the shop called it a pamper hamper.' He pulled a face and I smiled despite myself. It was so good to see him.

'What's so bad that you couldn't tell me over the phone?' he asked, once we were sitting at my tiny kitchen table with a cup of tea.

I picked at a loose piece of skin by my thumbnail. 'I'm pregnant.'

Miles blinked. 'Pregnant?'

I nodded. 'From, you know—'

He set his mug on the table and reached for my hand. 'And how do you feel about it?'

'Terrible. Worse than terrible. Absolutely shit. Like being raped wasn't bad enough.' My voice wobbled. 'I don't think I can have this baby.'

'But abortions aren't legal in the UAE,' he said. 'You'd go to jail, and that's if you even managed to find a doctor who would agree to help you.'

'I can't go home until I know what I'm going to do,' I told him emphatically.

Miles squeezed my hand and was quiet for a while, thinking. Eventually, he said, 'You know, I could have a solution. The cottage in Kinkirk we used to stay in when I was a kid is up for rent. It's in the middle of the Cairngorms. You could move there while you decide what to do.'

'In the Cairngorms?'

'Plenty of fell running on the doorstep,' he joked.

'But I don't know anyone in the Cairngorms.'

'I could ask for a transfer back to Aberdeen. I could help you.'

'What about Lucy?' I asked, drawing my hand away.

'Ah, well, there's something you need to know about me and Lucy.' He scratched his chin. Only then did I notice the stubble. It looked like he hadn't shaved for days. 'We've decided to separate.'

I couldn't hide the shock from my face. 'You've what? Why?'

He sighed. 'It hasn't been working for a long time. It's no one's fault. Just one of those things.'

'Why didn't you tell me?'

He looked sidelong at me. 'I didn't want you to think I was hitting on you.'

'I would never think that,' I said, thinking, *I wish you had*. But I also knew it was too late for me. Who wants a woman carrying the child of a rapist? No one, that's who. But Miles was still talking.

'...so I could stay with you when I'm onshore,' he said a little self-consciously, then his voice turned serious. 'Let me help you, Rae. Please.'

'Why would anyone want to help me?' I said in a small voice.

'Because we're friends.' He took my hand again. 'Aren't we?'

Friends. Disappointment settled in my stomach like sediment. If only he knew how much I longed for more. But having Miles as a friend was better than nothing, so I nodded and he squeezed my fingers.

'Good girl. And you know I said I didn't want you to think I was hitting on you?' His Adam's apple bobbed up and down as he swallowed. 'How, um... God, this is difficult... How would you feel if I did?'

I gazed at him, my heart in my mouth. 'I would like it very much.'

We grinned at each other foolishly for a moment, our fingers laced together, until I remembered why it could never happen.

As if he could sense I was faltering, Miles frowned. 'What is it?'

'The baby,' I said, glancing at my flat stomach.

'What about the baby?'

'You won't want another man's child.'

'Ah,' he said, his eyes fixed on mine. 'That's where you're wrong.'

53

RAE

I was still in Dubai, hiding out in my apartment, when I handed in my notice at work.

During my exit interview, conducted over a video call, I reported John Westfield for sexual harassment. I didn't tell the woman from HR about the rape. I couldn't trust my memory. If she'd asked for details, I couldn't have given her any. I had no proof. She might have suspected I'd made it up to incriminate him. She tried to talk me out of quitting, worried, no doubt, about a claim of constructive dismissal further down the line, but my mind was made up.

I was packing for the flight home when Miles rang from the rig with some shocking news.

'You don't have to worry about Westfield any more,' he said, after he'd asked about my morning sickness – terrible – and my hormones – completely haywire.

'Has he been fired?' I asked hopefully.

Miles laughed. 'Not exactly. He's dead.'

At first, I thought I'd misheard. 'He's what?'

'Silly prick jumped off the rig last night. He'd just come out of a meeting with HR.'

The colour drained from my face as I remembered Westfield had a wife and a little boy. A wife who was now a widow and a little boy who no longer had a father.

'That's awful,' I gasped.

'I thought you'd be pleased,' Miles said, almost accusingly.

'I would never have reported him if I thought he'd do something like that.'

'It wasn't just you, Rae. Claims were stacking up against him left, right and centre. It's not your fault he was too much of a coward to face them.'

My hand slid to my stomach. 'Do people know what he did to me?'

'Only HR, and they only know what you told them. I haven't breathed a word to anyone about what happened that night.'

That was something, I supposed. I realised Miles was still talking.

'Word is he'd just been told he was facing a gross misconduct hearing. Let's face it, he did everyone a favour.'

'I guess,' I said, as the news sank in. But although in some ways I was glad no one else would have to endure the living hell John Westfield put me through, I couldn't shake the feeling I had his blood on my hands.

I suppose I could have changed my mind about leaving the rig after Westfield died. But I could already feel the pure, soft air of the Highlands on my skin. I was done with Dubai.

I should have told Shona what I was planning. What I did, disappearing like that, was truly unforgivable. But I was too wrapped up in myself to give her or Mum a second thought, if I'm honest. I will carry the burden of my guilt for as long as I live.

Miles drove me to the airport, guiding me through check-in and taking me for a coffee when we saw my flight was running late.

'Lucy couldn't touch the stuff when she was pregnant,' he said, nodding at my cup.

I stared at him in astonishment. 'You never told me you and Lucy had kids.'

'We don't,' he said. 'She had a miscarriage.' A flicker of regret crossed his face. 'There were complications. She can't have children now.'

'I'm so sorry. That must have been awful. Poor Lucy. How did she cope?'

His expression hardened. 'By drowning her sorrows.'

I didn't know what to say to this, so I sipped my coffee and told Miles how excited I was to finally see the cottage. When he'd shown me the details on the rental website, I have to admit my heart had plummeted. The place was run-down, unloved, little more than a bothy. But it clearly meant a great deal to him so I found myself raving about its rustic charm and idyllic views, and this seemed to please him.

We made our way to the security gate and I riffled through my bag looking for my passport and boarding pass, suddenly gripped by panic. How would I cope, pregnant and alone in the middle of nowhere? I told myself I should forget all about Miles's crazy plan and call Shona the minute I arrived at Edinburgh Airport. I knew my kind, sensible sister would be there like a shot. She would know exactly what to do. The thought of letting her take charge was so, so seductive.

Just then, Miles lifted my chin and gazed into my eyes with such an intensity my heart skipped a beat.

'I'll be there in a week or so. I just need to sort out some stuff this end. Everything's going to be all right, Rae.' He bent down and kissed me lightly on the lips, sending darts of pleasure zipping through me. His hands slid down to cup my belly. 'You don't need anyone else. You and the baby have me now.'

54

RAE

Despite Miles's promises, I almost called Shona when the plane finally landed at Edinburgh. I'm still not sure why I didn't. Maybe it was the fleeting memory of his lips on mine, his assurances he would look after me and the baby. More likely, it was because Miles had spent the days before I left Dubai telling me how disappointed Shona would be, convincing me she would march me straight to the nearest police station to report the rape, when he knew this was the last thing I wanted. He was always so sure of himself that I believed every word he said. It's only now I can see my infatuation blinded me.

Miles had arranged for a car to pick me up from the airport and take me to Kinkirk. I dozed in the back, exhausted after the flight, only waking when we pulled into the big Tesco in Aviemore.

The driver waited in the car while I pushed a trolley round the aisles, filling it with everything on the list Miles had sent me, from long-life milk and pasta to a breadmaking machine, yeast and flour. Enough to keep me going for at least a couple of weeks.

The driver helped me load the shopping into the boot, and we set off on the twenty-minute drive to the croft.

The wild beauty of the place blew my mind. It was every bit as breathtaking as Miles had promised, and such a contrast to the dusty heat of Dubai. I fell head over heels in love with the place.

I spent the next week in a frenzy of activity, scrubbing and polishing, dusting and vacuuming until the neglected cottage sparkled. I worked until my muscles ached and my fingers were sore, but it was worth it to see the look of delight on Miles's face when he arrived ten days later with the biggest bouquet of roses you've ever seen in your life.

He took me in his arms and told me he loved me, and in that moment, I felt like the luckiest girl alive.

We quickly established a routine. Miles had managed to get a transfer to a rig off Aberdeen. When he was offshore, I didn't stray far from the cottage. I felt safe there. I could have called Shona, and there were times I almost did, because I knew how worried she must be. But it was as if I was bound to Miles and the cottage by a spell, a spell I couldn't risk breaking, because who else would look after me and the baby but Miles?

I never consciously decided to keep the baby. I just took each day as it came, and before I knew it the leaves were turning golden and I was beginning to show. The day I felt tiny kicks inside me was the day I knew my mind had been made up for me. John Westfield was dead. As far as I was concerned, the baby was mine and Miles's.

I gave birth at the hospital in Inverness to a bonny little boy on the fifth of February. He was eight pounds and nine ounces and worth every minute of the horrendous sixteen-hour labour. Miles was by my side the entire time, missing his helicopter ride back to the rig, changing the first meconium-filled nappies without so much as a wrinkle of his nose.

Those first few days are still a bit of a blur. The baby slept in his Moses basket on the floor by the side of my bed, and when he woke in the night Miles would scoop him up and hand him to me, along with a glass of water, then watch us as the baby fed. I was exhausted but so, so happy.

When we came to register the baby's birth, Miles was adamant he would put his name down as the father 'because there's no way that prick Westfield's name's going on the birth certificate'.

We still hadn't agreed on a name. I wanted to call the baby Rowan, after the trees that thrive in this beautiful corner of the Highlands. Miles said Rowan was a ridiculous name for a boy. He wanted to call him Max after a guy in some film called *Gladiator*.

Miles's snort of derision when I told him I'd never heard of it stung, but I was barely one when the film came out. How was I supposed to know?

We called our boy Max in the end. I didn't mind the name, and I owed Miles so much it seemed right to let him have his way.

I sensed a shift in Miles after that. Nothing I could put my finger on, but he was less attentive towards me and not as helpful as he had been with the baby. It was as if the novelty of being a new parent was wearing off. He loved Max, there was no question about that. And Max adored him. It was me he seemed to lose patience with, criticising me for the smallest of things. When it was time for him to return to the rig, I would kiss him goodbye and tell him how much I was going to miss him, while inwardly breathing a huge sigh of relief.

The first time he actually lost his temper with me was the day he found me with my phone in my hand, about to call Shona to let her know she had a nephew.

'I thought we agreed there was to be no contact with your family?' he said. I stared at him, trying to work out if he was joking, but his face was completely expressionless, as if he was wearing a mask.

I bit my lip. 'I know we did, but I just wanted to let Shona know I was all right, and I wanted her to tell Mum about Max. I wouldn't have told her where I was.'

'Give it to me,' Miles said, holding out his hand, and I gave him the phone. He slipped it into his pocket and I never saw it again.

I found a way of telling Mum and Shona, though. I took the photo of me and Max that Miles kept in his wallet, next to the picture of Max's twelve-week scan. I walked down to the village and posted it to Mum's nursing home so they'd both be sure to see it.

Living with Miles was like walking a tightrope. One wrong word, one less than perfect meal, was enough to trigger a black mood that could last for days. But the more I tiptoed around him, the more I tried to please him, the angrier he became. The kind, generous man I'd fallen in love with had disappeared, leaving a scowling, mercurial tyrant in his place. It was as if the reality of living in the cottage with me and Max had spectacularly failed to live up to his exacting expectations.

Sometimes, I sense a fury in Miles that I'm not even sure he's aware of. A barely suppressed rage bubbling just under the surface.

And it terrifies me.

LUCY

The page I'm reading flutters from my trembling fingers and drifts to the floor. I pick it up and reread the last few paragraphs.

Sometimes, I sense a fury in Miles that I'm not even sure he's aware of. A barely suppressed rage bubbling just under the surface.

And it terrifies me.

And so I have decided to leave. I will tell Miles tomorrow, when he comes back from the rig. I will ask him to drop me and Max at the train station in Aviemore and I will come to you, Shona. All being well, we will be with you by teatime.

So why am I writing you this long, rambling letter that I may never even get the chance to post?

In case all isn't well.

If something happens to me, I want to know that you'll look after Max. He is the sweetest baby, despite his start in life. Take him to Mum, tell her she's a granny. I know she'll adore him. He looks just like you as a baby.

I love you.

Rae x

I slump on the sofa with my elbows on my knees and Rae's letter in my hands. Thoughts are whirling in my mind as I try to process everything I've read.

It's clear that when Miles left Chilham for each four-week stint on an oil rig somewhere in the North Sea, he was actually spending part of the time here, in this tiny croft in the Cairngorms, playing happy families with Rae and her baby.

It's also clear that I was right. John Westfield did rape Rae. My flesh crawls with disgust for this married man who thought he could just take what he wanted. And then my disgust turns to horror as I realise what this all means. For Wren, my angelic, beautiful, perfect Wren.

I jump up from the sofa and stride across the room to the window, resting my forehead against the glass. I'm shocked Miles was willing to take on another man's child, if I'm honest. I would never have thought his ego would've allowed it. Especially the child of a creep like John Westfield. I glance guiltily at Wren as I think this. But he isn't defined by his parents. He is his own person.

I steer my mind back to the letter. I believe everything Rae says. Not just because she has no reason to lie, but because I recognise the Miles she writes about, the Miles she fell in love with. He is the same man who swept me off my feet almost a decade earlier by the sheer force of his personality. A knight on a white charger. A protector. A hero.

And I recognise the Miles he became, too. Impatient. Exacting. Contemptuous. Looking back, I can see that I lived with this version of Miles for years. I was so used to his scorn and derision it was normal.

It's like he has this idyllic image of how life should look, and everything in it must be nothing less than perfect. And when people or events don't live up to his expectations, he is disappointed. No, not disappointed. Angry and resentful. And, as Rae discovered, Miles can sulk for England. It's a power thing. Everything about Miles comes down to control, I know that now. Like the way he used to encourage me to drink, then have a go at me when I did.

Alcohol was my coping mechanism and Miles was right: drowning my sorrows was the only way I survived. All those years down the drain because I didn't have the courage to walk away from our toxic marriage. What a waste.

Rae saw the truth about Miles far sooner than I did. Maybe it was because she had Wren to think about. Perhaps she's more emotionally intelligent than me. More likely it's because she hasn't spent half her life drunk. But she sensed the anger in Miles, and she took the brave decision to leave him.

I can't see Shona from here: she must be in the back garden. Perhaps she's sitting on the bench that looks out over the glen, drinking her tea and waiting for me. How the hell am I going to tell her what happened to Rae?

I stumble back to the sofa, flicking back through the pages of Rae's letter until I've found the first sheet. I'm looking for a date, but there isn't one. She could have written the letter last week or last month for all I know.

I try to work it out. Wren was born on February the fifth. It must have been the day Miles didn't turn up for work. He was probably at the hospital with Rae while his boss was trying to contact him.

How had he been when he'd next come home to Kent? I try to cast my mind back but I can't remember. It's true he'd seemed generally dissatisfied with life since we moved back to the UK, but I'd put that down to the fact that he missed the ex-pat life. Perhaps it was Rae and Wren he was really missing.

So why had he stayed with me? He told Rae we'd separated,

but why hadn't he sat me down and announced he was leaving me? It wouldn't have been a huge shock. I realise now our marriage has been limping along for years.

And then a light bulb pings in my head and I feel sick to the core. Miles was broke. He was using Grandad's money to pay for his double life, and when that ran out, I have no doubt he would have talked me into selling the cottage. I once caught him looking up similar properties on Rightmove. He knew it had to be worth at least four hundred grand. Enough to keep us all going while he worked out what to do.

The lengths he's gone to, his sheer effrontery, takes my breath away. But it doesn't get me any closer to working out when Rae wrote the letter.

I skim-read the final couple of pages again. Rae talks about sending the photo of her and Wren to her mum's nursing home. According to the carer Shona spoke to, the photo arrived a month or so ago. Maybe the beginning of May? Rae said she planned to tell Miles she was leaving when he came back from the rig. I can narrow this down, because it would have been the same day he left Kent. I check Miles's rota on the calendar on my phone. He was in Kent with me from Friday, 19 May until Friday, 2 June. He would have left straight after an early breakfast, as he always does, aiming to be in Aberdeen by about nine o'clock. Just enough time to have something to eat and get his head down in the bed and breakfast he always stays in before the helicopter flight to the rig the following morning.

Only he wasn't going to Aberdeen at all. He was coming here.

I push the thought aside. It doesn't matter. What matters is finding Rae, reuniting her with Wren. I check the calendar again. It stands to reason Rae must have written this letter on Thursday, 1 June, planning to tell Miles the following day.

Yet she never posted the letter. Instead I found it jammed at the back of a kitchen drawer. Is it because she changed her mind about sending it, or is it because, as she suggested, she never had a chance to post it. And if she didn't... why?

And then, a week later, I wake to find Wren sleeping in a drawer in our cottage six hundred miles away.

I might have worked out the timings, but I'm no closer to discovering where the hell Rae is.

56

Shona is where I thought I'd find her: sitting on the bench with her knees clasped to her chest, gazing out across the glen.

'I saw some red deer. A stag and a couple of hinds,' she says, pointing towards the heather-clad foothills of the mountain dominating the skyline. 'They've gone now.'

The irony is not lost on me. Two poor hinds blindly following their faithless leader. But not any more. I hand Shona Rae's letter.

'What does it say? Just the headlines. I'll read it properly later.'

I sit beside her and relay the contents of Rae's letter as concisely as I can. How John Westfield set his sights on her, and when she turned down his advances, crept into her room and raped her. How Miles convinced her to move to the Highlands with him when she discovered she was pregnant, promising he would help her look after her baby. How she had desperately wanted to call Shona to tell her where she was, but was worried how Miles would react. And how, eventually, she'd plucked up the courage to leave.

'That's why she wrote to you. To tell you she was coming

home.' I look across at Shona, horrified to see tears rolling down her cheeks. I hold out my hand and she clasps it tightly. We sit like that for a while, until Shona pulls away, fishes a tissue from the pocket of her dungarees and blows her nose.

'Poor, poor Rae,' she says finally. 'If only she'd told me what happened. I could have... could have...' She trails off, because what could she have done to save her sister from a predatory man on an oil rig in the Persian Gulf nearly five thousand miles away?

'I've worked it out. I think Rae wrote the letter on Thursday, June the first, and was planning to catch the train down to Edinburgh the next day,' I say.

'But she never did.'

'No.'

'So where is she?'

'I don't know.' I rest my chin on my knees and gaze at the cloud-studded sky. A huge bird of prey is riding the thermals. It's much bigger than the buzzards we get at home, could even be a golden eagle, I suppose. I wonder if Arthur's remembered to feed Percy, and if Miles has crawled out of his sickbed yet. It's been less than twenty-four hours since I left Kent but it feels like a lifetime. 'Maybe Rae wanted to cut all ties with Miles and knew he'd find her if she moved in with you, so she hid the letter in the kitchen drawer. Maybe she's gone scouting for somewhere else to live and left Wren with Miles while she looks.'

Shona snorted. 'You think?'

I sigh. 'Not really, no.' But the alternative is too awful to contemplate.

57

We sit like that for a while, gazing at the view, lost in our own thoughts. Eventually, I shuffle to the edge of the bench.

'We should probably make a move.'

'So soon?' Shona asks.

'Wren's going to wake for a feed any minute, and I only brought two spare bottles.'

'Oh, OK.'

There's a reluctance in her voice and I ask, 'What's wrong?'

She starts to speak, then stops.

'What is it?'

'You'll think I'm being silly.'

'I won't, I promise.'

She shrugs. 'I don't know. I just feel close to Rae here, you know? Like she's sitting over there, just out of sight.'

I think of Grandad and a lump forms in my throat. 'I don't think you're silly at all. C'mon, let's check on that nephew of yours.'

I offer her my elbow and we amble arm in arm to the cottage. As we reach the back door Rae's letter flutters out of Shona's hand and she tuts and bends down to retrieve it.

I continue into the kitchen, rinse our mugs under the tap and dry them with a tea towel I find hanging from a hook by the side of the cooker. I'm putting them back in the cupboard when I realise Shona's still on her knees in the doorway, examining the skirting. She looks up at me, her face ashen, and I feel the colour drain from my own cheeks.

'Look.' She points to a series of ruby-red splatters on the skirting. 'I think it's blood.'

'Blood?' I repeat slowly. 'Are you sure?'

'Of course I'm not sure. I'm not a forensic bloody scientist. I'm just telling you what it looks like. Spots of blood. Christ.'

I squat down beside her. The red droplets speckle a tiny area of the white skirting board. I'm not sure I'd have seen them if Shona hadn't pointed them out. She lets out an anguished groan.

'Oh, Rae, what happened to you?'

'Come on, we don't know anything's happened. It could have been there for years for all we know. It might not even be blood. It's probably tomato ketchup.'

'It hasn't been there for years.' Shona's voice rings with certainty, and I remember that although she might not be a forensic scientist, she *is* a theatre nurse and has seen more than her fair share of blood in her life. 'And what about the bleach? The place reeks of it.' So she had noticed. 'Someone has gone to great lengths to scrub the place clean. Why would they do that if there was nothing to hide? We need to call the police. I still have the name of the inspector I spoke to when I reported Rae missing. I'll ask for him.'

Shona's right. We should call the police, show them the red splatters and the photo of Rae and Wren in front of the cottage. Let them decide what to do next.

She pulls her phone from the pocket of her dungarees and shakes her head as she stares at the screen. 'No signal. What about yours?'

It's only after I've turned my phone on that I remember Find My iPhone. But I'll have to take the risk. Miles is almost six hundred miles away. Even if he did see where I am it would take him at least ten hours to get here. We're safe.

'One bar,' I say, relieved. I give her the phone, but as she dials, her face creases into a frown. 'What's wrong?'

'The bloody bar's gone. I'll see if I can find a signal outside.'

It's as we're filing along the narrow hallway that we hear the low rumble of a car's engine. It'll be the owner, I tell myself. This Patrick Ryan guy. We'll ask him to call the police and everything will be fine. Not fine exactly, because Rae's still missing, but it will be out of our hands. The police can deal with it. Behind me, Shona has stiffened, her head cocked to one side. We listen in silence as the engine cuts out and a car door slams. I steal into the living room and peer through the gap in the curtains.

I gasp. Parked at the top of the slope next to Shona's Fiat is a silver Audi. Miles's silver Audi, to be precise. And he is standing by the bonnet staring at the cottage with an intensity that makes my heart skitter in my chest. I shrink back from the window and scurry into the hallway.

'It's Miles,' I whisper to Shona, even though there's no way he can hear me in here.

'Miles?' she hisses. 'I thought you said he didn't know where you were.'

'He didn't. I was so careful.' I clutch my cheeks. 'What are we going to *do*?'

Shona hands me my phone and pushes her shoulders back. Once again she is the decisive, focused woman I met in Edinburgh. 'We're going to find out what the hell he's done with my sister, that's what we're going to do.'

58

Before I can stop her, Shona throws open the front door. If Miles is surprised to see her, he doesn't show it.

'Lucy. There you are,' he says, spotting me lurking behind Shona's left shoulder. He speaks so matter-of-factly it's like he's just searched Grandad's cottage and found me in the garden watering the tomatoes, not followed me all the way from Kent to an isolated croft in the Scottish Highlands.

'Miles, what are you doing here?' I squeak.

'I could ask you the same thing. I thought you were handing yourself in to the police in Canterbury, not Aviemore.' His voice is light, almost amused. But a muscle twitches in his jaw. He is angry but trying his best not to show it.

'Who are you?' he asks, turning to Shona.

'Shona MacDonald. Rae's sister.'

He stares at her for a moment. 'I can see the likeness. Though Rae clearly got the looks.' The corners of his lips curl in a sneer. 'May I?' he says, gesturing to the open door. And before Shona can answer he is pushing past us and turning right into the living room. Wordlessly, Shona and I follow.

Wren squeals in excitement when he sees Miles, his face

split by the biggest grin. Miles drops to his knees, unclips the straps of the car seat and scoops the baby into his arms.

'Hey, Maximus,' he says, blowing a raspberry into Wren's neck. 'I've missed you, bud.' He looks over Wren's head to me. His expression is flinty. 'Don't ever, *ever* take him without my permission again.'

'He's not ours, Miles,' I begin, but he cuts across me.

'Of course he's ours. Well, he could have been if you'd done as I said. Why can't you ever just do as I say?'

Indignation rises in me like a riptide. 'I've spent my entire married life doing as you say, Miles. I chucked in my job and followed you halfway across the world. I played the dutiful wife and then I followed you back home when you'd grown bored of Dubai.'

'Here we go again.' He turns to Shona and rolls his eyes. 'My wife has always been under the illusion she was going to be the next big thing in publishing, until I ruined her career.'

'I gave up a job I loved for you.'

'Don't make me laugh. You were a flunkey at a publishing company no one's heard of. You weren't going anywhere. And you've been quite happy to sponge off me ever since.'

Shona, who's been watching this exchange in silence, clears her throat. 'Where is Rae, Miles? What have you done to her?'

'I haven't done anything to her.'

'Then where is she?'

'She fucked off, didn't she? Walked out and left us.'

'She wouldn't do that.'

'Sorry to disappoint. Perhaps you don't know her quite as well as you think.'

'I know there's no way she would have left her baby.' Shona glares at Miles. 'Especially with you.'

'What the fuck's that supposed to mean?'

Shona reaches into the pocket of her dungarees. Miles stills, watching her like a hawk, visibly relaxing when she produces a photo and thrusts it under his nose. It's the one of Rae and Wren outside the croft.

'How did you get that?'

'Rae sent it to Mum.'

'I thought your mum was doolally,' he scoffs.

Shona shakes her head angrily. 'She has dementia. But that aside, Rae loved little Wren, anyone can see that. She would never have left him.'

'His. Name. Is. Max,' Miles says through gritted teeth. 'Max Quinn. And Rae didn't care about him. She wouldn't have walked out on me if she did, would she? She wouldn't have split up our little family.'

The words slice through my heart like a knife, even after everything Miles has done. All I ever wanted was a family, and it seems it's what Miles wanted too, only not with me.

'I don't believe you,' Shona says.

'Believe what you like. It's what happened. She never wanted Max.'

'Then prove it.'

'How can I prove it if I don't know where the fuck she is?'

Shona looks as if she's about to speak and I'm gripped by a feeling of dread. If she mentions the splatters on the skirting board Miles will know we suspect him of harming Rae. And a cornered animal's first line of defence is attack.

'Why don't we all sit down?' I say desperately. 'Miles, you must be exhausted. You were on death's door last night. Are you still running a temperature?' I go to feel his forehead but he slaps my hand away.

'Stop fussing, woman,' he growls.

'Sorry. I tell you what, I'll make you a nice cup of tea, shall I?' Without waiting for an answer, I dart into the kitchen and fill the kettle.

When I return a few minutes later, Miles is on the sofa with Wren on his lap and Shona is standing by the fireplace. They both have thunderous expressions on their faces and Shona, to my horror, is holding Rae's letter.

Please don't, I silently will her. Either she doesn't notice my pleading face or she chooses to ignore it, because she holds the letter out, stabbing the pages with her index finger.

'Rae wrote to tell me she was leaving you.'

A flicker of uncertainty crosses Miles's face, the tiniest of facial tics that only someone watching him closely would notice. I am watching him *very* closely. Then his expression clears.

'Which is exactly what I told you. She fucked off and left us, didn't she, Max?'

Miles cups Wren's head in his hand as he says this, and I realise just how easy it would be for him to take Wren's life. A twist and a snap and it would be over. Mine too, because without Wren I have nothing.

'Do you know what I think?' Shona says. 'I think that when Rae told you she was leaving, you decided to stop her because you couldn't bear the thought of her rejecting you. It was too much for that monster-sized ego of yours to cope with.'

'You want to watch what you're saying,' Miles says, his voice dripping with menace.

Wren's face crumples and he starts to cry. My heart flips and I step forwards. 'You're upsetting him, Miles. Give him to me.'

Miles glances at me. His face is expressionless, but his dilated pupils give him away. He is a breath away from losing it completely.

'Miles,' I say again, holding out my arms.

After what seems like an age he hands Wren to me, and I retreat to the corner, soothing him as best I can, wondering if I can leave the room under the pretext of fetching a bottle from the car, and call the police.

'I've met psychopaths like you,' Shona continues. 'Charming, manipulative risk takers who expect to be treated like gods, who can detach themselves from human suffering. Of course, the ones I come across are all surgeons, but I know one when I see one. Where is Rae, Miles? What have you done to her?'

Miles springs up off the sofa, his face twisted with fury. I watch, horrified, as Shona reaches behind her and draws the cast-iron poker from the companion set on the hearth.

'Shona, no!' I cry, as she raises it above her head.

'Where is she?' she screams. 'Where is my sister?'

Before she can bring the poker down, Miles pushes her so hard in the chest that her legs buckle and she topples backwards. There's a leaden-sounding thump as the back of her head hits the mantel over the fireplace, and she slumps to the ground in a tangle of limbs.

'Oh my God. Shona. Shona!' She doesn't move a muscle and I gape at Miles over Wren's head. 'Christ, Miles. What have you done to her?'

'Silly bitch was trying to attack me.' His breathing is hard and fast, but his voice is filled with righteous indignation.

'I need to call an ambulance.' I pull my phone out of my back pocket and turn for the door, but before I've taken a step Miles is in my face, grabbing my wrist, his hand like the jaws of a vice.

'Not so fast,' he says, flecking my face with spittle. 'You're going nowhere.'

59

'Sit,' Miles commands.

'Let me at least check on her,' I beg.

'Give Max to me first,' he says, but there's no way I'm handing him over so, after glancing wretchedly at Shona's lifeless form, I perch on the end of the sofa, Wren clasped to my hip like a limpet.

'What are you doing here, Lucy?'

'I could ask the same of you.' I can't for the life of me think how he knew I was here, unless he was looking for Rae, not me. Which would mean he's telling the truth about her walking out on him.

But if there's one thing the last week has taught me, it's that Miles is a pathological liar.

'I came for Max,' he says.

'But how did you know we were here?'

He narrows his eyes. 'Not with Find My iPhone, because someone forgot to turn their phone on, didn't they?' he says in his best isn't-Lucy-stupid voice. 'Nice try, Luce. But you forgot about the tracker on your car.'

I stare at him in bemusement until the penny drops. When

we bought the Mini the garage offered us a deal on an anti-theft tracking device that used GPS to locate it if it was ever stolen. My phone was almost out of storage so Miles downloaded the app onto his. It would have been ridiculously easy for him to follow my journey all the way to Scotland. And I'd been so careful about not using my phone. What an idiot.

'I tracked you to Shona's address and when you weren't there, I just had a feeling that you would be here.'

'You were fast asleep when I left,' I say.

He laughs nastily. 'So you thought. But I suspected you were up to something. You're so fucking easy to read. And when you started trying to force Night Nurse down my throat, I knew I was right. I spat the last lot out.'

So much for my clever escape plan. Miles was a step ahead of me at every turn.

'Don't look so surprised. You lied to me, Lucy. Of course I was going to keep tabs on you.'

'What about you? You've been lying to me for months,' I cry. Miles shrugs like he couldn't care less but I have to get this off my chest. 'You didn't hand your notice in last week. You were sacked in February for not turning up for work because you were with Rae at the hospital, wiping her brow while she was giving birth!'

'I don't know what you're talking about.'

'Don't lie to me, Miles. I know it's true. Charlie told Tess. You were too traumatised to be there when I had my baby, but you were happy to be there for Rae.' It's petty, I know, but the words tumble out of my mouth before I can stop them.

'How many times do I have to say it? Ours wasn't a baby, it was a collection of cells. I don't know why you're still going on about it.'

Tears are streaming down my face, but my heart has turned to steel. 'He would have been a baby if you hadn't pushed me down the stairs.'

'*What?*'

'You heard me. I know you pushed me, Miles. And I'm pretty sure you drugged me too. I know I wasn't drunk that night.'

'Well, *that* makes a fucking change,' he sneers.

'Why did you do it? You said you were looking forward to being a dad.' I know I didn't imagine this. He had been surprised when I told him I was pregnant, yes, but once he was used to the idea he was pleased, I know he was.

Or was it all an act?

'I never wanted a baby with you,' he says. 'Couldn't take the risk it would end up with foetal alcohol syndrome.'

His words are a slap in my face. 'I stopped drinking when I found out I was pregnant.'

'Yeah, well, we'll have to take your word for that, won't we? And now I have Max, who's a chip off the old block, aren't you, son?' He reaches for Wren but I swerve out of the way before he can take him from me.

'Why did you bring Wren to Kent?'

'Because I knew you'd look after him.'

'He should be with his mother!'

'How many times do I have to tell you? She left him. She never wanted him.' He looks sidelong at me. 'And I knew you would.'

'You sneaked home and left him in the living room while I was asleep upstairs.' I frown. 'Did you slip me something that night too, just to keep me quiet?'

'Didn't need to. You were out of it.'

'You let me think I'd stolen him, Miles. Have you any idea how cruel that was?'

'I thought I was doing you a favour,' he says sulkily.

'No wonder you stopped me going to the police. Did you really think we could bring Wren up as our own, or was I supposed to be a caretaker mum until Rae decided she wanted him back?'

Rae had a baby she didn't want. I lost the baby I wanted more than anything. And at the centre of it all is Miles. Fixing things, dictating what happens, mapping out our futures.

'She's never coming back,' he says with the tiniest catch in his voice. I look at him sharply. He sounds so sure Rae's gone for good. How does he know? Unless...

'What did you do to her, Miles?'

He frowns. 'I didn't do anything.'

I don't believe him. I remember the hatred in his eyes as he threw the glass of water in my face before he pushed me down the stairs. Yet moments earlier he'd pecked my cheek and told me I was overdoing things. Living with Miles is like living with Dr Jekyll and Mr Hyde.

But which is the real Miles?

'Miles?' I repeat.

He steps towards me. His breath is so rank I gag.

'What happened with her was an accident, right?' He jabs his thumb in Shona's direction. 'I never meant to hurt her.'

'Of course you didn't,' I soothe. 'She came at you with a poker. You were only trying to defend yourself.'

His face clears. 'That's right. It was an accident. Just like Rae. It wasn't my fault.' He glances at me, as if reaching a decision. My scalp tingles.

'I'm on your side,' I remind him. And that's when I realise that although Miles might have physical strength and cunning on his side, he has an Achilles heel. His ego. Because he believes every single lie that trips off my tongue.

'I'd driven all the way up from Kent. Twelve bloody hours in the car. Stopped off at the supermarket to buy her flowers and wine. I even bought her a box of her favourite chocolates. When I finally arrive at the cottage, she's waiting by the front door with her bags packed. And then the next thing I know,

she's telling me that she's leaving me and taking Max with her.'
He snorts.

'I told her she wasn't going anywhere, and I went inside and
fetched Max and locked him in the car so she couldn't do
anything stupid. She went ballistic, screaming and shouting at
me to give her the car keys.' His hands curl into fists at the
memory.

We stare at each other. My heart is jumping in my chest.
'What happened then?'

Miles breaks his gaze first. 'I went to hold her, to talk some
sense into her, but she screamed. Screamed, Luce, as if I would
hurt her.' His laugh is high-pitched and it chills me to the core.
'I wanted to talk to her but those screams, they were messing
with my head. She was hysterical. So, I followed her into the
kitchen and tried to shake some sense into her but she hit her
head on the wall. She hit her head and she fell to the ground
and she didn't get up.'

'Then it wasn't your fault.'

'That's what I said,' he says impatiently. 'None of it was my
fault.'

'And Wren, I mean Max. Max was still in the car?'

He nods, his eyes lighting up when his gaze falls on Wren.
'My boy,' he says softly. 'Yes, he was safe. I kept him safe.'

'Where's Rae now?'

Miles looks away.

'Miles, you said there's to be no more secrets, remember?'

'Cesspit,' he mumbles. 'She's in the cesspit.'

My stomach swoops and I tighten my hold on Wren. Of
course Rae would never have left her baby. Miles killed her, and
whether it was deliberate or an accident, the result is still the
same. Miles killed Rae and flung her body into the cesspit like a
piece of trash.

60

Miles is watching me, waiting for a reaction. Waiting to see what I'll say before he decides what to do with me.

His ego is his Achilles heel, I remind myself.

'It must have been awful. You poor thing.'

The muscles in his face relax and he nods. 'It was. You're right. I was so stressed.'

'And that's when you decided to bring Max home?'

'We stayed here for a week, just the two of us. And then, yes, I brought him home. I gave you the child you always wanted,' he says, like he deserves a medal for his altruism. His grasp on reality is laughable, but I keep playing along. I don't have a choice.

'You did. Thank you.' I kiss the top of Wren's head.

'I thought you'd be a better mum to him than Rae anyway. She was too highly strung, you know? And she was always going on about phoning her bloody sister. Couldn't she see it was better it was just the three of us?'

'Especially as his dad was already dead,' I agree.

'Dead?'

'John Westfield,' I say. The man who'd raped Rae and then killed himself because he couldn't live with the guilt.

Miles's eyes widen a fraction but he doesn't speak. The silence stretches between us, so thick you could slice it with a knife.

'Miles?'

He glances to the left. As I stare at his sweat-stained T-shirt a memory comes to me. Whispers at the beach club. Someone overheard Westfield having an altercation with Miles the night he jumped off the rig. Another memory pushes its way into my head. Miles, squaring up to the guy with the tattoos at the club in Hackney all those years ago. Grabbing the man's T-shirt and calling him a fucking coward for picking on me. Miles had been apoplectic that night. Afterwards I'd wondered what he would have done to Tattoo Guy if he'd found him in a deserted alleyway and not in a crowded club with dozens of witnesses.

'What aren't you telling me, Miles?'

'He had it coming, the prick.'

'Westfield?' My stomach lurches. 'What... what did you do to him?'

'You don't treat women like that,' Miles continues, as if I haven't spoken. 'You should treat them with respect. But that prick wouldn't know what respect was if it came over and punched him in the fucking face.'

'Is that what you did, Miles? Did you punch John Westfield in the face?'

He shakes his head, frowning. 'Didn't need to.'

Scenes spool before my eyes. Miles pushing me down the stairs, shoving Shona against the fireplace. One sharp push enough to change the course of someone's life.

'Did you push Westfield off the rig?'

He shrugs, but makes no attempt to deny it. White noise fills my head, crackling and fizzing like an untuned radio, because it's obvious now I think of it. Miles pushed John Westfield from the rig as payback for raping Rae. I try to imagine what it must have been like. The feeling of weightlessness as Westfield fell, his arms and legs windmilling as he fought to grab hold of the towering metal legs of the rig. The impact of the water knocking the breath from his lungs. Saltwater like a chokehold around his neck as he gasped for breath. Sinking, sinking... and then nothing.

'You don't treat women like that,' Miles repeats, and I have to bite my tongue, literally clench it between my teeth, to stop a bark of bitter laughter escaping, because Miles genuinely believes he's the perfect gentleman where women are concerned. He has no idea. Not a fucking clue.

I realise he is talking. 'What did you say?'

'How did you know Rae was here at the cottage?'

I think on my feet. Better for him to think Rae somehow managed to contact Shona and give her the address of the croft than to realise I was the one who led Shona here.

'Rae must have told Shona. Perhaps she walked down to the village and called her while you were in Kent.'

His face tightens. 'Backstabbing bitch. C'mon.' He nods towards the door. 'We should get going.'

'Going? Where?'

'Home.'

'What about Shona? We can't just leave her here.'

He pauses, then gives a curt nod. 'You're right. Start putting Max's stuff in the car. I'll be right out.'

'What are you going to do with her?'

'I think it's best you don't know, don't you?' He grips my arm and begins to chivvy me from the room.

'But Miles—' I glance at Shona while his back is turned. Her eyes are open and she is staring intently at me. I blink, wondering if I've imagined it, but when I look again her eyes haven't left mine. She raises her eyebrows in Miles's direction. She's trying to tell me something, but what? I keep my expression blank. Miles thinks she's dead and it's best it stays that way if we are to have any chance of overpowering him.

I let Miles propel me along the hallway towards the front door, then stop.

'I've forgotten the car seat. You take Max and I'll fetch it.' I hand him Wren before he has a chance to argue. 'Honestly, I'd forget my own head if it wasn't screwed on. Won't be a sec.'

In the living room, I go straight to Shona, dropping to the floor beside her.

'Are you OK?' I whisper.

'Felt better.' She grimaces. 'You need to stop him, Lucy.'

'How?'

'I don't know, but you need to think of something. He can't be allowed to get away with this.'

'Lucy!' Miles shouts from the front of the house.

'Just coming,' I call back.

Shona grabs my wrist. 'You can't let that monster raise Rae's baby. Think of something, for Wren.'

'LUCY!' Miles yells.

Shona releases her grip and I force myself to my feet, picking up Wren's car seat as I leave the room. Shona's right. I can't let Miles bring up Wren. I *won't* let Miles bring up Wren.

But how the hell am I going to stop him?

'At last. What the fuck were you doing in there?' Miles growls as I join him outside the cottage. He pings the lock of the Audi and we traipse up the slope to the two cars.

'What are you going to do with Shona's car?' I ask, holding out my arms for Wren. After a moment's hesitation Miles hands him to me.

'I'll worry about that when I've dealt with her. Have you got everything?'

'I think so.' A plan is beginning to form in my mind. 'I just need to change Max and give him a feed, then I'm ready.'

'Do it in the car,' he orders. 'I don't want you going back inside.'

I look around in Wren's changing bag for the last bottle of milk, then make myself as comfortable as I can in the passenger seat of the Audi. Wren babbles away as I give the bottle a shake and pull off the lid. Miles tries the doors of the Fiat but Shona must have locked it, because he gives one of the tyres a vicious kick and disappears back down the slope and into the cottage.

When he reappears a few minutes later, he has Shona's keys balled in his fist. I can't let him get rid of the Fiat. It's now or never.

I open the passenger door, and, clutching Wren, scramble out. 'Miles,' I yell. 'Shona's at the window!'

He stops in his tracks and looks up at me.

'Shona,' I repeat, pointing. 'Look!'

He turns and walks towards the living room window. I lean back into the car and my fingers curl around the handbrake. I hold my breath and wait. I need to make sure Miles's back is turned.

When it is, I freeze for the briefest of moments, knowing there's no going back from this. And then I remember the contempt on his face in the seconds before he pushed me down the spiral staircase. And I release the handbrake.

61

At first nothing happens and I panic. I don't have a Plan B. It's this or nothing. And then the car begins to move, infinitesimally slowly at first, but gaining momentum as gravity takes hold. Miles is peering into the living room, his hands cupped against the glass to cut out the glare of the sun. If he hears the crunch of tyres now, he still has time to jump out of the way. What will I do then? I'll have to pretend I knocked the handbrake by accident and panicked. I'm not sure he'd believe me.

I clasp Wren to my chest. Even if he's too young to remember, I don't want him to see this, can't risk the scene unfolding in front of us imprinting on his memory.

Miles finally hears the car and he turns to face me, his expression startled, uncomprehending, as if I've just shaken him awake from a deep sleep.

For a moment he doesn't move, then his face twists with fury and he tries to leap out of the way. But it's too late. The car hits him, dragging him under the bonnet. The windscreen shatters, the resulting thunderclap echoing around the glen. I think of Rae's broken mirror, the shards of glass like her splintered memory of the night she was raped. Like my memory of the night I lost my baby. My gaze darts from left to right, looking for Miles, but he has disappeared under the car. I feel no guilt, but no relief either. Just empty and bone-achingly tired.

I walk down the slope and yank open the passenger door. I undo Wren's bib and lean in, running the clean side of the bib up and down the handbrake half a dozen times. I'm not worried about the rest of the Audi. My prints will be everywhere but why wouldn't they be? It's my husband's car.

I pick up Wren's bottle and check the back seat to make sure I haven't left anything else. Then I wrap the bib around my hand, lean over and tug the bonnet release handle. The bonnet clicks open. When the police eventually come they will assume Miles must have left the handbrake off when he went to check the oil or wiper fluid.

I sidle around to the front of the car. All I can see poking out from underneath the Audi's low-slung bonnet is Miles's right arm. I squat down and feel for a pulse. There isn't one.

'Come on, angel,' I say to Wren. 'Let's find your Auntie Shona.'

62

In the living room, I prop Wren on the sofa between some cushions and help Shona to her feet. She is clutching the back of her head, and when I prise her hand away there's a lump the size of a hen's egg on the base of her skull.

'Where's Miles?' she croaks.

'Outside.'

She licks her lips as her gaze tracks slowly to the door.

'It's all right, I've taken care of him. He won't bother us.'

She turns back to me. 'What about Rae? Did he tell you where she is?'

'You didn't hear?'

She shakes her head, then winces. 'Must have been knocked out cold.'

I pause. I have two choices. I can stick to Miles's narrative, that Rae walked out on him and Wren, that she is out there somewhere, building a new life for herself, alone but alive. Or I can tell Shona the truth, that she died after hitting her head as Miles tried to 'shake some sense into her' and that he disposed of her body in the cesspit.

Which is it to be: leave Shona with false hope, or break her heart? But I don't have a choice, not really. I have to tell her the truth.

'You'd better sit down,' I say, guiding her to the sofa. Her knees buckle and she lands heavily next to Wren. He watches her with round eyes, his thumb in his mouth, an innocent bystander in this twisted, fucked-up nightmare. 'I'm so sorry, Shona, but Rae is dead.'

She listens wordlessly as I repeat what Miles told me, that Rae had announced she was leaving him and taking Wren with her. That a furious Miles was trying to reason with her when she fell and hit her head.

'He said it was an accident. He didn't mean to kill her,' I finish, as if that makes it any better.

'Do you believe him?'

I wish I could accept Miles's version of events. It would be so much easier to come to terms with Rae's death if he was telling the truth, that it was all an unfortunate mistake, but the naked hatred in his eyes the night he pushed me down the spiral staircase still haunts me.

'No,' I say.

'What did he do with her?'

I pick Wren up and motion her to follow me out of the room. In the hallway I turn right, passing through the kitchen to the back door. We both avert our gaze from the blood splatters on the skirting and step outside into the warm summer evening.

When I reach Rae's flowerbed, I hand Wren to Shona and pick a posy of cornflowers, campion and poppies. Nettles sting my hands, but I welcome the pain.

'Where are we going?' Shona asks.

'Just over here.' I head for the manhole cover and stop, the flowers clasped in my hands like a bride's bouquet. Shona frowns, then her face crumples as understanding dawns.

'She's in there?' she whispers.

I nod.

'Jesus.'

I pull the hair tie from my ponytail and fix it around the stems of the flowers, then squat down and place the posy on the cast-iron cover.

'Do you want to say anything?' I ask Shona.

She shakes her head and disappears into the cottage with Wren. I wait a few more minutes, breathing in the scent of the Scots pines and drinking in the view of the glen. I imprint the wildness, the vastness of it all on my memory, because I have no wish to ever return. I think about Rae and how she sacrificed her own safety, her own *life*, for her son. And then I think about my husband, the man who gave her everything, then took it all away. The man whose life I have taken so we can both be free.

'I did it for you, Rae,' I murmur. And it's true.

But I also did it for me.

Shona's sitting at the kitchen table, Wren on her lap. She looks up with puffy, red-rimmed eyes when I arrive.

'We should go,' I tell her. 'I'll drive.'

'You still haven't told me where Miles is?'

'You'll see him soon enough.' I run two glasses of water from the tap and hand one to Shona. 'Drink up. I don't want to stop on the way.'

She does as she's told, as meekly as a child. Hatred for Miles and the misery he has caused her hits me anew. 'Come on,' I say gently. 'Let's get you home.'

She sways when she sees Miles's arm sticking out from under the car, and I grab Wren from her, worried she'll drop him.

'It was an accident,' I say, matter-of-factly. 'He was checking the windscreen wiper fluid but can't have fixed the handbrake properly.'

Her gaze flickers to the space at the top of the slope where Miles had parked his heavy Audi next to her little Fiat. A look of understanding passes between us, then she shrugs. 'That's... unfortunate,' she says.

'Shit happens,' I agree.

63

We don't talk much on the long drive back to Edinburgh, but when we reach the outskirts of the city Shona asks, 'What happens now?'

'I'll report Miles missing in the morning. I'll tell the police he'd rented the cottage on a long-term let for us to use as a holiday home. I'll say we travelled up to Scotland separately yesterday, and that he'd gone on ahead to get the place ready while I stayed with a friend. That's you,' I say, glancing at Shona. She nods.

'I'll tell them I was due to follow him up to the Highlands in a few days' time, but when I didn't hear from him, I began to worry.'

'And what happens when they send an officer up to the cottage?'

'They'll find him, won't they?'

'Are you sure they'll think it was an accident?'

'What else could it be? People get crushed by their own cars all the time.'

Shona raises an eyebrow.

'OK, maybe not all the time, but it does happen. And the police have no reason to suspect foul play. And if they do... well, I'll just have to deal with it.'

'What about Rae? If we tell them where her body is they'll know we were there.'

I suck in air through my teeth. 'It's up to you. At the moment, there's nothing to link Miles to Rae's disappearance. Other than you and me, the only person who suspected they were having an affair is dead.'

'John Westfield?'

I nod.

'And Miles killed him, too,' Shona says, shaking her head in disbelief.

I'd told her back at the croft that Miles as good as admitted he'd pushed Westfield off the rig.

'Jesus.' She groans. 'What the hell did you and Rae see in him?'

I shrug. 'We saw what we wanted to see.'

It's still light when I pull up outside Shona's bungalow. We tramp up the path to her front door like battle-weary soldiers returning from the Western Front: sweaty, dishevelled and scarred with sights we wished we'd never witnessed, but grateful we've made it back at all.

Shona rummages around in her freezer for pizzas while I give Wren a quick bath and feed him. Once he's settled in the middle of the double bed in Shona's spare room, I join her in the kitchen.

She pushes a glass of red wine across the worktop towards me and I'm about to take it, anticipation making my stomach clench, when I remember.

'Not for me, thanks. I'm trying to lay off the stuff.'

She winces. 'I'm sorry, Lucy. That was thoughtless of me.'

'It's OK.'

'D'you want me to—?' She mimes tipping the wine down the sink.

'No, that would be a waste. You have it.'

'Are you sure you don't mind?'

I give her a rueful smile. 'I'm going to have to get used to it.'

I find plates and fetch myself a glass of water while she slices the pizzas. It's not until she places the plate in front of me that I realise how ravenous I am.

We eat in silence for a bit, then Shona says, 'One of my oldest friends is an alcoholic.'

A piece of pizza is wedged in my throat. I take a sip of water and swallow hard. 'I'm a social drinker, not an alcoholic.'

Shona gazes at me so intently it's as if she can see straight into the deepest chambers of my soul. And it's true. I am a social drinker. That's how it started, anyway. Drinks after work. Friday night drinks. Saturdays down the pub. A bottle of wine on a Sunday night to fend off the end-of-weekend blues. A merry-go-round of drinking. Friends, boyfriends and drinking buddies all came and went. The one constant was the glass in my hand. Alcohol was my best friend.

I was a social drinker until I started drinking alone. I should have realised things were spinning out of control that first time I was on my own and opened a bottle of wine. The warning lights should have been flashing like mad that day. Maybe they were. Maybe I chose to ignore them.

I steal a look at Shona. She's still watching me. There's no judgement in her expression, only empathy. She's just found out her sister is dead, yet she's still concerned about me.

I push my plate away. My appetite has deserted me. 'I was a social drinker,' I admit. 'Until I wasn't.'

'Have you ever sought help?'

I shake my head. 'I never thought I needed to. I could always stop when Miles was home, you see.' And I could, until the day I started keeping a bottle of vodka in the shed. I rarely touched it, but it made me feel safe knowing it was there if I needed it.

'And now?' she asks gently.

'I want to stop. For Wren.'

She reaches out and squeezes my hand. 'I think it would be better if you wanted to stop for you. I can ask Polly to drop by tomorrow, if you like?'

'Your friend?'

She nods. 'We were at school together. She's been sober for over a decade and she's very easy to talk to.'

I think for a moment, then say, 'I'd like that. Thank you.' I fiddle with the hem of my T-shirt. 'But, never mind me. How are you feeling?'

Shona runs a hand across her face. 'Oh. Numb. It'll hit me at some point, I'm sure. But I started grieving for Rae the day she walked out of our lives. I think a part of me always knew she was never coming home.' Shona's eyes glisten. 'At least we have Wren.'

Her words pierce my heart, because Shona might well have Wren, but I have no claim to him. He wasn't my husband's son. I have no blood ties, nothing. Tears are rolling down my cheeks before I even realise that I'm crying.

'What is it, Lucy? What's wrong?'

I shake my head. I want to tell Shona she shouldn't be comforting me. I should be comforting her. She's the one who lost her sister today, whereas Wren was never mine to lose in the first place. But I can't force the words past the lump in my throat.

· · ·

Later, there's a tentative knock at the door.

'Are you asleep?' Shona whispers.

I had been lying in the dark, staring blankly at the ceiling, listening to Wren's steady breathing beside me. Sleep was impossible.

'No.' I drag myself out of bed and open the door. 'Is everything OK?'

Shona has changed out of her dungarees into charcoal-grey lounge pants and a matching top and she smells of lavender and bergamot. Wishing I'd had the energy to wash away the day's grime, I let her into the room. She wanders over to the bed and watches Wren for a moment.

'Look at his arms,' she murmurs. I glance down. They are flung wide by his head, cactus-style. 'How can that be comfortable?'

'He likes it here.' I smile at her. 'He likes you.'

Suddenly, Shona looks awkward, her gaze darting to the ceiling. She clears her throat. 'That's what I wanted to talk to you about, actually.'

'Oh. Right.' Here it comes, I think. Shona's going to tell me she'll be looking after Wren from now on. It's the obvious solution. She's his aunt, his closest living blood relative, after all. I was right. I was just a caretaker. Even though I knew it was coming, it doesn't make it hurt any less.

'I hope we can still keep in touch,' I say in a small voice.

Shona frowns. 'What are you talking about?'

I squirm. 'Oh, I see. You think it's better for Wren if I don't see him at all?' I swallow. 'Yes, you're right. A clean break is probably best for everyone.'

'A clean break?'

'Perhaps you could let me know how he's doing every so often?'

'Lucy—'

'Send me a photo now and again?'

'Lucy! Just listen to me for a minute. Wren can't live with me. I mean, he's very sweet and everything, even I can see that, and he's all I have left of Rae.' Her voice cracks and she closes her eyes for a moment, then gives her head a little shake. 'But I meant it when I told you I don't do babies. I can't take him in. I work full time and I don't have a support system. It wouldn't be fair on him.'

I stare at Shona in horror, because if she can't have Wren, he'll end up in the care system, and although he might wind up in a loving home, there's always a chance he might not.

'It's clear from Rae's letter who Wren should live with.'

I look at Shona in confusion. 'Is it?'

'You did see her postscript?'

'Postscript?'

'I didn't think so. Wait here, I'll be right back.'

I spoon around Wren's sleeping form while I wait, watching his tiny fists curl and uncurl as he dreams. I need to remember this. Remember the love and the happiness he brought me. Remember it and treasure it always.

Shona reappears, Rae's letter in her hand. She flicks through the pages, and hands me the last sheet of paper. I quickly scan the final paragraph.

If something happens to me, I want to know that you'll look after Max. He is the sweetest baby, despite his start in life. Take him to Mum, tell her she's a granny. I know she'll adore him. He looks just like you as a baby. I love you. Rae x

'On the other side,' Shona says.

I turn the sheet over and there it is. A postscript. Rae's final words are messier than the rest of the letter, as if she scrawled them in a hurry.

PS I know I'm asking a lot, especially after all the shit I've put you through this last year. And so, if you feel you can't look after Max yourself, I will understand. Just promise me one thing, Shona. Find someone who can look after him, someone who loves him. That's all I ask. I just want him to be loved. x

64

I look up at Shona. She is smiling.

'You love him, don't you?' she says.

'Of course.'

'How would you feel about bringing him up?'

'You mean it?'

'He adores you. If I didn't know better, I'd never guess he wasn't yours.'

'But I'm nobody. Social services would never let him live with me.'

'Miles put himself down as Wren's father on the birth certificate, didn't he?' Shona says, waving Rae's letter at me. 'And you're Miles's wife, well, widow. I've had a quick look on some family law websites. We'd need to get it checked out, but from what I understand, step-parents can apply to the courts for parental responsibility for their stepchildren. And there's also the legal guardian route. There are options, Lucy.' She holds my gaze. 'If you feel able to do this.'

Happiness fizzes through me, as effervescent as champagne. But this shot of pure joy is better than any alcohol-induced high.

. . .

The next morning, I call the police to report Miles missing. The call handler runs through a list of questions: When did I last see him? Have I checked to see if he's been in touch with friends and family? Is his disappearance out of character? What state of mind was he in? I answer as best I can, and she says someone should get back to me within a couple of hours. As it is, it's early afternoon when there's a knock at the door.

'I'll go,' Shona says, jumping out of her chair like a scalded cat.

She is back moments later, followed by two uniformed police officers, both wearing solemn expressions.

'Mrs Quinn?' the older officer asks. He is in his early thirties and has muscular forearms and a strong Glaswegian accent.

I nod and say tremulously, 'Have you found Miles?'

He exchanges a look with his companion, a slight girl with round tortoiseshell glasses and sandy-coloured hair fixed in a low bun.

'I'm sorry to say I have some bad news, Mrs Quinn,' he says. 'Following the missing person report you made this morning, an officer carried out a check at the address in Kinkirk.' He clears his throat. 'It seems your husband had an accident.'

My hand flies to my mouth. 'An accident?'

'Does your husband own a silver Audi A4?' He reels off Miles's registration plate.

'Yes, that's Miles's car.'

'I'm afraid he appears to have been hit by it.'

'By his own car?'

'Obviously there'll be a full investigation, but the officer who found him believes the Audi's handbrake either wasn't on, or wasn't working, and the car rolled down the drive, knocking him over.'

'Oh my God.' I jump up, looking for my handbag. 'Is he all right? Which hospital's he in?'

The officer laces his hands together and exhales. 'He's not. In hospital, I mean. I'm afraid he died from his injuries.'

'Died? Don't be ridiculous. He can't have.'

'The officer called an ambulance, but Mr Quinn was pronounced dead at the scene. There will be a post-mortem examination, but it's likely he died from crush injuries. It's rare but it does happen,' the officer says.

I collapse back in the armchair and bury my face in my hands. The last time I was given news like this was the day a doctor told me I'd lost my baby. Tears course down my cheeks at the memory.

'Is there anyone we can contact for you?' the female officer asks gently.

'It's OK. I'll look after her,' Shona says.

'We'll be in touch in the next day or so to explain what happens next. There'll be a fatal accident inquiry to establish the circumstances of your husband's death, but it sounds pretty clear-cut to me. It was a tragic accident.'

Once the police have gone, Shona and I take Wren for a walk around the Royal Botanic Gardens. The gardens are stunning, and as we meander past swathes of rhododendrons and stroll along the colourful herbaceous border, I picture Grandad in his shirtsleeves, turning over his vegetable patch. For the first time since he died, I'm not floored by grief. He would be proud of me. He'd have hated all the moping.

'My grandad was a gardening fanatic,' I tell Shona as we stop to admire clusters of dainty powder-pink flowers on a cotoneaster that sweeps elegantly over the path like the sculpted arm of a ballerina.

'Was?'

'He died last year. He left me his cottage. I've been trying to look after his garden, but I don't have his green fingers.'

'That's where you lived with Miles?'

'Yes.' Since Grandad died his cottage has been my sanctuary, a rock to cling onto. I used to describe it as my happy place, but I wasn't happy there, not really. I told myself Miles was like he was because he cared about me. But I was living a lie. The only thing he cared about was himself.

Rae saw beneath his shiny veneer and I admire her for that. She had the backbone to stand up to him, something I'd never managed to do.

I touch Shona's arm. 'Have you decided what you're going to do about Rae?'

She stops, rubs the acid-green leaf of a fern between her thumb and forefinger, and sighs. 'I've thought about little else. If we tell the police where her body is, they'll know we've been at the croft. What if they decide to look more closely at Miles's death? We can't risk them suspecting it was anything other than a freak accident.'

'I suppose.'

'And all the while she's still missing, Mum can hold onto the hope she's still alive. We'll leave her where she is. It's kinder this way.'

'What will we tell Wren when he grows up? That his mum walked out on him when he was a baby? He'll be devastated.'

'I don't pretend to have all the answers, Lucy. We'll have to cross that bridge when we come to it.'

'But, still—' I hate to think of Rae alone in the cesspit. It's beyond awful that someone so beautiful, so intelligent and full of life, will rot in that hellhole. It could be decades before her remains are found.

'I know what you're thinking,' Shona says. 'But I've always

believed our bodies are just vessels.' She shrugs. 'Rae's soul isn't down there. Rae's soul was set free when Miles died.'

We head towards the rock garden in the far east corner of the gardens. As we pass through a small area of woodland Shona beckons me into the trees and I step off the path and follow, wondering where she's taking me.

Branches form a canopy above our heads, blocking out the sun and muffling all sound. We could be in the middle of a Caledonian pine forest, miles from anywhere, not in the heart of the city. Just me, Shona and Wren.

'Where are we going?' I call to Shona, who is flitting through the trees ahead of me, a woman on a mission.

'You'll see,' she calls back. The hairs on my arms stiffen. It's chilly here, out of the sun. I drop a kiss onto Wren's head and grab his feet. He giggles as a shaft of sunlight lights our path.

Shona is standing in the middle of a circle of enormous trees. She pats the bark of the nearest one. 'Giant redwoods,' she says. 'Rae loved it here. Our parents used to bring us for picnics when we were younger. She used to say it reminded her of a cathedral.'

'Wren likes it too,' I say. He is chattering excitedly to himself, a baby babble only he can understand. I gaze up. The redwoods tower over us. Their sheer size is breathtaking.

I think of how fond of Shona I have become in the last couple of days. I'm going to miss her.

As I stare at the green-leaved roof of Rae's cathedral, I have an epiphany. I don't want to go back to Kent. Grandad's cottage is just four walls surrounded by some grass and flowers without him in it. When he left it to me, I assumed it was because he wanted me to live there. Now I can see I was wrong. By leaving me the cottage he gave me freedom. Independence. Choices.

I glance at Shona. Her face is upturned, her eyes closed. There's a trace of a smile on her face. Is she picturing past picnics? Remembering a carefree girl with pigtails the colour of burnt sienna?

'Shona?'

'Mmm?' she says, without opening her eyes.

I take a deep breath. For the first time in my life I feel in charge of my own destiny. Mine and Wren's.

'How would you feel about me moving to Edinburgh?'

65

SIX WEEKS LATER

There are fewer than a dozen of us at the funeral. Miles's siblings found excuses not to come and he didn't have many close friends. Correction: he didn't have *any* close friends. That should have been another red flag. All those warning signs I was too blind to see.

Wren is outside, being pushed around the churchyard in his new buggy by Arthur, Grandad's old friend and neighbour. It's the one designed for running we ordered before Miles followed me to Scotland. Arthur turned up on the doorstep with it the morning after Wren and I arrived home. Wren watched in amazement as I tore off the plastic wrapping, and gurgled in excitement when I strapped him in.

'It's a fancy pants running one,' I told him. 'I could go running with you if you wanted. Not until you're six months old though.'

As I said the words, I pictured myself clad in Lycra, pounding the lanes with the wind in my hair, my legs toned and strong, one hand guiding the handlebar, a grin on Wren's face.

That afternoon, while Wren was napping, I pulled on some yoga pants and an old T-shirt and went next door to ask Arthur if he'd sit with Wren while I went for a run.

I was shocked at how unfit I was, barely managing five minutes before I was bent double, gasping for breath. But when I arrived back at the cottage, red-faced and wobbly-legged, I realised I had actually enjoyed myself. Since then I've been out three or four times a week when Arthur can mind Wren for me. I can run for half an hour without stopping now, and in a couple of weeks' time Wren'll be old enough to come with me. Running gives me a natural high. I sleep better, eat better, keep sober. It gives me mental clarity and stops my thoughts slipping into a dark place. And although it's only been six weeks, I can already see my body changing, becoming stronger. And strong is good.

I check my watch. The vicar is running late. I use the opportunity to glance around the church. I am flanked on either side by my parents, who flew in from Portugal a week ago to lend a hand with the last-minute funeral arrangements. They're also going to help me pack up the cottage, which is going on the market in the next couple of weeks.

They were surprisingly unfazed when I told them that while they may have lost a son-in-law, they'd gained a grandson. A grandson called Max, although everyone knows him as Wren. When he's older, he can choose whichever name he prefers. I don't have a problem with that at all.

To the outside world, Wren is Miles's child, conceived during an extra-marital affair I knew nothing about. Miles's name is on the birth certificate, after all. His birth mum, a young chemical engineer Miles worked with in Dubai, walked out when Wren was four months old, and that's when he came down to Kent to live with us.

This is the narrative Shona and I have agreed upon, because if John Westfield's widow learns her late husband fathered a child, there's always a chance she might show up and fight for custody. And hell would have to freeze over before we let that happen.

We have instructed a solicitor experienced in family law and she is optimistic that as Wren's stepmother – and with Shona's blessing – the courts will grant me parental responsibility, which will pave the way for me to legally adopt Wren further down the line.

I have to pinch myself every single day to make sure I'm not dreaming.

My mother-in-law is sitting to Dad's left, her walking sticks propped against the pew between them. Faye is only in her early seventies but looks ten years older and has the crackly breathing of someone with chronic emphysema. She cried when I phoned to tell her about Miles's accident. Wheezy sobs that tugged at my heartstrings, because no mother deserves to lose a child. But last night, as I helped her up the stairs to the spare bedroom, she admitted her tears were for the boy she'd lost, not the man Miles had become.

'It pains me to say this, Lucy, love. But he was a stranger to me. My own son, a stranger.'

Shona is sitting behind me. She drove down from Edinburgh in her little Fiat 500 a couple of days ago. I can't decide if she's here to give me moral support or to bid good riddance to the man who murdered her sister. Whatever her motivation, I'm glad to see her. Wren and I are flying up to Edinburgh to stay with her the week after next. She's already found a couple of houses within walking distance of her bungalow for me to look at.

The organist is playing *Air on the G String* and the air is heavy with the sickly scent of lilies. Faye insisted on a fussy arrangement of them for the top of the coffin and, as I couldn't give a toss what we had, I gave her free rein. When we arrived at the church she produced a couple of framed photos from her voluminous handbag and tucked them in among the waxy white petals. I'll have a look at them when this circus is over. I'll give her a hug and tell her what a lovely send-off Miles has had. It'll make her happy, and God knows she deserves that.

I smooth the skirt of my black shift dress, then sneak a glance over my shoulder to see who else has turned up.

There are a couple of broad-shouldered men with weathered faces who must have worked with Miles on the rigs, and two elderly ladies from the village who never miss a funeral, according to Arthur.

To my surprise, Sarah and Toby are sitting in a pew at the back of the church. Sarah catches my eye and gives me a sympathetic smile. Colour races up my cheeks as I remember the last time I saw her, staggering out of her beautiful garden as drunk as a lord. But it seems she's forgiven me. I smile back. Maybe I'll phone her and arrange a playdate before we move to Scotland. Theo and Wren are roughly the same age, after all.

Pete has forgiven me too, after I summoned the courage to track him down a couple of weeks ago. I found him on Facebook and messaged him, telling him how sorry I was for my appalling behaviour that afternoon at the ABode. I explained I was finally seeking help for my drink problem and would really appreciate it if Sophie could put me in touch with a couple of support groups after all.

He messaged straight back, saying there was nothing to forgive, and a flurry of messages pinged between us. I told him about Wren and what happened to Miles. He told me about the twins he and Sophie lost, Thea and Elijah, and how he still struggled to talk about what happened.

After a few days the messages petered out, and that is how it should be. My future is in Scotland with Wren and Shona, not back in Kent, trying to cling onto the past.

It seems crazy now to think I ever wondered if Wren was

Pete and Sophie's poor lost Elijah, or Sarah and Toby's little Theo.

Looking back, I *was* a bit crazy. Thanks to Miles.

There's a shift in the atmosphere and the vicar glides in, his robes wafting behind him. He takes his place at the lectern, his voice grave but full of sympathy as he welcomes us.

We sing Faye's favourite hymn – *All Things Bright and Beautiful* – before the vicar reads out the eulogy I cobbled together last night. The picture he paints is of a loving husband and son, a devoted father, a man who was tragically taken before his time.

Miles's post-mortem examination found he died of crush injuries to his chest. Accident investigation officers concluded he must have forgotten to pull up the handbrake properly when he went to check the windscreen washer fluid level. The reservoir was almost empty, which is hardly surprising after the long journey up from Kent, but it helps our narrative, nonetheless. The officer liaising with me said the fatal accident inquiry should be straightforward when it is heard later this year. I am off the hook, it seems.

But that doesn't mean I got away scot-free. Guilt hits me like a hammer blow when I least expect it. I could be wandering up an aisle in the supermarket when I reach for a packet of the shortbread biscuits Miles loves, then remember he's not here to eat them. Wren and I might be lying on the picnic blanket under the apple tree when I sense Miles's presence so strongly, I swear I catch a whiff of his aftershave. I often wake in the middle of the night, my heart thumping in my chest, the image of his broken body slumped under the bonnet of his car etched on my mind. I know the guilt will never leave me. I have taken a life, after all. But Miles took three, and I tell myself the world is a better place without him in it.

The vicar invites us to stand for the commendation and

farewell, and, heads bowed, we listen as he entrusts Miles to the love and mercy of God.

It's nonsense, all of it. For a start, Miles was a raging atheist. But you have to play the game. And, besides, Faye wanted a church service.

I look round briefly and catch Shona's eye.

'You OK?' she mouths. I nod, wondering if she regrets her decision not to tell the police where Rae's body is. Because Rae will never have the funeral she deserves. I will find time once we're back at the cottage to check in with her properly, make sure she's all right.

People start to file out of the church. I wait at the end of the aisle for Faye.

'Shall we look at the flowers?' I ask.

She nods, slips her arm in mine, and we walk slowly to the coffin, the cloying scent of the lilies growing stronger with every step.

'They're beautiful. You chose well,' I tell her. I reach for one of the photos she slipped between the flowers. 'I haven't seen this one.' It's a school photo, taken, I'm guessing, when Miles was eight or nine. His hair wasn't as dark then, and flopped untidily over his forehead. 'He doesn't look very happy,' I remark. It's an understatement. He's glaring at the camera as if the photographer has just announced Christmas is cancelled.

Faye takes the photo from me. She sniffs, and tears spill down her cheeks. I find her a tissue and she dabs her face, then reaches for the second photo frame.

'Who does this remind you of?' she says, passing it to me.

I roll my eyes inwardly. Faye has been chuntering on about Wren being the spit of Miles since she arrived yesterday afternoon. I suppose it's understandable. She believes Wren is Miles's son, and she sees what she wants to see.

I take the photo anyway, just to keep her happy. I'm also intrigued. I've never seen any pictures of Miles as a baby.

I look down at the photo, then step back, confused. 'Where did you get this?'

Faye smiles fondly. 'I brought it with me.'

I look at the photo again. It's Wren, lying on his tummy, looking up at the camera and laughing. But something's not right. I don't recognise the babygrow he's wearing. Or the blanket he's lying on.

'Told you, didn't I?' Faye says. 'They could be peas in a pod.'

'I don't understand.' I stare at the photo until Wren, no... *Miles*, grows blurry. Faye was right. Wren *is* the spit of Miles, from the colour of his hair down to the shape of his ears.

Which means one thing. It wasn't John Westfield who crept into Rae's cabin and raped her. It was Miles.

I remember with growing horror Rae describing in her letter how Miles had fetched her a cup of tea; how she'd been hit by a wave of exhaustion and taken herself off to bed soon after.

Miles drugged her, just as he drugged me the night he pushed me down the stairs. It was his modus operandi. All his life he manipulated, lied and coerced, stopping at nothing to get what he wanted. And Wren, a beautiful, innocent little boy who has become mine by default, is the result.

The contents of my stomach heave as I am hit by a wave of dizziness. I close my eyes and force myself to breathe. I can't afford to lose it now. Wren needs me.

I feel a hand on my arm, and my eyes snap open. Faye is peering at me, her brow creased in concern.

'Lucy, love, are you all right?'

I'm not, but I will be.

A LETTER FROM A J MCDINE

Dear Reader,

Thank you so much for reading *The Baby*. If you enjoyed the book even half as much as I loved writing it, then that's a win for us both!

If this is the first of my books you've read, thanks for taking a chance on me and I hope you liked it enough to dip into my others. If you've been with me from the start, a million thank yous. Your support means the world to me.

If you would like to keep up to date with all my latest releases, just go to the link below and I'll let you know when I have a new novel coming out. Your email address will never be shared and you can unsubscribe at any time.

www.bookouture.com/a-j-mcdine

The Baby is my sixth psychological thriller and people often ask me if it gets any easier the more books I write. The answer is, not really! There are so many thrillers out there now that it's almost impossible to come up with a truly original idea.

So with *The Baby*, I decided to take a popular trope – a missing child – and turn it completely on its head, exploring what might happen if a woman who'd never had children woke up one day to find a baby in her house.

I first came up with the idea a couple of years ago, but at the time I shelved it because I couldn't work out who the baby belonged to, which was fairly crucial to the plot.

And then, one magical evening, the answer just popped into my head and suddenly I had the makings of a book.

I love it when that 'eureka moment' happens. Sadly it doesn't happen nearly as often as I'd like! But my subconscious mind must have been hard at work, whirring away as it mulled over the problem, and delivering the solution just when I least expected it.

After that, the writing process was fairly straightforward, and I finished the first draft in just under four months, which is pretty quick for me.

If you did enjoy Lucy's story, I would be very grateful if you could spare a moment to write a review. I'd love to hear what you think, and reviews make such a difference in helping new readers discover my books.

I absolutely love hearing from readers, so please feel free to get in touch by emailing me at amanda@ajmcdine.com. I promise to reply!

You can also visit my website or come and say hello over on Facebook or Instagram.

All the best,

Amanda x

www.ajmcdine.com

facebook.com/ajmcdineauthor

instagram.com/ajmcdineauthor

ACKNOWLEDGEMENTS

Firstly, I would like to thank my lovely editor, Billi-Dee Jones, whose enthusiasm for *The Baby* has been unwavering from the moment I explained the very basic premise to her.

Thank you, Billi, for your insights and wisdom. This book is all the better for your input and it has been a joy to work with you.

A massive shoutout to the rest of the wonderful team at Bookouture. You have all made me feel so welcome and I absolutely love being part of the Bookouture family.

Thanks to my copyeditor, Jane Eastgate, and my proofreader, Jenny Page.

I would like to thank my readers and all the brilliant bloggers who take the time to read, review or recommend my books. Your support means the world to me.

Finally, I would like to thank my husband and fellow author, Adrian, for always being happy to talk books, and to our boys, Oliver and Thomas, whose eyes glaze over every time we do.

PUBLISHING TEAM

Turning a manuscript into a book requires the efforts of many people. The publishing team at Bookouture would like to acknowledge everyone who contributed to this publication.

Audio
Alba Proko
Sinead O'Connor
Melissa Tran

Commercial
Lauren Morrissette
Jil Thielen
Imogen Allport

Data and analysis
Mark Alder
Mohamed Bussuri

Editorial
Billi-Dee Jones
Nadia Michael

Copyeditor
Jane Eastgate

Made in the USA
Coppell, TX
06 May 2024

32097779R00180